W9-BRX-408

Berkley Prime Crime titles by Kathleen Bridge

BETTER HOMES AND CORPSES
HEARSE AND GARDENS
GHOSTAL LIVING

Ghostal
Living

KATHLEEN BRIDGE

BERKLEY PRIME CRIME
New York

BERKLEY PRIME CRIME
Published by Berkley
An imprint of Penguin Random House LLC
375 Hudson Street, New York, New York 10014

Copyright © 2017 by Kathleen Bridge
Excerpt from *Better Homes and Corpses* copyright © 2015 by Kathleen Bridge
Penguin Random House supports copyright. Copyright fuels creativity, encourages
diverse voices, promotes free speech, and creates a vibrant culture. Thank you for buying
an authorized edition of this book and for complying with copyright laws by not
reproducing, scanning, or distributing any part of it in any form without permission.
You are supporting writers and allowing Penguin Random House to continue to
publish books for every reader.

BERKLEY is a registered trademark and BERKLEY PRIME CRIME and
the B colophon are trademarks of Penguin Random House LLC.

First Edition: May 2017

ISBN: 9780425276600

Printed in the United States of America
1 3 5 7 9 10 8 6 4 2

Cover art by Marjorie Muns
Cover design by Diana Kolsky
Book design by Kristin del Rosario

To my mother and best friend, Judith Mae Anderson Drawe, with my eternal love. I don't know how I got to be so fortunate to have such a beautiful and wonderful mom as a role model. This one's for you!

ACKNOWLEDGMENTS

I want to thank Dr. James L. W. West III, Fitzgerald biographer, book historian, and scholarly editor for his invaluable advice and guidance about an unpublished F. Scott Fitzgerald novel-length manuscript turning up in Montauk, NY. I got the idea from an article titled "A Fleeting Era's Timeless Chronicle" in the *New York Times* in which Dr. West was quoted in reference to Fitzgerald's short story that takes place in Montauk, *The Unspeakable Egg*, of which Dr. West was the annotator and editor.

Lon Otremba, once again, you came through with wonderful recipes from your archives that I am honored to share with the world.

Lee Goldstein for her expertise on fortune-telling and handwriting analysis.

My agent extraordinaire, Dawn Dowdle, thanks again for all your help and support.

My stellar new editor Bethany Blair, I have really enjoyed the journey and the collaboration.

As always, thanks to my early readers, Ellen (Elle) Broder, Ann Costigan, Michelle Mason Otremba, Marc and Daddy John, my words couldn't be in better hands. Nancy, Ann, Maura, Eunice,

Gayle and Ro at Backstreet Antiques for your knowledge, support, and friendship.

My family, Josh, Lindsey, and Marc—I would be lost without your loving support.

As always, Montauk—thanks for the inspiration!

CHAPTER

❧❧❧

ONE

It was an understatement to say that I, Meg Barrett, had too much on my plate. My plate, a new cottage in Montauk overlooking the Atlantic, was piled so high I couldn't see under the minutiae of zoning permits and small-town politics. Luckily, the ready-to-topple cake on top of my plate was layered with rich chocolate ganache consisting of romance with two men, a major score at a recent estate sale, and a temperate Long Island August deserving a place in the history books—notwithstanding the hurricane that planned to make landfall at 1300.

The vintage boat—or "yacht," as I was told to call the *Malabar X*—listed from side to side, making it impossible to balance the crate holding Jo, my twenty-three-pound, one-eyed feline. Thanks to one of my aforementioned love interests, the sixty-foot, circa 1920 vessel had been my summer abode while I waited for zoning approval on my new cottage.

While I'd spent the past three months living on a yacht moored at the ritzy East End Yacht Club in Montauk, Jo had bunked with Georgia, proprietor of The Old Man and the Sea Books. Septuagenarian Georgia was on a weeklong bike tour in Maine, and I was left with the task of confining my Maine coon to the cabin of the yacht. The vintage sailboat had been my cat's home for only a week. A very long week.

I placed Jo on the cracked pleather front seat of the Wrangler and took one last look at the *Malabar X*. Gargantuan waves pounded her hull. Due to the hurricane barreling up the East Coast, a mandatory evacuation had been issued in Montauk for anyone living south of Route 27. The yacht club was north of the highway, but I wasn't taking any chances. In the Great Hurricane of 1938, water flooded across the Napeague dunes and turned Montauk into an island. The entire downtown had to be moved three miles south.

Once inside the Jeep, I said, "I promise, Miss Josephine, soon you'll be on solid ground."

She wasn't going for it and started howling. The decibel level was higher than when I'd switched her gourmet cat food for another brand on sale.

In Montauk, police cars were stationed at every beach entrance, barring surfers lugging heavy boards from partaking in the record-breaking waves. On South Elmwood Avenue, The Fudge Shop and A Little Bit of Everything had wisely boarded up their plate glass windows. I was happy I'd found a safe port for Jo and me in Sag Harbor.

In East Hampton, Jo's mewing intensified, along with the gale-force winds. On Main Street, a herd of five-foot-ten sun-kissed models window shopped, daring the hurricane to grace the gold-paved streets. *As if!*

Seven miles and thirty minutes later, we arrived in Sag Harbor. I turned onto Hollingsworth Avenue, went through the iron gates at the side of the Bibliophile Bed & Breakfast, and parked in the lot. The Victorian was the largest and most ornate in Sag Harbor. Franklin Hollingsworth owned the Bibliophile B & B. He shared the ten-acre estate with his brother, Ollie. For the past fifty years, the mansion had sat in disrepair. Working side by side with the Sag Harbor Historical Society, and without his brother Ollie's help, Franklin invested over a million dollars into the mansion's renovation. As a tribute to his favorite American authors, he transformed the old homestead into the Bibliophile Bed & Breakfast.

My one-woman interior design firm, Cottages by the Sea, had been in charge of the décor in each of the inn's guest suites. During the past few months, the project had taken up most of my waking hours. I couldn't have done it without the help of my best friend and former coworker at *American Home and Garden* magazine, Elle Warner. Elle had a thriving antiques/vintage shop in Sag Harbor called Mabel and Elle's Curiosities and was occasionally called in by First Fidelity Mutual, a local insurance company, to inventory art and antiques in the Hamptons area. We'd recently completed each American-author-inspired suite, with the exception of the third floor Emily Dickinson loft.

The inn wasn't officially open to the public yet. A rare book collector, Franklin Hollingsworth had carefully chosen only a few upper-echelon bibliophiles to be his guests. Franklin had timed the inn's unofficial opening with the first annual Sag Harbor Antiquarian Book and Ephemera Fair, of which he was a founding father. The book fair was sure to be a success due to all the press surrounding Franklin's purchase of an unpublished F. Scott Fitzgerald manuscript.

Franklin Hollingsworth had bought the F. Scott Fitzgerald manuscript, *The Heiress and the Light*, for the bargain price of five million dollars at a local auction. The F. Scott Fitzgerald Trust was the only one with the right to publish the manuscript in novel form. However, Franklin, according to an article in *Dave's Hamptons*, said the ownership of *The Heiress and the Light* had been the pinnacle of his fifty-year career. And what a career it had been. It was rumored Franklin spent a good share of his multimillion-dollar Hollingsworth inheritance on rare, first edition books and manuscripts, making him one of the top book collectors in the United States. Even the Smithsonian had tried to buy some of Franklin's items for their collection. Franklin refused to sell, not even granting a short exhibit, which was probably the reason there was so much buzz about the viewing of *The Heiress and the Light* at Saturday's kick-off cocktail party for the book fair. The 1920s-themed gala was to take place at Hollingsworth Castle; Franklin's brother Ollie's newly-built monstrosity. It was ostentatious with a capital *O*. Just like Ollie himself.

I was a huge Fitzgerald fan and looked forward to the book fair on Sunday. However, I had another reason for attending. During the time I worked on the interior rooms at the Bibliophile B & B, I'd gone to a nearby estate sale and found a signed, first edition, first printing of the John Steinbeck novel *The Winter of Our Discontent*. A few days ago, I gave the book to Franklin's go-to rare-book broker, who was staying at the inn. Jordan Innes valued my John Steinbeck book at twelve thousand dollars. She told me the price could go even higher because the author had once been a resident of Sag Harbor. The fictional setting in Steinbeck's book, New Baytown, had been modeled after Sag Harbor.

I'd found the Steinbeck buried in the bottom of a trunk, under a stack of old newspapers covered in mouse droppings. Vintage picking wasn't a glamorous job, even in the Hamptons. I felt less guilty about paying only fifty dollars for a book valued in the thousands because the owner of the house was a billionaire Wall Streeter, and for each treasure I profited from, there were always a few gambles that didn't pay off. But wasn't that the thrill of the hunt? With the low interior design rates I charged my Cottages by the Sea clients, the karmic scales seemed evenly balanced.

I switched off the ignition. Jo was uncharacteristically quiet. Not a peep or a howl. It was the calm before the storm. The cat's and the hurricane's. The Bibliophile B & B's parking lot was empty, except for one car, a navy-blue Fiat. Perhaps the inn's guests were stocking up on snacks and board games to keep them busy while they were holed up inside. There wouldn't be any need to visit the bookstore on Main Street. The Bibliophile's obsolete greenhouse bloomed with a lending library of books. There were plenty of rare editions inside the inn, but most were locked behind glass bookcases.

I got out of the Jeep, took my suitcase from the back, and admired the Victorian's architecture. The exterior was painted teal blue with white trim. Lush, wedding-white hydrangea bushes bordered the sprawling wraparound veranda. The mansion was topped with a gold-leaf cupola reminiscent of the Taj Mahal's. Under the dome was an open perch with a circular wood railing offering 360-degree views of Sag Harbor. There were four turrets, one at each corner of the house, and fretwork decorated every wooden gable.

I craned my neck and looked at the copper whale weathervane. The verdigris arrow determining the wind's direction spun frenetically left then right and back again. Dusty mauve clouds moved toward me from the harbor and the wind lashed my face. It whistled and tunneled in and out of my hearing aids, producing an eerie soundtrack: "Storm a'comin'. Storm a'comin'." Next to me, a flock of sparrows left a huge magnolia tree, scattering in all directions. These birds of a feather weren't sticking together.

The sky darkened, and I jumped when I saw movement from behind a lace curtain in the Edgar Allan Poe suite.

I'd designed the suite for atmosphere—apparently I'd done a stellar job.

CHAPTER

TWO

I opened the Jeep's passenger door and Jo gave me the evil eye through a hole in the crate. She only had one, but she sure knew how to use it. I thought we'd come a long way from when I'd been tricked into adopting her. However, the past week on the yacht had set our relationship back a few notches. I was thrilled we were staying in the unfinished Emily Dickinson loft. I could only imagine what damage Jo would do if I let her loose in one of the guest suites filled with antique and vintage linens.

The inn's guests had been at the Bibliophile for two weeks. The suites booked were: the F. Scott Fitzgerald, the Herman Melville, and the Edgar Allan Poe. The empty suites included: the Louisa May Alcott, the John Steinbeck, and the Edith Wharton. Only seven suites, including the Emily Dickinson loft, but when the inn officially opened, each suite would go for eight hundred dollars a night off-season, with meals extra.

Jo mewed as I grabbed the handle of the crate. A single talon poked through one of the holes.

"That's the girl I know and love."

Brenna, Franklin's niece who ran the B and B, waited on the veranda at the rear entrance. Brenna was my age, in her early thirties, with coffee ground–brown hair and olive skin. Her appearance was average in every way, except for one: she stood six feet tall. She reminded me of a young Julia Child, in looks and cooking ability. "Hurry, Meg, before someone sees your cat."

Guests weren't allowed pets. The inn came with its own "well-behaved" tortoiseshell feline named Catterina. "Well-behaved" and Jo would never be used in the same sentence.

I leaned to the right, Quasimodo-style, holding the crate in one hand while I dragged my suitcase over the gravel with the other.

Brenna came toward us. She always dressed in khaki pants and a preppy, insignia-clad polo shirt. "Welcome back. We've missed you. Sorry it had to be the same day as a hurricane. I don't think it'll hit too hard in Sag Harbor. I heard the south shore will bear the brunt of it."

"Great."

"Don't worry. Your cottage will be fine."

My little Montauk bungalow sat on a half acre of land and included a glass folly and a centuries-old garden. The panoramic ocean views from the cottage included the Montauk Point Lighthouse, the same "light" referred to in the title of Fitzgerald's unpublished manuscript *The Heiress and the Light*.

I gave Brenna a quick hug, and we walked to the rear entrance of the inn. Brenna grabbed the handle of the suitcase, pulled it up the wooden steps like it weighed nothing, then held open the door. We stepped into the rear vestibule and I was immediately comforted with the sweet scent of beeswax. The inn served honey from its own apiary and made beeswax candles and furniture polish. I also noticed the distinctive smell of cardamom. When I'd worked on the guest suites at the Bibliophile, I enjoyed an array of memorable meals that Brenna had prepared from recipes she found in one of her vintage cookbooks. The book-collecting apple hadn't fallen far from the Hollingsworth tree. And like my foodie-snob, gourmet cook father, Brenna added her own spin to each recipe she followed.

Brenna carried my suitcase up to the Emily Dickinson loft then left to make sure there were enough supplies in case we had a power outage.

The beast was set free in the loft, which at one time had been a nursery/schoolroom. Jo spent the first few minutes doing a cursory inspection, then plopped down on the single bed under a long rectangular window. The loft spanned the entire width of the mansion, with ceilings that rose almost two stories high. Like every other room in the Victorian, it had its own fireplace. Also in the loft was a door that opened to stairs leading up to the cupola. I couldn't wait to climb them and check out the harbor view.

A branch slammed against the window and Jo gave me a look like, "What have you gotten us into now?"

It seemed I'd have to wait for my bird's-nest view of Sag Harbor until *after* the hurricane.

On the east wall, I'd stacked antique and vintage furniture and accessories similar to those I'd spied at the Emily Dickinson Museum in Massachusetts. The center guest suite on the second floor started out as the Emily Dickinson suite. After Franklin's purchase of F. Scott Fitzgerald's *The Heiress and the Light* manuscript, the contents of the Dickinson guest suite were banished to the attic loft, and the F. Scott Fitzgerald suite was born.

Elle and I'd had only a one-month deadline to scour Long Island for items to the fill the Fitzgerald suite. We traveled eighty-five miles west to Great Neck, where the Fitzgeralds once lived and F. Scott penned *The Great Gatsby*, then back east to the Hamptons, where F. Scott and Zelda most likely once romped, visiting every resale and vintage shop along the way. Elle and I had an unspoken rule of shopping mostly at local antique/vintage shops and estate and garage sales for our furniture and accessories. We preferred our treasure hunts to be just that.

In each author-inspired suite, I'd made the desk the focal point—like the author had just stepped out for a bit of air. The only items not of period in the rooms were the king-sized down-topped mattresses. I was confident that when the Emily Dickinson loft was completed, even shy Emily would have preferred the cozy attic space to the second-floor guest suite.

A replica of Miss Dickinson's cherrywood desk sat in front of an oriel window that faced the harbor. The Bibliophile B & B had six oriel windows, which Elle had explained were a type of bay window supported by brackets that jutted out from a wall with side windows designed to catch cool summer breezes before the advent of air-conditioning. The harbor vista outside the window would have provided Emily with enough inspiration to pen a few hundred more poems to add to her bountiful repertoire. Like Emily's, the desk I'd chosen was more of a square-top writing stand. Small tables of this kind were usually used as worktables or sewing tables in the nineteenth century. At the end of the single bed was a flat-top trunk. On top of the trunk was a basket, its handle tied with a rope. The charming story went: Emily Dickinson would lower freshly baked gingerbread out her window for the neighborhood children of Amherst, Massachusetts, to enjoy. A docent at the museum had told us Emily was a passionate baker and spent a good part of her time in her kitchen, occasionally writing lines of poetry on the backs of Parisian chocolate wrappers.

On the west wall, in a cupboard under the rafters, was a storage space that housed trunks and boxes filled with antique items dating as far back as the mid-1800s. Franklin Hollingsworth said to toss anything that wasn't book related—if it didn't have to do with books, he wasn't interested. His niece, Brenna, told me to feel free to rummage through the storage space for family heirlooms or small items that could be used in the Bibliophile B & B's suites. Anything left over would be donated to the Sag Harbor Whaling & Historical Museum.

Wind rattled the shutters. I went to the window and pushed up the sash. Then I leaned out, grabbed first the left shutter then the right, and pulled them toward me. After latching them together, I closed the window. I'd used similar shutters as décor in many of my cottages but had never before thought of their functional purpose during a storm.

Through all the commotion, Jo's eye remained closed. Wanting to go out before the storm hit and we'd be quarantined indoors, I took advantage of the cat's sanguine position. I removed my hearing aids, knowing they'd be useless in the high winds, and placed them on top of an antique dresser. I grabbed my hoodie, then snuck down the back stairs and went out the rear door.

The sky matched the color of the choppy bay. The scent of roses drew my gaze to a latticed trellis leaning against the north side of the inn. The roses were a pale yellow tinged with peach. They were so full and fragrant, I'd have bet they were heirloom blooms. Brenna had told me the Hollingsworths had been in Sag Harbor since the 1700s. They were one of the few Sag Harbor families who had come out unscathed after the collapse of the whaling industry because they'd wisely invested their fortune in railroads and factories. In the mid-nineteenth century, Ezekiel Hollingsworth, Franklin and Ollie Hollingsworth's great-great-grandfather, was the one who had transformed the white clapboard Greek revival house into a ginormous Victorian.

As I passed the inn's parking lot, I saw it was now filled with four vehicles, including mine. I ignored the NO TRESPASSING and PRIVATE PROPERTY signs posted on the second set of ornate iron gates at the back of the B and B and dashed through—thankful I didn't get zapped by an electric current.

I had three choices on which way to go.

The first path led to a decrepit, falling-in ruin Greek revival mansion I'd discovered on one of my wanderings. Scrimshaw House had been built so close to the eroding land above the harbor, it had been condemned by the village and had sat empty for the past hundred years. Scrimshaw House had belonged to the only Hollingsworth ancestor who'd been a whaling captain. The story went like this: when Captain Isaiah Hollingsworth's wife, Sarah, heard her husband's ship, *Manifest Destiny,* had sunk in a squall on its way to Honduras, she had a miscarriage. A day later, she wandered out into a storm and threw herself off a piece of land that jutted fifty feet above the rocky harbor. Sailors saw her floating in the water, her white nightgown spread around her like angel's wings. Supposedly, Captain Isaiah's widow haunted the bluff next to Scrimshaw House, ever searching the horizon for the safe return of *Manifest Destiny*. The locals renamed the piece of land from where Sarah had jumped Widow's Point.

My second choice was a gravel drive that ended at Ollie Hollingsworth's castle. No thank you. Ollie's castle didn't meld with the beautiful harbor-front land it sat on. Hollingsworth Castle had aluminum siding that mimicked large gray bricks, multiple Juliet balconies, ramparts, and turrets. Through the trees I saw the castle's double towers. I'd heard Ollie had cut down forty-five oaks, maples, and elms to make room for his not-so-humble abode. He must have had a Sag Harbor councilman in his back pocket in order to get that, and the aluminum siding, passed. And here I was waiting for zoning approval on a tiny six-room cottage.

My third choice was a dirt trail I'd never taken that led into the woods.

I chose the woods.

As I stepped onto the path, a huge branch from a forty-foot oak swept the ground like a gentleman asking a debutante for a dance. Then a voracious blast of wind ricocheted the branch upward. The limb severed, landing inches in front of me. The ground, along with my knees, shook. The wise thing would have been to turn around and go inside.

No one ever said I was wise.

I kept walking until I saw a red Japanese pagoda at the top of a hill. The pagoda had a slatted, triple-tiered, ogee roof with ornate wood carvings at each corner. Three of the four sides of the pagoda had glass walls trimmed in red. My kind of cozy structure. A waterfall trickled down the side of the hill and emptied into a pond filled with neon-hued koi. Surrounding the pond were double begonias, perfumed ruffle-edged lilies, and ferns. I suspected that landscape architect Byron Hughes had something to do with its magnificence.

Byron had recommended Cottages by the Sea to Franklin Hollingsworth. Byron was the number-one, top-man-on-the-totem-pole Hamptons landscape architect and my occasional Saturday night date. If I hadn't had Byron's competition, Cole Spenser, in my life, things would have been much easier. But not much fun. I couldn't ignore my feelings for both Byron and Cole. And why shouldn't I date two guys at the same time? My ex-fiancé had cheated behind my back with his ex-wife, Miss Fancy Pants, Paige Whitney of Whitney Publications.

Lately, things had been a little easier on the man front because Cole was delivering one of his vintage sailing yachts to a client in Saint Thomas. I pulled out my cell phone to see if he'd left a message. He hadn't. I put my phone back in my pocket, noticing it had only one bar of battery left, and hurried over a small stone bridge, then climbed the steps to the top of the hill.

In front of the pagoda were a rock garden, bonsai trees, and two weeping cherries. A light glowed from inside. I crouched under one of the weeping cherries and looked in. Violet Hollingsworth, Franklin's wife, sat at her sculpting table. She held a tool consisting of two small handles with a wire stretched between them and was in the process of slicing off the top of a large clay head. She removed the scalp portion and placed it next to her. As she worked, she conversed with the head, even pinching its cheekbones, like she wanted to inflict bodily harm. Then she reached inside the head and removed a wad of crumpled newspapers and slid the scalpless head off a metal pole. Next, she went to work hollowing out the interior of the head with a tool that had a metal loop at its end, like something a dentist might use to torture his patients.

In the past, when I'd worked at the inn, I rarely saw Franklin's wife. Violet left everything concerning the B and B in her niece Brenna's capable hands. Franklin and Violet lived in a small cabin behind the inn. The cabin had once been used as the main house's kitchen and cook's residence. Franklin was usually sequestered inside, nose-deep in books, or in his private reading lair: a gutted smokehouse, windowless and temperature- and humidity-controlled. The smokehouse had enough high-tech security to keep his prized rare books and manuscripts, including *The Heiress and the Light*, safe. Brenna told me Violet spent most of her time in her studio. She and Franklin seemed a good match. Neither was boisterous or commanding. They were the complete opposite of Franklin's brother, Ollie.

A drop of rain landed on my nose. Not wanting to disturb Violet, and feeling like a voyeur, I turned and sprinted down the hill. In front of me was the inn and beyond it, a turbulent Sag Harbor Bay. The wind picked up—if that was even possible. I looked toward the Bibliophile. It was the perfect backdrop for a Hitchcockian film. The landscape surrounding the estate seemed sopped of color by the black storm clouds. I'd believed Brenna and her mild Sag Harbor weather prognostication. But now I wasn't too sure. I hurried over the stone bridge then broke into a run.

The wind whipped my hair in front of my eyes and I tripped over something on the rocky path.

A book.

Wow. Books just grew in the woods on the grounds of the Bibliophile B & B.

I picked it up. It was a bound copy of F. Scott Fitzgerald's short stories, originally published in the *Saturday Evening Post*. I opened the book. The pages fluttered violently back and forth. I shoved the book under my jacket and pulled up my hood. The sky let loose its deluge. Rain, mixed with hail, pelted my head like a hydraulic jackhammer.

The pagoda was closer than the inn. I turned and sprinted toward it.

The hurricane had arrived.

THREE

I hurried along the path. It felt like I was inside a Whac-A-Mole arcade game. Small tree branches flew in horizontal trajectories then dive-bombed to the ground.

At the top of the hill, I climbed the three wooden steps and pounded on the glass door. Violet Hollingsworth's back faced me. Twigs and other forest shrapnel clawed at my bare legs. I rapped harder with the side of my fist. Violet turned, surprise showing in her pale gray eyes. She hurriedly placed the scalp on the head and covered the sculpture with black fabric. She floated toward the door, in no hurry to rescue me from the storm. She wore a caftan made of a diaphanous material in iridescent purples, greens, and blues. As she reached for the sliding glass door, her sleeves morphed into huge wings and I couldn't help but think of the lead in the opera *Madama Butterfly*.

I stepped—more like flew—inside, pushed by the unrelenting wind. There wasn't a chance I'd be able to get back to the Bibliophile until the storm let up.

"Ms. Barrett. What are you doing out on a day like this?" She had short lemon-blonde hair. Two shiny curls were flattened against her cheeks like they'd been lacquered with decoupage glue.

Still holding the book under my jacket with one hand, I used the other to help Violet close the sliding glass door. The cuticles on her short nails were caked with clay.

Violet noticed my stare and apologetically folded her hands into her sleeves. "I fear we'll become better friends in the next few hours, my dear."

Her choice of using the word "fear" seemed slightly odd.

The space was open and airy. I felt like I was on a different continent. An indoor fountain at the west-facing window emptied into a rock-filled pond glittering with goldfish. Flanked on both sides of the fountain were potted, dwarf bonsai trees and orchids, their mouths gaped open to catch the moist air. The room smelled of damp earth and something sweet and familiar I couldn't make out.

I said, "I hope the storm doesn't damage any of these beautiful windows."

She walked to the only solid wall in the pagoda. It was faced in river rocks, accented with a long copper counter, farm sink, and refrigerator, and a gas stovetop on which a copper kettle simmered. Along the counter were ten clear glass jars filled with either pipe tobacco or tea—I was banking on the tea—although, her husband, Franklin, smoked a pipe. Next to the stove was an appliance in the same size and shape as the huge iron bank vault Elle had in her carriage house workroom.

Violet spoke to me, but I couldn't make out her words.

When she turned, I said, "I have a hearing loss and left my hearing aids at the inn. If you don't mind, it helps if you face me when you speak."

She gave me an unfocused look and after a few beats said, "We'll be fine. Mr. Hughes installed special shatter-proof glass panels in the teahouse after the last big storm."

At the thought of *my* Byron as her Mr. Hughes, I smiled. He'd made quite a first impression on me last October when I'd hired him to draw up landscape plans for my newly purchased property in Montauk. At our first meeting, he'd brought Montauk daisies and an out-of-print book called *The Illuminated Language of Flowers*. I'd been putty in Byron's hands—like the rest of the female population in the Hamptons.

I unzipped my jacket and put the Fitzgerald book on a wooden bench. The book was dry and damage-free. I couldn't say the same for my formerly white sneakers, or tennis shoes as we called them in Michigan. Puddles formed beneath me on the slate floors. After I hung my jacket on a hook, I placed my shoes on a mat next to Violet's child-sized ballet flats. I picked up the book and padded in my stockinged feet toward the center of the room.

At the copper table that held Violet's shrouded work-in-progress, it took everything I had not to tear off the sheet to get a better look at the sculpture. My father was a retired homicide detective in the Detroit Police Department, and I was naturally inquisitive about all things covered. Curiosity was something inbred, but as Elle would attest to, it was also my Achilles' heel, especially if you counted my two recent near-death experiences since I moved to Montauk—which I wholeheartedly did.

Violet waited until we made eye contact, then beckoned

me forward. On a round bamboo table with two chairs, she'd placed a tray holding a blue willow teapot and two matching cups and saucers. A sterling silver tea strainer topped each cup. Steam escaped the teapot's spout, scenting the air—rose hips, if I wasn't mistaken. That was the scent I'd noticed earlier.

I handed her the book. "I tripped over this on the path to the teahouse. I assume it's Franklin's, seeing it's about F. Scott Fitzgerald."

"Oh, yes. He must have dropped it earlier after he stopped here for his cup of tea. He'll be thrilled you rescued it."

I sat at the table. The wind and rain swirled around us. Violet seemed unconcerned, so I followed her lead. Byron had landscaped the area around the teahouse with small trees and bushes. The teahouse sat on a hill, so there was little threat of one of the numerous oaks or maples falling on us. A lightning storm would be a different story.

Violet reached for the teapot. "Shall I be mother?"

She and Franklin had no children. So, of course, I let her.

Violet held the teapot with her long sculptor's fingers, not spilling a drop as she poured it over the strainer. "I mix the tea myself and I'm afraid I am a bit of a purist. I don't add milk or sugar. It muddles the benefits of my elixirs." Violet took the strainer off her cup and placed it on the tray next to the teapot.

Not up on tea etiquette, just tea consumption, I did the same. The tea was too hot to drink, so I positioned my nose over the cup and inhaled the bouquet. "It smells yummy. I'm surprised you don't use honey, seeing you have an apiary on the grounds."

"Like I said, it muddles the benefits of the tea leaves. This blend is rose hips with a pinch of a centuries-old artisan green tea from Kanazawa, Japan. It contains gold leaf."

"Gold leaf?"

"Gold is a mineral, my dear, and thought to have numerous healing properties. If I had to guess, I'd say you're still hurting from a broken heart. If you want, I can read your tea leaves. I was taught tasseography by Misho Maguro, a half-Indian, half-Japanese swami from Tibet."

My friend Elle collected vintage fortune-telling teacups, so I knew the definition of tasseography. "*Tasse*" is a French word meaning "cup." However, Elle didn't read tea leaves; she just collected the cups. She'd instructed me that fortune-telling teacups were produced from the late nineteenth century until today, most given as advertising premiums when buying bulk tea. The three most popular designs for the interior of the cups were: zodiac signs, playing cards, or occult symbols.

I said, "Sounds like an interesting swami. Does she drink gold leaf tea and have a fulfilling love-life?"

Violet showed me her first smile. "You remind me of Franklin. There are things inside us that can't help but surface in our current lives—things we keep repeating over and over again when we revisit this earthly plane."

I didn't know how to respond, so I took a gulp of tea, hoping not to get gold stuck between my teeth.

Outside, the hurricane was at its peak. Hail hit the glass, along with branches stripped of their foliage. Debris swirled in funnel-shaped mini-cyclones. As I asked myself if a tornado could mix with a hurricane, one of the weeping cherries uprooted itself and slammed against the window. I thought of my cat, alone in the loft at the inn, and hoped she was safe from the storm. The darn beast was growing on me.

Trying to keep my voice steady, I said, "We better move the table closer to the solid kitchen wall. Is there a bathtub? We may need to take shelter."

Violet stood slowly. "As you wish, my dear." She didn't offer to help me move the furniture. Instead, she walked to the indoor fountain, placed her hand on top of the water in a calming gesture, and murmured some kind of mantra. I was a huge fan of meditation. Every morning I sat on the beach and repeated a simple chant that worked wonders: "Thank you. Thank you. Thank you." I didn't know if Violet helped calm the goldfish, but with *The Perfect Storm* hullabaloo going on outside, her calmness anchored me.

After we finished our tea, I got up and reached for Violet's empty cup.

She put her hand on my arm. There was strength in her grip. "You can take mine. But leave yours and bring me that large alabaster cup and saucer on the counter. I might as well read your tea leaves."

I wasn't a huge fan of fortune-tellers. I planned to make my own fortune and didn't want any soothsayers planting negative seeds in my head. I did what I was told because we were shipwrecked with nothing else to do. Also, I had to play nice. There was still the little matter of Franklin, Violet's husband, paying me for the work I'd done at the B and B.

The cup, the size of a soup bowl, was on the copper counter next to the farm sink. Unlike the cups in Elle's collection, this one had a blank interior. Inside the sink was the cup's twin, a pattern of tea leaves clinging to its sides. Did Violet read her own tea leaves or did the cup belong to her husband, Franklin?

There was a door to the left of the copper sink. I made

sure Violet wasn't looking and quickly opened it. Inside
was a large, windowless room. Behind a translucent folding
screen, I spied a puffy white duvet on top of a mattress that
sat on a wooden platform. Through an open door, I saw a
bathroom with a Jacuzzi we could hide in, if needed. That
was one problem to check off my worry list.

After I closed the door, I brought the cup and saucer to
the table and placed it in front of Violet. She reached for my
blue willow cup. There was a small amount of liquid at the
bottom. She emptied the contents of my cup into the larger
one. Then she took my tea strainer from the tray and handed
it to me. "Using your fingers, flick a small amount of leaves
into your cup, about a tablespoon, then hand it back to me."

I did as I was told and passed her the cup. "What are you
looking for?"

She inhaled, then slowly exhaled and looked inside.
"Patterns in the reverse of the tea leaves. Most people look
at the shape the leaves make against the white background.
Instead, I like to see what the white, negative spaces inside
the cup reveal."

I looked from Violet's face to the teacup. Her eyebrows
rose and lowered as she twirled the cup three times, from
left to right in a fast motion. She turned the cup upside
down over the saucer, drained the liquid, then flipped the
cup right-side up.

She looked inside. The corners of her mouth tightened
and she muttered, "Oh, my dear. Oh, my dear."

That didn't sound good.

Violet pushed the cup to the center of the table. "Look,"
she whispered.

CHAPTER

FOUR

The tea leaves clung to the interior of the cup. The white open spaces reminded me of clouds. Childhood memories of Michigan flooded back. Mom would pack a picnic basket and we'd go to the park on Lake St. Clair. Our picnic basket wasn't filled with just peanut butter-and-banana sandwiches and Vernors ginger ale. There would always be four or five picture books wrapped in red-checked cloth napkins, like gifts waiting to be opened. I'd randomly pick one and she would read it to me. Afterward, we'd lie on our backs and look up at the sky and call out names of things we saw in the cloud formations.

I looked again at the inside of the cup. "I don't see anything. Wait. It looks like a little house." I pointed to the side closest to her.

Violet pulled the cup toward her and glanced quickly inside, then shoved it back. "Yes, a house. But look next to the house."

I squinted my eyes and scanned the interior. "Sorry. What am I looking for?"

She stood and walked over to me. "The raven."

Ah, Poe's raven. Franklin must be rubbing off on her.

She said, "Not just a raven. A snake with the head of a raven."

I couldn't find anything, even though she kept pointing.

"It's there. See the beak and the serpent's long, dark body."

"Dark body? Thought we were only looking at the white part of the cup?"

"When something like this appears, you have to take notice."

There it was. Not like any flossy cloud design I'd ever seen. "What do the raven and the snake symbolize?"

For the first time, Violet startled when a branch hit the window. She began rubbing her thumbs and forefingers together in a repetitive motion.

By the pricking of my thumbs, something wicked this way comes.

She left my side in a hurry and grabbed an aquamarine shawl from a hook next to where I'd hung my jacket. She tightened it around her, then took agonizingly small steps back to the table, her toes pointed like a tenuous ballerina. "The snake represents falsehood or hostility and the raven is a harbinger of death or bad news. I've never seen the two together."

"Yes. But like you said, you only read the white part of the cup. What about the cute little house?"

"A house usually means change and success."

I stood. "Well, that's the fortune I'm going for. I'm sure what you're seeing is my past. I've had my fair share of death and falsehood in the past year."

I cleared the table and put my cup in the sink and turned on the faucet. *What a bunch of hooey.* With a tremor in my hand, I picked up the other alabaster cup at the bottom of the sink and looked inside, hoping to spy a "raven-snake"—thus proving the whole thing had been a parlor trick. But that wasn't the case. When I turned to go back to the table, I looked again at the weird appliance next to the stove. It had a star insignia with the words GEIL KILN circled around it. Of course. A kiln to fire her sculptures.

When I returned to the table, Violet had a white tablet of paper and a pen in front of her. She pushed them toward me. "You may be right. Perhaps the leaves were telling us about your past. I'm also proficient in graphography—handwriting analysis. If you write your name in script, I'll be better able to get a feel for the history of your spiritual self."

I wrote "Megan Barrett" in my best penmanship, trying to not let my hand drag across the paper. I'm a lefty and my pinky always gets slathered with ink. I handed the pad back to her, feeling like a bored sorcerer's guinea pig.

"Add today's date below."

I did.

"Now hand it to me." Violet moved her head from left to right. Then added a few clicks of the tongue.

"Well?"

"The *g* in Megan is very telling, as is the capital *A* in August. But I need to see more before I can do a proper assessment." She tore off the page with my signature and handed it to me. "Take this with you, and when you come back, bring other samples of your handwriting, an old note or even a canceled check."

How about a handwritten invoice for my design ser-

vices? I folded the sheet and put it in my shorts pocket. My stomach growled. I couldn't hear it, but I felt it.

Violet glanced at my midsection. "I have nibbles in the fridge. I can't believe we didn't lose power."

Of course, two seconds later, the electricity went out.

We sat for ten minutes before moving. The bad mojo from my teacup reading clung to me like the cloying, humid air. To kill time, I asked Violet about the history of Scrimshaw House, pushing the candle toward her so I could read her lips.

Violet had grown up in Sag Harbor. Since a child, she'd heard about the numerous sightings from ships in the harbor of Sarah Hollingsworth's ghost and mysterious lights in Scrimshaw House. Of course, what other lights could there be in an abandoned house but mysterious ones?

She told me about Sarah's love story with Captain Isaiah, and the building of their home—Scrimshaw House—as well as all the parties and dances at Captain Isaiah's brother's house, now the Bibliophile B & B. Then the tragic tale of Captain Isaiah's ship, *Manifest Destiny*, disappearing on what was supposed to be its last voyage as a whaler. Captain Isaiah had promised Sarah, because of the upcoming baby, that he was going to work with his brother on dry land. When Sarah learned of the sinking of *Manifest Destiny* she had a miscarriage and the next day threw herself off the point.

Violet said, "Sarah was a gifted portrait miniaturist. Sailors' wives and loved ones from Sag Harbor would come and sit for her. Sarah would send them away with portraits painted on chips of ivory or bone, a memento for the sailors to hang in their berths or stick in their pockets.

Sometimes the portraits would be mounted on miniature frames enclosed in glass, like the daguerreotypes that came out during the Civil War. The painted miniatures were a reminder of what was waiting at home when the sailors returned, months, sometimes years, later."

Violet stood and stretched her legs, then sat again. "Sarah even painted one of herself. It's in a locked case in the drawing room. They found it on the bluff after she threw herself onto the rocks. I've always wondered why the miniature wasn't with her husband when his ship went down and I swear I've seen her white form at Scrimshaw House many times."

I shivered in the now-oppressive heat. I had no idea of the time, because my cell phone had died a while ago, right after I'd texted Elle: *All okay. I'm with Mrs. Hollingsworth in the teahouse.* Violet told me earlier that she never brought her cell phone when she sculpted.

The storm weakened at the same pace as our waning conversation. I was willing to venture back to the Bibliophile B & B alone, but Violet wasn't going for it. She left me sitting at the table and went into the other room. Through the open door, I saw her candlelit silhouette on the bed behind the translucent screen. Violet flipped and flopped on top of the mattress, visions of ravens, snakes, and Sarah's ghost no doubt dancing in her head.

After an hour of dozing upright in a chair, I woke with a huge crick in my neck. The sky had turned dark. I got up and pulled the long wooden bench that was next to the sliding glass doors to the middle of the room. I removed the cushions from the bamboo chairs and placed them on top, making my own little bed. It felt as comfortable as if I were in a holding cell. Not that I'd ever spent the night in jail. Unless you counted that time I was digging through a pile of boxes on the curb in front of a Southampton estate and the gatekeeper called the cops. Doc, a retired Detroit coroner and my dad's best friend, was there to bail me out within the hour. If only he hadn't related my exploits to my father. Apparently, watching over me was Doc's assignment since he'd moved to Montauk.

Countless hours passed until Brenna came to our rescue. She stood outside the glass door in a black hooded raincoat, holding an electric lantern in her right hand and two others in her left. For a minute, I'd thought she was Sarah's ghost or the Grim Reaper.

After I let Brenna inside, Violet shuffled in from the other room.

Brenna stopped next to the table where Violet had lit a dozen sage-scented votives—something about clearing the bad vibes in the air. She placed the three lanterns on top of the table and said, "I've been in a tizzy worrying about you two." She went to Violet and gave her a big hug. "And you, Aunty, you knew the storm was coming. I suppose you were working on the Steinbeck and couldn't tear yourself away?"

Brenna must have seen my puzzled look. "Aunt Violet has been working on her John Steinbeck sculpture that will go in the Steinbeck suite. She is becoming quite famous in the Hamptons. Her pieces have won juried first place ribbons at local art shows and she also displays some of her work in Sag Art on Main Street."

"What an honor," I said, thinking about how I was supposed to fit the huge head into the suite's décor. "How's Jo?"

Brenna laughed. "I kept checking on her because you said she could be a terror. Every time I looked, she was fast asleep. I left her some of Catterina's kibble."

Brenna had told me she'd named Catterina after Edgar Allan Poe's real-life tortoiseshell cat. Poe never mistreated his cat, like the narrator in his story "The Black Cat" did of Pluto. In fact, Poe was a huge animal lover.

I asked how the inn had fared in the hurricane and Brenna said everyone was safe. With one exception: Randall McFee. Randall was one of Franklin's chosen guests. He'd been the authenticator of *The Heiress and the Light* before it went up for auction. Brenna told us Randall's Fiat was in the lot, but he hadn't returned to the Bibliophile. Until Elle told Brenna about my text message, everyone assumed Randall was with Violet or me.

Brenna handed each of us a lantern. "The inn lost power. The old emergency generator only provides enough electricity for the kitchen."

When I took the lantern, I noticed a tattoo of a skull with a knife in its teeth on the underside of Brenna's forearm. Brenna must have covered the awful thing with makeup and the rain had washed it away. I was surprised about the tattoo. It didn't coincide with Brenna's cozy bed-and-breakfast-innkeeper's persona and preppy style of dressing.

We made it down the hill from the teahouse without mishap. Brenna grabbed onto Violet's elbow for support and I followed. The desecration of flora and fauna, and a slew of downed trees, made it rough going in the dark.

Within sight of the inn, the front half of my tennis shoe got stuck under a log. I pitched forward and landed face-first in the bushes. I rooted in the underbrush for my lantern, stood, and went back to where I'd lost my shoe. I rolled the log to release it and the light from my lantern highlighted a small, folded piece of paper.

Brenna called out, "Meg, you okay?"

I stuck the paper in my pocket. "I'm good," I shouted back. I grabbed my shoe, then continued down the lane with one shoe on and one shoe off.

At the back entrance to the Bibliophile, Brenna and Violet stood next to two familiar figures holding lanterns: Elle and Detective Arthur Shoner of the East Hampton Town Police.

Elle ran toward me. Her short frame torpedoed into mine and she squeezed me like there was no tomorrow.

After Elle unglued herself and was satisfied I was in tip-top shape, I held my lantern at eyelevel and scanned the exterior of the inn. There were branches everywhere. A pear tree had collapsed the side veranda railing on the front porch. I aimed my lantern in the other direction and startled when I saw someone dressed in a white beekeeper's suit and hat standing next to the door to the greenhouse—the elusive Kortney Lerner.

Kortney Lerner was Franklin and Ollie's grounds- and beekeeper. I'd rarely seen her up close. Unlike her twin brother, Ken, the Hollingsworths' butler and concierge, Kortney didn't share meals at the inn. What was she doing in the middle of an eighty-degree night dressed as a towering Ghostbuster? I took a step toward her and she darted into the shadows.

Detective Shoner said something I couldn't make out. Even in the sweltering heat, he was dressed in a suit and tie. When he saw me looking at his mouth, he repeated, "Ms. Barrett, were you with Randall McFee?" He knew about my hearing loss.

"No. He wasn't at the teahouse with Mrs. Hollingsworth and me."

Elle introduced Detective Shoner to Violet and he asked her the same question. Clutching her shawl tighter to her body, she gave him the same answer.

He stepped closer. "When was the last time you saw Mr. McFee?"

I said, "I haven't seen him since last Friday. We shared cocktails on the veranda and talked about the upcoming book fair."

Violet said, "I haven't seen him since breakfast. Did you ask my husband?"

He said, "Who's your husband?"

I took a step toward the stairs at the back porch and said, "Franklin Hollingsworth. Do you think we could get out of this wind? I need to feed my cat."

CHAPTER

〜✦〜

FIVE

When we entered the Bibliophile, the smell of freshly brewed coffee lingered. I hoped Brenna had homemade pastries to go with it. Violet's nibbles had been exactly that. No wonder she was so thin.

Detective Shoner followed Brenna and Violet into the dining parlor. Elle and I planned to join them after we checked on Jo and I changed into clean clothes.

I opened the leaded-glass-panel door that led to the back vestibule. The design in the glass was a colorful geometric pattern that matched the floor tiles.

"Wow! These tiles are awesome!" Elle's ever-changeable chestnut eyes loomed large in her fine-featured face. "They're original nineteenth-century encaustic. Popular in the Victorian period and copied from medieval art," she recited in her Sotheby's voice. Before our stint at *American Home and Garden* magazine, Elle had worked at the Manhattan auction house.

We went up to the third floor and caught Miss Josephine

red-handed, or should I say red-pawed. Her claws were
caught in the not-so delicate weave of my first knitting
project—a crimson scarf made with size fifty knitting
needles. The scarf grew two feet every time I wore it. It
came in handy, even in August. Staying on Cole's yacht,
I'd experienced more than a few cool summer nights.

Because Jo's paws were otherwise occupied, I rubbed
her squishy belly. Jo and I had a yin-yang relationship—I
was yin, she was yang. We were two opposing forces in
the universe, with the occasional complementary intersection of affection—just enough to keep our relationship
interesting. Shadow couldn't exist without light.

While Elle played with Jo, I grabbed a pair of jeans and
a Detroit Tigers T-shirt from my suitcase and changed behind a Victorian folding screen. I'd found the screen on the
side of the road in Water Mill. After I'd beeswaxed the
screen's cherry wood frame and added vintage fabric panels in a pattern similar to those I'd seen at the Emily Dickinson Museum, I was confident I'd hit the mark. Never
thought the screen would be functional in the twenty-first
century. The only downfall about the loft space was I had
to go to the second floor to use the bathroom—it was just
a stumble down the stairs in the middle of the night away.

I said, "Feeding time."

Elle snapped into action. She covered the writing stand
with a painter's tarp, put her lantern on top, and moved it
next to the bed. I took out a mini-can of three-dollar organic gourmet cat food from my suitcase, opened it, and
placed it on Jo's special china plate. Along with Jo's adop-
tion papers came strict instructions for her dietary needs—
of which there were many.

After I put the plate on the writing stand, Jo stared straight ahead.

"Sorry, missy. I got caught in a little ole hurricane." I reached for her plate. "If you don't want it, I'm sure Catterina will."

Without blinking her eye, Jo swiped her left paw in my direction. After I backed away, she started eating. It didn't take her long to finish. Thirty seconds. Tops.

Elle laughed hysterically at the unfolding circus act. I shot her a dirty look. She was the reason I was saddled with the wayward pet. She and her sidekick, Detective Shoner.

I removed the tarp and moved the writing stand back under the window. Jo was already nestling on the bed. "So, why is your boyfriend, Detective Shoner, here?"

"I got your text that you were with Mrs. Hollingsworth and told Brenna. Brenna mentioned Randall was missing, so I called Detective Shoner. He was in Montauk, overseeing the evacuation."

"Montauk? Break it to me gently."

"The hurricane was almost a nonevent. The worst happened out at sea. But the East End Yacht Club got hit pretty hard. Sorry. I hope Cole's boat survived."

So did I. Especially since it was under my guardianship. "When you're talking about Detective Shoner, you can call him Arthur. I'm onto your little tryst."

Elle's cheeks were rosy. But not from makeup. She never used it. Elle was a connoisseur of all things vintage, even her hairstyle, which was cut in a pixie style emulating Scout's in the movie version of *To Kill a Mockingbird*. Her brown hair, freckles, and scrubbed face made her look like she was in her twenties, not early thirties. I quickly told her about my tea party with Violet, leaving out the whole "death and damnation" part. Stuff and nonsense.

I crossed the room and set my lantern on the dresser, opened the case to my hearing aids, and put them in.

Elle walked over and stroked the dresser's satiny top. "Do you believe I found this? Right in our 'hood. And I love that you filled the bottom drawer with Emily Dickinson's poetry books. Nice touch." I'd left the drawer slightly open to show the books. Elle pulled out the drawer, withdrew one, and held it to my lantern. "I wonder if this is a sign? This poem, 'The Heart Has Narrow Banks,' talks about a hurricane."

I said, "I love that poem. It's pretty amazing she uses the sea analogy, especially for someone who rarely, if ever, saw it."

"I was talking about the word 'hurricane.'"

Elle and I had taken a road trip to the Houghton Library at Harvard University in Cambridge, Massachusetts, stopping at every vintage and antique shop on the way—which numbered quite a few. We'd drooled over Emily's authentic circa 1785 cherrywood bow front chest of drawers with inlaid mahogany veneers. It was the same dresser in which Emily Dickinson's sister found piles of poems in the bottom drawer after her death. In Emily Dickinson's lifetime, only about eight to ten of her poems were published—all anonymously and without her permission.

I said, "I'm thrilled you found a similar dresser. The only thing I'm not thrilled about is the price you had to pay at Grimes House Antiques. Rita saw you coming. I feel bad because you're the one who had to shell out the cash."

Elle sat next to Jo on the bed and scratched under her white chin. "Have you received any payment from Franklin?"

"Not a dime." I said, as we headed downstairs.

A marble-topped "whatnot" table stood next to leaded-glass French doors leading into the dining parlor. On top of the table was a cone-shaped Victorian flower basket. Even though it was well past dinnertime, Elle and I had to drop our cell phones inside. The Bibliophile had a strict rule about dining with cell phones—don't.

We stepped into the room and Elle whispered, "It looks like we're just in time for the séance."

Violet Hollingsworth sat at one end of the table. The tapers in the candelabra in front of her dripped rivers of beeswax. Even though the temperature in the room was in the eighties, Violet still wore her gypsy shawl. My mind flittered back to our eerie tea party. Maybe the ravensnake was a precursor to Randall McFee's destiny. Not mine. I shivered and Elle gave me a questioning glance. I'd never let on to scaredy-cat Elle that I believed in omens—bad or otherwise.

Franklin Hollingsworth, owner of the Bibliophile and Violet's husband, wasn't seated at the table. He sat between two ornate mahogany glass-fronted curio cabinets topped with an assortment of sandwich glass. The curios weren't filled with china—only books. Every room at the Biblio-phile, with the exception of the bathrooms, had at least two locked cases of books. On top of one curio was a small desk lamp highlighting Franklin's shiny bald head. The lamp was attached to a thick orange extension cord that led to the kitchen. Reddish gray tufts of hair shot upward above his ears. With his thin mustache, he reminded me of the mayor of Munchkinland. And in pure bibliophilic style, Franklin wore round wire spectacles. He clutched a gilt clothbound volume in his right hand and in his left, an unlit pipe. The Bibliophile's guests, with the exception of Randall McFee, were seated on either side of an eighteen-foot-long mahogany table topped with a delicate Belgian lace runner. I'd found the runner in a box in the attic. An overnight soaking in my top-secret whitening potion had restored it to its original milky shade.

Brenna sat opposite Violet, stroking Catterina. The cat sat with perfect posture, pretending she wasn't interested in the humans in the room.

It was a scene from *The Age of Innocence*. But maybe that was because of the candlelight, along with the fact I'd just finished decorating the Edith Wharton suite. The majority of the furniture in the Bibliophile B & B had been in the Victorian since the mid–eighteen hundreds. Brenna had told me that after her grandfather died, his inheritance was split in half. Her Uncle Franklin bought out her father's interest in the Victorian, including its contents, and owned the inn and the land it sat on, free and clear. Her father, Ollie, used his money to build his castle and finance his stable of equestrian horses. Condemned and haunted Scrim-shaw House belonged to both brothers.

"Meg, we're so happy you and Violet survived the storm." Jordan Innes said. Her sparkly, almond-shaped eyes and long, glossy blue-black hair contrasted with her husband Hal's fair all-American look.

Hal and Jordan were staying in the Herman Melville suite. When I'd first met the couple, I'd been struck by how companionable they seemed. At meals, they held hands

under the table like newlyweds, which they weren't. Jordan
and Hal ran a used bookshop in Williamsburg, Brooklyn,
called Carpe Librum, Latin for "seize the book." Jordan
was the one who procured the majority of Franklin's acquisitions through her exclusive connections. She'd rented
a space at Sunday's Antiquarian Book Fair and graciously
promised to sell my John Steinbeck, *The Winter of Our
Discontent*, for me.

Hal got up and pulled out the two chairs to the right of
Jordan and we sat. After we thanked him, Elle reached for
the last pastry on the tray. I raised my foot to kick her, just
as she broke the almond horn in two and handed me half.

I had let my hunger think the worst of my sweet friend.

Hal said, "Meg, any sign of Randall while you were out?"

"I wish we'd been with him." I looked over at Violet.
Her gaze followed the flame on one of the candles. She
was tuned in to another dimension.

Hal Innes worked for the publisher who acquired the
rights for the manuscript from the F. Scott Fitzgerald Trust.
Hal would be the person transcribing *The Heiress and the
Light* into book form—a very prestigious assignment. Last
week, Elle overheard Hal and Franklin arguing. Hal
wanted to stay in the Fitzgerald suite, not the Melville.
Franklin didn't back down. The F. Scott Fitzgerald suite
was definitively Randall McFee's.

On the other side of the table, surrounded by seven empty
Chippendale chairs, was Allan E. Wolfstrum, America's pre-
mier spy novelist. Allan didn't have cooties; it was more that
his grand presence deserved the extra space. In the late '80s,
Allan Wolfstrum's books had topped the *New York Times*
Bestseller List the day they came out. Today—not so much.
He was still a force to be reckoned with, especially in the

Hamptons, where he'd spent over four decades in true Americanized James Bond style. In his late sixties, he had a long face with deep laugh lines that formed rutted parentheses on either side of his mouth. His thick dark hair glistened with hair product, accentuating the strands of gray at his temples. Allan was eccentric in his style of clothing—Hugh Hefner with more taste. Elle had sold him a few silk smoking jackets from her store. I'd contributed a basket of vintage ascots I'd found at an estate sale. Elle and I made a "BFF" for life. Allan had been so charming, I hadn't charged him a mark-up.

Elle's salesperson, Maurice, told me Allan had fallen on hard times. His hard times coincided with his divorce from his fourth wife, Nicole. Nicole was an award-winning actress and the star of the films *Twilight Mission* and *New Moon Mission*; Allan Wolfstrum had written the screenplays based on his books. Both movies were box office disappointments. There were even rumors that the Twilight Saga franchise went after him for plagiarizing their titles. It didn't matter in the long run. You couldn't make a good movie out of a bad book—or a catchy title.

In the divorce settlement, Allan lost his prized beachfront home in Southampton. Moonraker was an ultramodern beach house built in the 1970s in the shape of a missile. It had floor-to-ceiling glass walls on each of its six levels. The structure sat on rippled white sand, giving it a very moon-esque vibe.

Allan banged the table with his fist. "Well, what are we waiting for? Gather the troops and let's search the woods. This Randall fellow might need medical assistance." He adjusted his ascot and stood. He was what would be described in a book as "tall and lanky."

A lumbering voice from under the doorframe said,

"Allan, my man. Let the police handle the situation. That's what we pay them for."

Brenna's father and Franklin's brother, Ollie, had entered the building.

Ollie wasn't my cup of tea. I'd rather drink from the cup in the teahouse plastered with a ravensnake. Byron had confided that he'd once witnessed Ollie mistreating one of his horses. There were even rumors of steroid injections. Hurt an animal and you hurt me. It was hard to believe easygoing Brenna was Ollie's spawn.

Ollie had white hair that he wore in a military buzzcut and a larger than average mouth. His square face, strong jawline, and dimpled chin reminded me of a plastic action figure. Ollie's unnaturally white teeth looked fake. Maybe a horse had kicked him and knocked out his real ones.

One could only hope.

Brenna didn't even glance in her father's direction when he took a seat next to Allan. I'd often wondered what had happened to Brenna's mother. Elle said, fifteen years ago, Brenna had showed up on her Uncle Franklin's doorstep. Not her father's. Brenna had lived in the Victorian before its renovation, but once finished, she shared the rooms over the stables with the Lerners. I'd overheard Franklin tell Brenna she was free to stay in the Louisa May Alcott suite when it wasn't booked.

As I stuffed the last bite of pastry inside my mouth, Ollie aimed his flashlight at me. "Remember, Miss Barrett: gluttony is one of the seven deadly sins."

I started coughing. Jordan used the heel of her hand to tap me between the shoulder blades.

I choked out, "I'm good."

A gravelly explosion of wheezing hee-haws escaped Ollie's piehole—his version of laughter.

Ollie Hollingsworth wouldn't see me sweat—which I was profusely doing now because of the heat in the room. I wanted to get up and give Ollie a few of my own slaps on the back—hard ones. Our feud started a few months ago when I caught him trying to sneak out a two-thousand-dollar French rococo revival writing desk from the Edith Wharton suite to put in his "castle." I didn't have to go to Franklin about the theft because Brenna had stepped in. She spewed a few expletives in her father's direction. After his daughter's tongue lashing, Ollie's right eye had teared. Just when I thought I'd misjudged the guy, he peeled off his contact lens, blinked, then flicked it onto the nineteenth-century rug. Ollie's baby-blue iris turned muddy brown.

Just like his soul.

Detective Shoner entered the room from the kitchen, followed by Ken Lerner, the B and B's bellhop/concierge/handyman. Ken split his time between the Bibliophile and Hollingsworth Castle. Ken and his twin sister, Kortney, the property's bee- and groundskeeper, lived over the stables next to Ollie's eyesore.

Ken wheeled a mahogany cart topped with a sterling coffee service next to Franklin. No pastries. As if I would eat more in front of Ollie anyway. Ken was tall and stoic, maintaining perfect butler posture. His hair and goatee were a light shade of gray. I guessed he was somewhere in his early forties. He wore khakis and a white button-down shirt, but it was easy to picture him in a black-tailed waistcoat serving a formal dinner party. Ken was profusely sweating. As he poured coffee into a blue nautical-themed transfer-ware cup, a drop of sweat landed on the saucer. He added three cubes of sugar to the coffee and handed the cup to Franklin.

Franklin shooed him away with a flick of his pipe. "Leave me be." He continued reading the small book in his hand.

Violet turned in her chair. "Franklin, you haven't eaten all day. Let Ken give you some coffee and something to eat."

Franklin didn't even look up. "Stop hovering. I'm fine."

Detective Shoner said, "I'll take the coffee." He took the cup from Ken's outstretched hand and placed it on the table. "I think it'll be rough going tonight with all the downed trees on the property. It's possible a friend picked up Mr. McFee before the storm and he's safe." There were blue crescents under the detective's bloodshot eyes. If it wasn't for Elle, I doubted he would have come all the way from Montauk in a hurricane, even a small one.

Jordan Innes said, "I saw Randall at breakfast before the storm hit. We were sitting here at the table. He said he needed to get out for a while, to clear his head. He told me he'd just received distressing news. I tried to press him further, but he seemed distracted. A few minutes later, I went outside to make sure the Prius's windows were closed and saw Randall's Fiat parked next to our car."

Hal took Jordan's hand in his and gave her a quick kiss on the temple. I could tell that whatever distressed his wife, distressed him.

Detective Shoner stood. "Ok, let's form a search party."

As we were leaving the room, I whispered into Detective Shoner's ear, "Where is Kortney Lerner?"

He said, "Who?"

"Ken's sister, the groundskeeper. Wouldn't she be helpful in searching the property?"

"She sure would."

Detective Shoner went over to Ken.

Ken shook his head like he'd no clue where his sister might be.

Had I been the only one who had seen her earlier near the greenhouse in the beekeeper's suit?

Brenna stayed at the inn with Violet. Detective Shoner broke the search party into groups of three: Hal, Jordan, and Franklin; Allan, Ken, and Ollie; and Elle, Detective Shoner, and me. It took our group thirty minutes to get to Hollingsworth Castle, usually a ten-minute walk. It was rough going because of all the branches and small trees that littered the gravel lane. When we stepped into the clearing, we found that every interior and exterior castle light was on. Leave it to Ollie to make us sit in the inn without air-conditioning while his castle sizzled with electrical current. The brightness from the floodlights accentuated the loss of trees sacrificed in the making of the castle. Such a pretentious building. The exterior was faced in a gray faux stone, similar to the rocks on mountain climbing walls at amusement parks. There were two towers in the shape of rooks from a chess set. The double front door was big enough to let in all the animals that boarded Noah's Ark. All that was missing was a moat and drawbridge.

Elle and Detective Shoner checked inside the castle. I went into the stables. There were six gorgeous horses, one with a new foal, but no Randall McFee. I was happy to see the horses had hay and that their stalls looked clean. I met Elle and the detective back in a cobblestoned courtyard that was the perfect size for a jousting match.

Elle said, "Have you ever been in there? The place is colossal, but the only area with furniture is Ollie's bedroom suite. There's a table in the banquet room and a throne, of course. That's about it."

"No wonder he was trying to steal furniture."

Detective Shoner said, "He was what?"

Elle pointed to above the stable where lights were on. "Look. It's Kortney. She might know where Randall is."

Detective Shoner scurried up the outdoor staircase, just as Kortney Lerner stepped onto the landing. She was dressed in a men's T-shirt that barely covered her undies, exposing generous thighs. Her over-processed blonde hair looked like a tower of cotton candy after someone had taken an eggbeater to it. Apparently, wearing a beekeeper's hat didn't make for a good hair day. Detective Shoner stood nose to nose with her and asked a few questions. She shook her head in the negative.

Disheartened, we trudged back to the Bibliophile to meet the rest of the motley crew. Detective Shoner took Elle home, Ken and Ollie left for the castle, and Franklin and Violet went to their cabin.

When Hal, Jordan, Allan, and I entered the inn, Brenna was waiting with individual trays topped with her signature cheddar-and-herb cheese straws, grapes, and chilled Perrier to take to our suites.

CHAPTER

SIX

After a few hours' sleep, I woke on Thursday to find all twenty-three pounds of fat cat splayed across my chest. She peered down like she wanted to suck out my last breath, the long hair from her ears brushing against my cheeks.

"Okay. I'm up!" I sat and waited for the sway of the ocean, then realized I was on firm ground. I hoped the same wasn't true of Cole's yacht, the *Malabar X*. Thankfully, the B and B's power had been restored during the night. Now, with the sun shining through the window, it was hard to believe there had ever been a storm.

I filled Jo's GROUCHY CAT bowl with dry food and took her water bowl with me to the bathroom on the second floor.

All the doors along the hallway were shut, with the exception of Randall McFee's.

In the bathroom, I rinsed Jo's bowl and filled it with water. Then, on autopilot, I brushed my teeth, washed my face, and added blush and mascara. My eyes were bloodshot. It must have been from staring at the ceiling all night, worrying about Randall McFee. I'd woken in the middle of the night—or should I say morning?—after I dreamt that someone had locked Randall in Violet's kiln in the teahouse studio. When I finally opened it, only his ashes remained. Were dreams about kilns ever mentioned in one of Elle's dream-interpretation books?

I exited the bathroom and stopped to appreciate the glorious color coming through a fan-shaped stained-glass window at the end of the hallway. The construction crew had wanted to toss the window because two leaves on one of the lily pads were cracked. In my not so subtle way, I'd intervened. I got Franklin to send the window to an expert stained-glass artisan. Now I couldn't tell which leaves had been replaced.

As I walked toward the back stairway, the open door to the F. Scott Fitzgerald suite called to me. Like a homing pigeon to its roost, I stepped inside. I hoped to find Randall McFee asleep in his bed, but everything looked the same as when I'd decorated it in monochromatic shades of icy blue and white, keeping to the Art Nouveau/Art Deco feel of the time period in which *The Great Gatsby* and *The Heiress and the Light* had been written. The only addition to the room was an open suitcase on a luggage stand.

A sterling silver cigarette case, similar to one F. Scott might own, was still on the Deco nightstand. Instead of Fitzgerald's initials, this one was etched with *PSF*. The scrolling *P* looked very close to an *F*. The cigarette case had been a lucky find at a Long Island antique store in Huntington, when Elle and I were trekking back from Great Neck to Sag Harbor.

Great Neck, a real town below Gatsby's fictitious West

Egg, was where F. Scott Fitzgerald wrote the first three chapters of *The Great Gatsby* in 1922 at a not-too-shabby home he rented for two years on Gateway Drive. It was also where he wrote "The Unspeakable Egg," a short story that took place in Montauk.

As I was leaving the suite, I noticed the key to one of the glass doors of the barrister bookcase was in its lock. The door was ajar and there were a few empty spaces where books had once sat. I hoped my John Steinbeck book, *The Winter of Our Discontent*, was safe in the Melville suite with Jordan Innes. I locked the bookcase, put the key in my robe pocket, and glanced at the burled wood clock on top of the mantel. Should I continue snooping or bring Jo her water?

My maternal instinct took over. I ran up to the loft and placed Jo's water bowl in front of her.

Of course, she ignored it.

I changed into one of Elle's birthday gifts—a vintage '40s sundress printed with oversized magnolia flowers, then grabbed a pair of two-dollar flip-flops from my un-packed suitcase. I added pearl earrings that had once been my mother's and put in my hearing aids. The mirror showed a sunnier version of my reflection than most people were used to. I wanted to distance myself from the doom and gloom of the last twenty-four hours.

Before leaving Sag Harbor to check on my cottage and Cole's yacht, I opened both oriel windows so Jo could take advantage of the fresh air and cross breeze. I took a deep gulp of herb-laced air—lemon verbena and basil wafted up from Brenna's kitchen garden, two levels below. I made sure Jo had a full bowl of food and her favorite cat toy. The toy was in the shape of a miniature tiger filled with catnip.

It was true what I'd been told when I adopted her: She was afraid of mice. Even toy mice.

I had planned on doing a little more digging in the F. Scott Fitzgerald suite, but when I got to the second floor, Jordan Innes was coming out of the Herman Melville suite.

"Meg, you look lovely. Where are you off to?"

"I need to see if there was any hurricane damage to my cottage."

"You live in Montauk, right?"

"Yes."

"Lucky you. Although, I wouldn't mind living in Sag Harbor. I wanted to ask you what you thought of the dress I picked out for Saturday night's party?"

"Of course." I stepped inside the Melville suite. I wanted to hit the road, but a few minutes wouldn't hurt.

"I must compliment you and Elle for the fantastic job you've done on all the author-inspired suites. The first time I walked into the Melville suite, I felt like I was entering the cabin of a whaling ship moored at the wharf in Sag Harbor."

I smiled and remembered a quote from Herman Melville I'd read in a book about Melville's home, Arrowhead. It had inspired me to give the suite a ship-like feel: "My room seems a ship's cabin; and at night when I wake up and hear the wind shrieking, I almost fancy there is too much sail on the house and I had better go on the roof and rig the chimney."

I said, "It was the easiest of all the rooms. Brenna told me most of the furniture and smalls had originally been in Scrimshaw House, from Captain Isaiah's old whaling days." I was proudest of the rectangular mahogany desk topped with a double quill-filled inkwell and scrimshaw carvings, some depicting sailors on tall ships harpooning whales. I walked over to the desk, noticing that the curved, dagger-shaped letter opener that was supposed to be next to an antique whale-oil lamp, was missing. The opener was on the macabre side. The end of its mahogany handle had a brass embossed head of a tattooed native with an open mouth and fang-shaped teeth. It had reminded me of the cannibals mentioned in Herman Melville's semiautobiographical book *Typee: A Peep at Polynesian Life*. *Typee* was Melville's first book based on his adventures on a South Seas island. He'd jumped overboard from a ship he'd signed onto to escape floggings and disease and ended up in a hotbed of cannibalism. The letter opener was on the desk last Friday when Jordan and I talked about the book fair. Maybe Elle had taken it out because it was too disturbing. It would be something she'd do. I made a mental note to ask her.

I glanced at the two bookcases flanking the fireplace in the outer room of the suite. They were filled with volumes I knew Melville would have had in his library: Shakespeare, natural history, and anything to do with travels on the open sea. There were also two books by James Fenimore Cooper, of *The Last of the Mohicans* fame. Not many people knew Cooper married a local and lived in Sag Harbor for a few years in the early 1800s, even investing in a whaling enterprise. The books *Precaution* and *The Sea Lions* were written while Cooper lived in Sag Harbor, and Franklin had included them in the locked bookcases. One of Cooper's iconic characters, Natty Bumppo, the hero of his Leatherstocking Tales, was based on real life Sag Harborian Captain David Hand. Most of the books in the Melville suite came from Franklin's family's bookshelves and trunks that had once been stored in Scrimshaw House.

Jordan held up a silver-sequined draped-back dress.

"It's gorgeous," I said.

Her ebony hair and sparkly dark eyes were a perfect match to the dress. "I still need a long necklace that I can knot, and perhaps a cigarette holder."

"Why don't you stop over at Mabel and Elle's Curiosities? I'm sure Elle or Maurice will have the perfect accessories."

We chatted for a few minutes about the book fair. After noticing the missing books in the F. Scott Fitzgerald suite, I was happy to see the spine of my Steinbeck book, *The Winter of Our Discontent*, in a box next to a freestanding Newton old-world globe. The box held other first editions to be sold at the Antiquarian Book Fair on Sunday. One of them, *To Kill a Mockingbird*, caught my attention. I bent to touch its clear-plastic-protected spine.

Jordan said, "It's yours. I'll give you a good price."

"I have a feeling it's well above my means."

"When I sell the Steinbeck for you, I won't charge a commission. Then you can put the proceeds toward the *Mockingbird*."

"I'll keep that in mind. Thank you. Who's minding the store while you're in Sag Harbor?"

"We closed shop. Business is slow until the colleges in the area begin classes. Actually, business has been slow for the past year."

"E-books?"

"No. It's more the skyrocketing rent in Williamsburg. If I had to depend on Carpe Librum to pay the bills, I'd be in bad shape. That's why Hal's job putting the Fitzgerald into novel form is so important. We don't just *need* the money, we need the prestige that comes with it so he can procure future jobs." She walked over to the box of books. "I brought an early *Moby-Dick* I had hoped to sell to Franklin, but I think he blew the motherlode on *The Heiress and the Light*. Did you know Melville mentioned Sag Harbor?" She gingerly removed *Moby-Dick* from the box and opened it to a bookmarked passage. "'Arrived at last in old Sag Harbor; and seeing what the sailors did there; and then going on to Nantucket, and seeing how they spent their wages in that place also, poor Queequeg gave it up for lost. Thought he, it's a wicked world in all meridians; I'll die a pagan.'"

"Ha," I said. "That quote would be fitting today when talking about all the excesses in the Hamptons."

"I'm going to ask thirty-five thousand for it at the book fair. It's the first American edition. Not in the best shape but better than a reading copy."

"Wow. Can I touch it?"

"With your pinkie finger."

She was probably kidding, but I wasn't sure, so I tapped it with my pinkie and thought I felt a shock from all the symbolism scholars and readers, myself included, had gotten from *Moby-Dick*—the nature of good and evil, class and society, and the existence of God. "Thirty-five thousand. Did you find it at an estate sale?"

Jordan laughed. "I wish. No, I got it from another dealer. I paid thirty-two thousand four years ago. Did you know in Melville's lifetime he only made three thousand dollars on *Moby-Dick*?"

"Amazing."

"I also have a copy of Steinbeck's *The Grapes of Wrath* to place next to your *The Winter of Our Discontent* at the book fair."

"How much are you asking for it?"

"Twenty-three thousand. It's a signed first edition."

"So is mine."

"You're right, but there is one distinction: Steinbeck added a flying pig illustration—a rare illustration he only drew for his very close friends."

"Hmmm. A flying pig."

I asked her again about her last conversation with the missing Randall McFee and she repeated what she'd told us last night.

What had Randall been upset about? And where was he?

I said, "I'd better run. See you at dinner."

"It's a date."

When I stepped out of the room, Brenna was coming out of the Edith Wharton suite.

I walked over to her. "How do you think the suite turned out?"

"It's wonderful. I can't wait until we have our first paying customer. I know how much went into the renovation and Uncle Franklin has all his money tied up in books and, of course, *The Heiress and the Light* manuscript. We have bookings all through fall, so that's a good sign. I better get downstairs. My dough is ready for its second kneading."

I looked at her large hands. Maybe that was the secret to her fabulous breads.

I walked into the Edith Wharton sitting room. There were two open bookcases, with only a few books and small items reminiscent of the period during Wharton's fame. The two chairs I'd placed in front of the fireplace were carved and covered in thick goldleaf. The needlepoint seat cushion had pastel scenes showing a pair of cherubic angels holding a banner. Edith Wharton and Henry James had been contemporaries. I could picture them sitting in front of a fire, discussing the social season or politics of the day.

Unlike the other suites, which had a fireplace in the outer room only, the Edith Wharton suite also had one in the bedroom. I specifically chose the two-fireplace suite because, of all the authors Franklin chose, Edith Wharton, a connoisseur of the gilded age, would expect nothing less than the royal treatment.

I stepped inside the bedroom. There was a gold bed tray on the bed, topped with a single bud vase, and Wharton's book *The Age of Innocence*. Edith Wharton had rarely written at the ornate desk in her library at The Mount, in Lenox, Massachusetts. She'd spent most of her mornings writing in bed, looking out through the French doors at the pine trees and mountains for inspiration. When I researched authors and their desks to find the appropriate décor for each suite, I found that, while Edith Wharton liked to write in bed, Ernest Hemingway, Virginia Woolf, Lewis Carroll, and Charles Dickens usually wrote standing up.

I went to a lacquered French bookcase enclosed in glass. There were definitely books missing. *The House of Mirth* and *Ethan Frome*. The first person I thought of was Ollie Hollingsworth. I wouldn't have put it past him, but it didn't fit his MO, and the one time I'd been inside his castle, I hadn't seen one book. Although, he'd steal sterling silver or a piece of furniture in a heartbeat. I quickly looked around at the grandeur of the room and didn't see anything else overtly missing, even after opening the mirrored wardrobe decorated with elaborate gold mounts and Sèvres-style porcelain plaques. Brenna said the wardrobe had once belonged to her grandmother when the room had been hers.

I left the room and met Jordan at the top of the curving main staircase that led down to the first floor's front vestibule.

"You haven't seen the letter opener I had on the desk in the Melville room, have you?"

Jordan stopped on the step above me. "No, I haven't. Do you think someone stole it? Brenna told me it came from Scrimshaw House. She said the whaling museum wanted it, because it had belonged to Captain Isaiah. It was there on Tuesday, because Hal actually used it to open some mail. I'd ask Ken. He's the one who just made up the room."

We went down the curving staircase and when we got to the entrance of the dining salon, Jordan asked, "Aren't you coming in?"

"I'm going to skip breakfast. I need to head to Montauk."

As I passed the dining salon, Brenna called out, "Meg Barrett, get in here!"

A few minutes later, I left the Bibliophile with sustenance for the road: a cup of coffee and four chipotle pork quichelets in cupcake wrappers.

By the time I got to the parking lot, only two quichelettes remained.

Randall McFee's car was still in its same spot.

Where was he?

CHAPTER

SEVEN

It took an hour and a half to get from Sag Harbor to Montauk. It had less to do with the hurricane and more to do with typical Hamptons summer traffic. Usually, I didn't mind snailing my way through the quaint villages and hamlets: Bridgehampton, Wainscott, East Hampton, and Amagansett, occasionally sighting celebs walking casually down the tree-shaded streets, but I had to make sure my cottage hadn't suffered storm damage. I also needed to go to the East End Yacht Club and check out the *Malabar X*.

My first stop would be 221B Surfside Drive. Cole had a dozen more antique sailing yachts at his disposal, but I only had *one* cottage. Finally.

In Montauk, a line of people—a mixture of the Hamptons elite and vacationing families with small children carrying sand buckets or wave boards—waited outside Paddy's Pancake House. Through the Jeep's open window, I inhaled the scent of suntan lotion and briny ocean air.

When I pulled onto Surfside Drive, I understood why my property wasn't littered with debris from yesterday's storm. Byron Hughes stood shirtless next to a sleek black pickup. There wasn't advertising on the side of his truck because he didn't need to advertise. Byron's architectural landscape services were legendary. He received clients by word of mouth only. Usually, that mouth was filled with a silver spoon.

Byron raised a gnarly rhododendron bush over his head. The bush's roots rained black dirt onto his sun-streaked, sandy brown hair. He tossed the bush into the bed of the truck, turned in my direction, and gave me that smile of his. I'm not one to swoon over tan, muscular, glossed with sweat, washboard-cut abs, but swoon I did.

A guilty breeze blew a vision of Cole Spenser's arctic blue eyes in front of my heated face.

I got out of the car and walked to Byron.

He said, "I wanted this to be a surprise. I was at the Clawson estate and thought I'd check on your bungalow."

"Well, that was extra wonderful of you, kind sir." I sat against the bumper of his truck.

Byron came and sat next to me. He needed to put a shirt on. It was steamy. And not from the humidity. The last two times I'd seen him, and in every society photo, he'd worn a suit.

"My pleasure, m'lady. I have to get back to the Clawsons', but I have a proposition for you."

"Umm. Sounds good. Yes."

"Ha. You don't even know what I'm asking."

"You've never led me wrong in the past."

"Would you like to go to the Artists and Writers Charity Softball Game at Herrick Park?"

I tried not to jump onto his lap. "I'd love to. Never been."
The East Hampton Artists & Writers Charity Softball Game
had been going on for almost seventy years. And when
they said artists, they meant famous actors and artists, and
when they said writers, they meant the cream of the crop.
The money raised at the event went to local Hamptons
charities.

In 1948, the first softball game was played in the front
yard of an artist, who lived in Springs. In the late '40s and
early '50s, Springs was the place to live if you were an
artist. Willem de Kooning and Jackson Pollock were a few
of the local artists who'd attended the game, along with a
couple of prolific writers. After the game, the participants
would partake in potluck dinners and bring-your-own bev-
erages, mostly alcoholic. The game became so popular, it
had to be relocated to Herrick Park in East Hampton. In
the sixties and seventies, the game expanded to include
musicians, actors, writers, and politicians. Past participants
included President Bill Clinton, Gloria Steinem, John Irving, Paul Simon, and Neil Simon—just to name a few.

I couldn't wait to see who would show up this afternoon.

After a not-so-brief kiss good-bye, Byron left, promising
to pick me up at the Bibliophile B & B at two.

A bluestone path led to my cottage. I'd thought of naming it but realized it was a bit pretentious to name a six-
room bungalow. The bungalow was perched on a cliff, with
views even Cathy and Heathcliff would envy. It hadn't been
an easy feat to own such a perfect home. But I'd have done
it all over again. Well, maybe I'd have left out the part
where I almost got murdered.

I climbed the steps to the wraparound porch and realized the keys to my cottage were back at the inn. I was

usually more organized, but with the distraction of Randall McFee's disappearance, the missing books from the F. Scott Fitzgerald and Edith Wharton suites, and the missing cannibal-head letter opener—along with my lack of sleep—I was understandably fuzzy-headed.

Half of the porch had been screened-in, fulfilling my wish to replicate the cozy beachfront rental I'd lived in for two years. The portion of the porch that wasn't screened-in had a wooden swing that faced the Atlantic. I peeked in every window. All looked calm and serene. I went down the porch steps and followed the short path to a covered wooden landing and looked out at the Atlantic. My property was only a mile from the rental I'd lived in for two years, but it seemed farther, more remote, mostly due to the height of the cliffs closer to the lighthouse.

To my west, more than the usual number of surfers were out at Ditch Plains Beach. The wave swells were still enormous from the hurricane. I couldn't wait for the day I could climb down to the ocean and explore the beach in front of my property, but that would have to wait until the stairs were finished. I'd thought of renting rock-climbing gear. After an accident I'd had on the cliffs, that wouldn't be happening too soon.

Patrick Seaton's beachfront cottage was also a mile west. The solitary author was my sometime poetry pen pal in the sand. Georgia, owner of The Old Man and the Sea Books, told me Patrick had subleased his cottage for the summer. Patrick Seaton's cottage and my former rental were nearer to town. That meant more summer tourists and less alone time on the beach. A majority of year-rounders, including myself, anxiously awaited the exodus of tourists after the Labor Day weekend. Soon we'd reclaim our sleepy little town and get back to our cathartic walks along the shoreline. For now, I felt blessed with the current trifecta: August, Montauk, and the sea.

I looked at my watch. I'd better get going. I still needed to check on the *Malabar X*. But first I would check out the rest of my property. The owner of the large cottage next to mine lived in California. In a few months, the owner's mother-in-law was coming to take up residence.

My next project, after I finished at the Bibliophile, was to decorate my neighbor's cottage with items from the packed attic. The owner promised that whatever I didn't use was free to go into my cottage or future clients' homes. I couldn't wait to go through the overfull attic's contents piece by glorious piece.

The path on the western side of my cottage brought me to the gate leading to my walled-in garden. Against the exterior walls were small trees, sturdy shrubs, and flowering hostas: hardy plants that could survive the cold and wind. Vines had been planted on both sides of the walls. Clematis, Boston ivy, and wisteria climbed a vintage pergola. I walked through the worn, shuttered saloon-style doors. The organized chaos of the interior of my walled-in garden had been created by Byron on paper and me in dirt. After all the grand plans I'd had for my garden, I'd settled on small and cozy. Like the rest of my life, cozy seemed the way to go. A few of the plants and garden ornaments had survived for a hundred years. There were tubs of double impatiens and begonias tucked in hidden spots. I'd originally told Byron I didn't want any annuals—too much upkeep—but because it was my first season, I'd agreed the garden needed some color until my perennials had a chance to take over. Phlox, heirloom roses, and coral bells had been planted for the sunny center of the walled garden, along with zinnias, black-eyed Susans, coneflowers, and rose of Sharon. My favorites—delphiniums—had already bloomed and most likely would have to be replanted next spring. Delphiniums were a biannual for some people, but an annual in Montauk.

There were peekaboo cutouts on the western and eastern cement walls of the garden offering magnificent ocean views. I'd placed an iron bistro table and two chairs in front of each cutout. When I got paid for my work at the Bibliophile B & B, I planned to buy an ultraexpensive set of garden furniture from Gildreth's in Bridgehampton to place in front of the outdoor fireplace. I had the inside scoop that the furniture would be included in their end-of-the-summer sale.

Byron had rebuilt the crumbling fireplace that came with the property and had even added a mantel. The fireplace was next to the back garden gate that led to my folly. He'd wanted to add a built-in Viking grill but seemed disappointed that I was fine with the small Weber that Elle had given me. I wasn't much of a cook, as my disappointed father would attest to. However, I liked grilling summer veggies: season, brush with olive oil, and melt a little herbed goat cheese on top. Three to four ingredients were usually my maximum for any recipe.

In the northeast corner of the walled-in garden, Byron had created a covered nook. He'd added an antique cement bench he'd excavated from nearby Morrison Manor. I'd bought thick cushions for the bench and transformed the nook into my favorite shady spot to read books and sip wine while sheltered from the wind. The alcove also provided a romantic candlelit make-out spot to share with either Cole or Byron.

After a year and a half of knowing him, I still found
Cole mysterious and moody. His company had him on the
high seas six months of the year. In the time left over, he
worked on his vintage yachts in North Carolina or came
to New York to be with me. Byron, on the other hand, was
fun and upbeat, but sometimes I felt like he was the same
with me as he was with other women. I wanted a glimpse
of his dark side or a chance to see him vulnerable, like I
had with Cole. Byron was more accessible during the
spring and summer. But the rest of the year he was out of
town, consulting on grand landscaping plans for his clients'
winter estates.

Byron didn't own a home in the Hamptons. He stayed
free of charge in the guest cottage of Suzy and Beauregard
Schlesinger's estate in East Hampton. Cole lived on one of
his boats and Byron in someone's guesthouse. No terra
firma for either of them. I liked having roots and someplace
to call my own. Apparently that wasn't important to the
men in my life.

With all the work I had to do at the Bibliophile B & B,
I hadn't had much time to concentrate on my love life, or
my garden's finishing touches. When Elle and I searched
for items to fill the author suites at the Bibliophile, I'd
purchased some fun decorative items for my garden. I was
good at multitasking when it came to vintage shopping.
Half of Elle's carriage house in Sag Harbor was filled with
garden ornaments, statues, out-of-the-box plant containers,
and even a triple-tiered cement fountain topped with a
statue of Demeter, the Greek goddess of the harvest. My
mind flashed to Violet and her bust of John Steinbeck.
Naturally, that thought segued to the ravensnake and the
missing Randall McFee.

Through the back garden gate, I followed the path to my folly. It was hidden behind tall spikes of bamboo. I'd turned the Queen Anne structure into my light and airy interior design studio. I removed the key hidden under a wrought-iron Chinese cricket and walked inside. Everything inside the folly was as I left it. Through rippled nineteenth-century glass at the back of the folly, I saw that even my herb garden flourished.

Happy everything seemed status quo, I locked the folly door and hid the key. There was a definite spring in my step as I walked to my Jeep. And it had a lot to do with my upcoming date for the Artists & Writers Charity Softball Game.

CHAPTER

EIGHT

On my way to the yacht club, I stopped at my favorite shop in Montauk, Rockin' Retro, for a few packs of Violets. Rockin' Retro sold vintage and vintage-inspired nostalgic gifts. I kept my purse stocked with at least two packages of the floral-tasting candy. Byron had once commented on how he loved their smell on my breath. Funny, so had Cole.

When I got to the East End Yacht Club, a security guard stood at the entrance. He glanced at the parking sticker on my windshield, then asked what slip I was going to. When I told him, he instructed me to pull to the side. Ten minutes later, I was escorted to the *Malabar X*—or should I say the now-shared slip of the *Malabar X* and *Misty Morning*. Both yachts were joined at the waist, tilted toward each other like Siamese twins. Compared to the other boats in the cove, the *Malabar X* had fared pretty well. But if I sent Cole a photo of his yacht, I had a feeling he wouldn't consider himself too lucky.

Two people were standing, or should I say leaning, on the deck—Doc Heckler, retired Detroit PD coroner and my father's best friend, and Sullivan Cooper, Doc's best fishing buddy. Sully was also the one who'd found the F. Scott Fitzgerald manuscript *The Heiress and the Light* hidden in a pile of his great-grandfather's papers.

The last time I'd been with Captain Sully, I'd caught my first striped bass. But that was back when he was five million dollars poorer.

Back in the day, Sully's great-grandfather had been mogul Carl Graham Fisher's yacht captain. Carl had been a wealthy Gatsby-era automobile and real estate tycoon. In 1925, Carl bought nine thousand acres of land in Montauk and built Montauk Manor, a rambling Tudor-style hotel. Fisher's goal had been to turn the easternmost tip of Long Island into a huge resort, like he'd done with thousands of acres of swampland in Florida. He'd planned for Montauk to be "The Miami Beach of the North." When the stock market crashed in 1929, so did Fisher's dream. He lost his fortune and ended up living in a modest cottage in Miami Beach. Not a major hardship, in my opinion. They even named an island off the coast of Miami after him. Today, Fisher Island had one of the highest per capita incomes in the United States. Carl's vision had been sound, his timing had just been off. And now that I called Montauk my home, I was selfishly thrilled Carl Fisher's plans had fallen through, leaving my town untamed and unspoiled.

Doc's familiar face, with its neatly trimmed white beard, leaned over the railing on the leeward side of the boat. "Meg. Don't come on board. It's not safe."

"Then what are you two doing on there? This is a disaster. What am I supposed to do?"

Sully hopped onto the dock and walked over to me. "Don't worry. We're on it. We just have to wait in line. As you can see, the yacht club got hit pretty hard. The *Malabar X* is tenth on the list for the towboat, and that's after I used all my clout with the commodore." He smiled, exposing two perfect rows of white teeth.

I breathed a sigh of relief. Sully had a way of simplifying things and instilling confidence in highly charged situations— the opposite of worrywart Doc, my father's snitch.

Sully helped Doc off the *Malabar X* and I went to him and kissed his furry cheek.

I said, "Tenth in line?"

"You wouldn't even be on the list   " Doc said.

"I'm not being ungrateful. I just   bearer of bad news. You know how   his yachts."

Sully said, "Touchy? I'd be touc   America's Cup winner latched ont   middle of a hurricane. The teak i   logged, and if we don't pump the water, all the metal will corrode."

I was happy to see Sully had stopped dying his hair shoe-polish black. Instead of him looking older, his salt-and-pepper hair made him look ten years younger. With his classic looks, tan sea-faring face, and five million dollars in the bank from the sale of the Fitzgerald manuscript, Sully made a fine figure of a man. He'd better be careful or he might get snared by one of the lionesses at Friday Night Bingo at the American Legion Hall.

I sighed. "Well, it's just a boat."

Sully and Doc both inhaled and looked at each other. Then they shook their heads.

Doc said, "What if your precious cottage got swept into the sea? It's 'just' a cottage."

"Point taken. Well, let's keep this between us until we know more about the damage."

Doc, Sully, and I decided we needed a good meal at Mickey's Chowder Shack to lift our spirits. I was a happy camper, because Mickey's was my favorite Montauk hole-in-the-wall eatery.

When we walked into Mickey's, my mouth dropped. It was packed to its rafters. The same rafters from which kitschy pirates' heads made out of coconuts hung. With all the nouveau, high-end food establishments on the ocean side of Montauk, I'd thought Mickey's would remain undiscovered.

Erin, Mickey's granddaughter, seated us immediately. A trio of female East Hamptonites, who might as well have had COUTURE ADDICT stamped on their foreheads, grumbled as we passed by. None of the usual fishermen and fisherwomen, wearing baseball caps and drinking yard-long lagers, were slumped over the bar.

We all ordered the fish special, and for the twenty minutes it took us to scarf it down, we forgot about the hurricane damage to the *Malabar X*.

I took my last bite of fish pot pie and wiped my mouth. "Randall McFee is missing."

Sully said, "The guy who authenticated my Fitzgerald manuscript before I sold it at East Coast Auctioneers?"

I put my napkin on the table. "The same."

Doc poured hot sauce onto the stub of a shrimp fritter. "What do you mean by missing?"

I explained about Randall's car still being in the lot of the Bibliophile and Randall's strange conversation with Jordan Innes.

Doc said, "Does he have any family? A wife? Kids?"

I didn't know, but I made a mental note to check with Brenna. "It's possible when I get back to the inn, he'll be sitting at the bar, safe and sound, holding a bee's knees."

Doc said, "What's a bee's knees?"

"It's a drink from the 1920s Jazz Age era, Sully's great-grandfather's era. Ever since Franklin bought *The Heiress and the Light,* it's become his five o'clock cocktail staple. Gin, honey syrup, and fresh lemon juice with a twist. Quite tasty."

Doc raised his white eyebrows. I would always be underage in his eyes.

Sully filled his takeout box with leftovers. I couldn't remember one time I'd had leftovers from Mickey's.

He said, "Oh, I know all about Jazz Age cocktails from my great-grandfather's ship's dining log. Let's see. There's the southside—gin, sugar, and lemon with muddled mint. The Mary Pickford—light rum, pineapple juice, grenadine, and cherry juice. And my great-grandfather's favorite, and possibly one of Fitzgerald's, a French 75—gin, lemon juice, powdered sugar over ice, then fill the glass to the rim with champagne."

I licked my lips. "They all sound delish. Nice watch, Captain Sully."

Sully smiled.

Doc said. "A Rolex Submariner, only twenty-seven thousand. Sully rolls in the big leagues now."

"Not exactly true," Sully said. "I got a good deal on it. Always wanted one. The rest of the dough is in the bank. It felt like I'd won the lottery after I sold *The Heiress and the Light*. But don't worry, I'm aware of all those stories about the curse of lottery winners, how they either end up dead or lose their families and all their winnings."

I rubbed the goosebumps on my arm.

Erin came over and placed a plate topped with a large slice of apple pie and a wedge of sharp cheddar cheese in the center of the table. She took three forks out of her apron pocket and plunked them on the plate. "On the house." She winked at Sully. "Even though I know you can afford it."

We, her adoring fans, blew kisses in her direction, then each grabbed a fork.

Erin's sister, Tara, was my arch nemesis and Cole's former teenage girlfriend. Recently she tried to clone my Cottages by the Shore business into her own interior design company. Too bad she'd been fired by her first client. I hadn't seen or heard from her in ten months—which was a good thing. I was sure Tara lurked somewhere in the Hamptons, up to her usual thievery like she'd been charged with in the past. I didn't ask Erin about her sister. I let sleeping dragons lie.

I said, "Sully, tell me more about your great-grandfather and his connection to Carl Fisher and F. Scott Fitzgerald."

"All I'm sure about is my great-grandfather's connection with Carl G. Fisher. I don't know of any relationship between Fisher and F. Scott Fitzgerald, but everyone agrees the timing was right for them to have met. The dedication on the manuscript was addressed to my great-grandfather. Something along the lines of: 'To Captain Cooper, a fine chap and great skipper. Hopefully, this try at penning a story about the magic of Montauk and its people will become a favorite on America's shelf. As always, much gratitude for your service on Carl's and my travels around the East End Egg and beyond. Your friend, Scotty.' The personalized note in F. Scott Fitzgerald's handwriting is what sealed the deal with the auction house, proving the manuscript was mine to sell. Seeing as I am the last of the Coopers, the rest is history."

I said, "I know 'The Unspeakable Egg' was a short story written by F. Scott Fitzgerald in the *Saturday Evening Post*, and that it takes place in Montauk. I wonder if there are similarities. It's a charming tale about two spinster sisters living in Montauk, their wayward great-niece, and a mysterious hermit on the beach."

Sully took a forkful of apple pie and cheese. I did the same.

He mumbled, "I'll have to check it out."

I threw in the fork. I couldn't eat another bite. "Did you read the manuscript before you sold it?"

Doc said, "Of course he read it. And I did too. Who do you think told him to contact East Coast Auctioneers?"

I said, "Did you make a copy? I'd love to see it."

Sully threw a fifty on the table. "No, I don't have a copy. The auction house wouldn't allow it. I had to hand over the manuscript and my photocopy to them. The Fitzgerald Family Trust already had a photocopy from Randall McFee after he authenticated F. Scott's handwriting on the title page, and his notes and whatever else he needed to do to prove it was legit."

I said, "Was any of it handwritten or was it all typed?"

"Typed," they both said at the same time.

Sully said, "There were lots of cross-outs, arrows, and notes in the margins."

Doc added, "It was like a religious experience to hold those pages. I don't understand why F. Scott Fitzgerald didn't have it published. There are some parallels to *The Great Gatsby*, but the story is more about romance, less about obsession." He patted his white beard with a napkin. "I actually liked it as much as *The Great Gatsby*. It doesn't have a narrator like Nick Carraway in *Gatsby*. You feel closer to the action. I was also surprised at Fitzgerald's level of comedic timing. His sardonic wit shines through loud and clear." Doc looked at Sully. "But there still was the running theme of how too much money can change your perspective on reality."

Sully let out a robust laugh. "Funny, Doc. I don't see you complaining about the new titanium fishing rod and reel I bought you."

Doc said, "'So we beat on, boats against the current, borne back ceaselessly into the past.'"

I said, "The last sentence in *The Great Gatsby*."

Doc said, "Yep."

I couldn't wait to read the book. Perhaps Franklin Hollingsworth would hand out copies at Saturday's gala.

CHAPTER

❦

NINE

The traffic from Montauk to Sag Harbor was horrendous. I doubted I'd have time to change clothes for my date with Byron. If the game took place in Detroit, cutoffs and a T-shirt would have been the perfect attire for the Artists & Writers Charity Softball Game. In the Hamptons, you never knew the proper dress code. Spectators in this 'hood could really glam it up, especially in the summer. But that wasn't me—never would be. The exception would be Saturday night's Jazz Age party at the castle to kick off the book fair. Two months ago, I'd chosen the perfect sheath dress to wear to the book fair's gala. Elle's salesperson, Maurice, helped me choose the gem from Elle's guestroom-turned–closet of vintage clothing and accessories. We'd decided on a beaded and fringed flapper dress in turquoise. It even had a matching headband.

When I pulled into the parking lot of the Bibliophile B & B, the clock on my dashboard said two twenty. No time to change.

Byron sat on the trunk of a white Maserati convertible. His NY plates read, BYRON 1. Now I knew what 1, 2, and 3 were: Maserati, Ford F-350 pickup, and Range Rover. Was there a BYRON 4?

I parked next to the Maserati, noticing Randall's Fiat was in its same position.

Byron came over to the Jeep and chivalrously opened my door. He took my hand and I climbed out. I leaned into the hollow of his neck and smelled soap and a touch of sandalwood.

Byron was dressed appropriately, per usual. He said, "I almost gave up. Thought you'd forgotten."

"Me. Never. You know Hamptons summer traffic."

"We'd better hit the road. I don't want to miss the first pitch."

"Neither do I." I'd read in *Dave's Hamptons* that Britain's top movie heartthrob, who happened to have the same intense blue eyes as Cole, was pitching for the Artists team. And the pitcher for the Writers team was no schlub either—just the top horror and suspense writer of all time, rumored to have a wicked underhand. The Artists & Writers Charity Game coincided with weeklong Hamptons events. The East Hampton Library hosted a Hamptons Authors' Night, a chance to listen to bestselling authors talk and get signed copies of their recent books. Franklin Hollingsworth had purposely coordinated this week with the first annual Sag Harbor Antiquarian Book and Ephemera Fair, hoping to attract some top celebs and literati who were attending Authors' Night and the Artists & Writers Charity Softball Game.

Byron opened the passenger door to the Maserati and I got in. Before closing the door, he leaned in and kissed me roughly on the lips—perfectly roughly. I had a case of the vapors and had to fan myself with my hand. When I turned my head toward the back of the inn, I saw Kortney, the groundskeeper. She was watching us from behind the wrought-iron fence. Byron reached over and secured my seat belt.

I said, "That's not a good sign. Are you some kind of crazy driver?"

"Not crazy, but I have been known to enter a race or two."

"Of course you have. Is there anything you don't do?"

Kortney was still peering at us. "What's the deal with Kortney the beekeeper? She's watching us right now."

Byron turned to look and all I saw was a flash of retreating white. "Never mind about Kortney. She's harmless."

The interior of the Maserati had soft white leather upholstery. I thought of all the ketchup stains on my Jeep's tan gearshift. This car wouldn't be practical for my lifestyle but was perfectly suited for Byron's. Maybe when he ate his fries from McDonald's he used the Range Rover? Or God forbid, he didn't use ketchup. We'd only been to top-rated restaurants. I'd have to take him to Mickey's Chowder Shack and see how he fit in.

Byron's foot was heavy on the gas pedal. Riding in his convertible was like riding on the back of Cole's Harley. It was hard to carry on a conversation, especially if you wore hearing aids.

He found a few shortcuts and we arrived in time for the "Star-Spangled Banner." We stood behind the chain-link fence, held hands, and watched the start of the game. Halfway through, Byron abandoned me to help out at the scorekeeper's table. It was just as well. There were so many female clients coming over to talk to him, it was hard to concentrate on the game.

After he left, I sat cross-legged on the grass near third base, arranging the skirt of my sundress as demurely as possible.

The game was a hoot. Everyone was low-key, even the spectators, with one exception. Next to me on a lounge chair was a bedazzled and bejeweled over-the-top wife or girlfriend of one of the players. Accompanying her were twin teacup-sized dogs yapping like windup toys inside their purse-sized Louis Vuitton crates. I wished I could flip the latches on their cages so they could breathe fresh air and not remain caged parakeets on the dry, dusty ground. I was all for dogs of every size and breed, but I didn't think they were meant to be a fashion accessory. The woman either talked on her cell phone or preened in front of the drone camera that hovered at the edge of the baseball field. I wasn't about to tell her the camera was only for capturing aerial views of the softball game, not celebrity pics for the glossies.

The last time I saw Cole's dog, Tripod's huge Saint Bernard size hadn't stopped my cat and him from bonding. I really thought the two of them were going to pack a little knapsack filled with catnip and liver treats and saunter off into the sunset. When Jo stayed on the *Malabar X*, I'd hoped her doggie boyfriend's sea legs would have rubbed off on her. But she'd hated every minute on the yacht. Tripod traveled the ocean with his master through all kinds of weather; pretty amazing for a three-legged dog.

When the teams switched places at the top of the last inning, I walked over to a food truck selling local bottled Lighthouse iced tea and bought a Montauk Mango. Gourmet food trucks were a staple in the Hamptons. Today there were three trucks parked on the grass. They offered everything from fresh lobster rolls to flank steak tacos with wine-glazed caramelized onions. I was still full from Mickey's but was tempted to try the barbeque duck sliders.

As I walked back to the field, I looked inside the cap

from my iced tea. Like another popular brand, it provided a fun trivia question: "What do you call a flock of ravens? Answer: An unkindness of ravens." A sooty cloud covered the sun, and I was chilled in the summer heat. If Byron decided to take me out for Chinese, I wouldn't open my fortune cookie. A ravensnake might pop out.

I made it back to the game in time to witness Allan Wolf-strum, the Bibliophile B & B's very own spy author, hit the game-winning home run for the Writers team. Final score: Writers 3, Artists 2. After the game ended, Allan walked toward me. I thought he was coming to say hi, instead, he addressed a woman standing behind me. She wore a floppy white hat that not only covered her head but also both shoulders. Two-thirds of her face was hidden behind dark-tinted sunglasses.

Allan said, "Nicole, what the hell are you doing here?"

Nicole, top-tier actress and Allan's ex-wife, took off her hat and pushed her Gucci-emblemed sunglasses onto her head. The crowd oohed. Nicole was as stunning in real life as she was on the screen. She had emerald eyes and mahogany hair streaked with shades of amber. Her hair color changed with her movie roles. So far, I'd never seen her in an unflattering shade.

She squinted at Allan. "I've been rooting Paulo on."

"Paulo the Peruvian polo player? What is he, about eighteen? That's rich!" Allan's face turned a mottled red. He stuck out his lower jaw so his bottom teeth covered his top lip, piranha-style. Then he whispered something menacing into Nicole's ear.

This was a side of genial Allan I'd never seen.

When Allan noticed me, he said, "Meg. What do you

think of my softball performance?" He added a chuckle, but his expression remained hard.

"Excellent. And I love the way you're dressed. Quite the dandy for a rough-and-tumble softball game."

His straw Panama hat had a snazzy plaid band. He took it off, then bowed toward me. "I have a rep to uphold."

I didn't want to say, *Yes, but it's eighty-five degrees, and your white linen blazer with its plaid silk pocket square and long patchwork plaid pants might be a bit much.* In all fairness to Allan, when he hit his homerun, he'd left his jacket and Panama hat behind.

Allan looked over at Nicole, who was now signing autographs. *If looks could kill . . .*

I was relieved when Byron came over.

He handed me a cup of Gatorade, then shook Allan's hand, "Great homer, my man."

Allan beamed at the compliment. "I've been playing for years and that was my first hit. Meg, you must be good luck." He made sure Nicole was looking and put his arm around my shoulders and squeezed. It wouldn't have been a problem, but I'd forgotten sunscreen and was worried my blistered flesh might stick to his blazer.

Byron didn't even notice my grimace. His focus was on Nicole.

He said, "Hey, Nic."

She opened her mouth to speak and swayed slightly backward. Apparently, Byron made her swoon, like he'd done to me. I stepped out of Allan's embrace and slipped my arm through Byron's, letting Nicole know who was boss.

Nicole said, "Hey, yourself. It's been a while."

There was an awkward pause, and I could tell by Allan's

expression that he didn't know Byron and Nicole knew each other.

Nicole walked toward a tanned young man who must have been Paulo, the polo player. The crowds parted like she was royalty. Nicole kissed her Latin lover. It was a longer than average kiss and a little too public for someone known to the press as a very private person. Was the display for Allan's or Byron's benefit?

A few minutes later, Nicole and her boytoy strolled arm-in-arm toward Newtown Lane, where a limo waited. Nicole didn't seem to be hurting for money. But if what Maurice had told me was true, Allan Wolfstrum was.

Allan left us without a good-bye and scurried toward his ex-wife.

Byron said, "Come on, Meg. It's tradition to hit a few balls before they pack up the equipment."

He took my hand and led me to home plate.

A young guy wearing a navy-insignia T-shirt loaded equipment into a large duffelbag.

Byron called out, "Tim, how about throwing us a few pitches."

Us?

"Sure thing, Mr. Hughes." He dug in the equipment bag, took out two mitts, then handed a catcher's mitt to a pimply teenage boy with braces.

Tim went to the pitcher's mound and the kid crouched behind home plate. After a few practice throws and catches, Tim called out, "Batterup!"

Byron took his stance. Instead of jeans, I wished he'd been wearing those stretchy pants the major-leaguers wore. Of course, on the first pitch, he hit it out of the park. The ball landed in the IGA parking lot.

Byron walked over and handed me the bat. "Your turn."

"I can't. I'm wearing a dress."

"Thought you were a Detroit Tigers fanatic? You're going to let a little dress stop you from taking a swing?" He tugged on the thin spaghetti straps.

"Okay, buster, you asked for it."

He handed me his bat.

I went to home plate and took my position: elbows up and rear end pushed out.

Byron shouted, "A lefty! Hit it outta the park!"

I didn't hit it out of the park. But I did belt it into left field. Byron said, "Run."

I looked at him. "Run? You didn't run."

He repeated, "Run."

So I ran.

I was almost to second base when Tim charged toward me, the softball peeking from the top of his glove. I slid underneath his mitt and my flip-flopped foot touched second base.

I heard Byron yell, "SAFE!"

My other flip-flop flew in the air and whacked Tim above his right eye. Good thing all the spectators had left the park, because the skirt to my sundress was bunched up above my thighs.

When I hobbled over to Byron, he was ready with bandages from an open first aid kit. He applied them to both of my elbows. I was proud of my boo-boos. But I had to wonder which type of woman Byron really preferred— tomboy me or glamorous beauty Nicole Wolfstrum? I heard my mother's voice: "Just be yourself and don't worry about others' perception of you."

After we helped Tim collect the equipment, we got in the convertible and headed back to Sag Harbor.

CHAPTER TEN

In Sag Harbor, Main Street was crowded with summer tourists. The centuries-old Early American downtown was lined with galleries, restaurants, and boutiques. Back in the day, from the mid-1700s to the mid-1800s, the view at the end of Main Street would have been a port full of tall ships. Today there was a marina where multimillion-dollar yachts and sailboats docked.

Byron waved to a couple coming out of The American Hotel. Did he know everyone in the Hamptons? The American Hotel was one of the oldest hotels in the United States, and a top dining destination. It was built in 1824 as a boarding house and still had its original Gothic Revival columns. Similar to the Bibliophile B &B, it had fallen into almost irreversible ruin before a smart native Long Islander renovated the building in the 1970s and opened it as a restaurant. The red-brick façade with its white-painted trim reminded me of the old hotel/saloons in the Wild West. There was a balustered porch on which you could spot summer diners who at various times included presidents, governors, singers, actors, yachts-men, or plain folk who wanted a top-rated meal or a bottle of wine from the eighty-five-page wine list.

Because of all the traffic in town, Byron was forced to drive at a safer, slower speed. I told him how pleased I was with the way his landscaping plans had come to fruition at my cottage. Instead of only ten months of ownership, the grounds looked like they'd been restored to heirloom status. I also asked if he had an inside track with anyone on Mon-tauk's zoning commission. He said he knew someone and he'd call them in the morning.

I hated discussing money with people I dated, but I had to ask, "When you completed your landscape plans for the Hollingsworths', did you get paid on time?"

"Franklin paid me for his share, but Ollie still owes me for plans I drew up that he didn't go along with. He wanted some-thing on a much grander scale. Why? You haven't been paid?"

"No. I've put my invoices into Franklin's mail slot with copies of my receipts, but he's never acknowledged them."

"That explains it. Brenna pays all the bills relating to the Bibliophile B and B."

"And Violet doesn't mind?"

"The only thing Violet might mind is all the money Franklin's invested in his books. I take that back. I don't think Violet cares about the money he's spent on books, more the time they take him away from her. Violet leads a pretty solitary life in her teahouse studio."

"How about Violet and Ollie? Does she get along with her brother-in-law?"

He said, "Like the rest of us, I think she could take him or leave him."

I looked at Byron's profile. His jaw seemed locked tight. I was happy he shared my dislike of Ollie Hollingsworth.

I said, "I could definitely leave him."

We passed the Sag Harbor Whaling & Historical Museum, a former Greek Revival mansion built by one of the town's most prosperous citizens during the height of the whaling industry. The front door had a huge whale bone on either side of its frame and a decorative blubber-spade wrought-iron rail that followed the roofline. Inside, a circular skylight shone down on a magnificent spiral staircase painted white with wood-carved moldings in a wave motif.

The traffic let up and the Hannibal French House whizzed by in a flash of white. The elaborate Italianate-style mansion with twisted baroque columns and fleur-de-lis trim over the upper windows had been built by one of Sag Harbor's premier whaling and ship-owning families around the 1830s, then enlarged in the 1860s.

We turned onto Hollingsworth Avenue.

An ambulance, fire truck, and an East Hampton Town patrol car with lights flashing, stood in front of the Bibliophile B & B.

Byron parked on the street, and we got out and sprinted toward the inn. A uniformed policewoman tried to stop us from entering the area beyond the front gates.

Detective Shoner called out, "It's okay. Let them in."

Elle came scurrying over. "Isn't this terrible?"

I looked at the Bibliophile. I didn't see a wisp of smoke.

Detective Shoner joined us. "Kortney, the groundskeeper, found Randall McFee's body."

"Body? As in dead?" I looked at the nearest ambulance, hoping I was wrong.

A single tear trickled down Elle's freckled cheek. "Yes."

Byron put his arm around me. "What happened?"

Detective Shoner said, "Kortney Lerner was checking on the grounds near Scrimshaw House and saw Randall McFee's body on the rocks below."

Bile rose. Randall McFee had been lying helpless, perhaps still alive, when we'd searched the grounds. How had we missed finding him? I tried to remember who'd searched the area near Scrimshaw House. "Does Franklin know?"

The detective wiped his brow with a handkerchief. "Yes."

Beyond the ambulance, Franklin sat on an Adirondack chair, holding his pipe. He looked like a specimen from the House of Wax. Violet, Brenna, Hal, Jordan, and Ollie stood next to him. I didn't see Allan. He was probably in East Hampton, stalking his movie star ex-wife.

Byron stayed until after Randall McFee's body was loaded into the ambulance. The paramedics hadn't covered Randall's face like they did in crime dramas. He had no marks that I could see, which told me he must have fallen backward off Widow's Point.

I voiced my theory to Detective Shoner. He didn't seem interested and went to the back of the ambulance and pulled up the body bag to cover Randall's face, then shut the back doors, and the ambulance pulled away.

Before Elle and Detective Shoner left in Detective Shoner's Lexus, I ran over and stuck my head in the open passenger-side window and told them about the missing books in the Edith Wharton and F. Scott Fitzgerald suites.

Elle said, "When it rains, it pours. I'll call First Fidelity Mutual."

I watched them pull away. Detective Shoner and Elle

made a good couple. Elle deserved to be happy and, of course, I was happy for myself because I liked the security of having a homicide detective as a friend of a friend, even if he could be a bit dismissive at times.

I wondered if Randall McFee had a girlfriend? He'd never been married. Had he suffered? Would he still have been alive if we'd found him last night? And how bizarre that he'd fallen on the same spot as the resident ghost, Sarah Hollingsworth.

Brenna came out on the front veranda and I walked over to her. She said, "I gave Uncle Franklin one of my sleeping pills and sent him to the John Steinbeck suite to rest. I've never seen him so distressed. He has a bad heart and a pacemaker. It runs in the family." She thumped at her chest. "Aunt Violet is in the drawing room drinking tea. Come join us."

"I will. I have to get Jo's cat bed from the back of the Jeep first. That twin bed isn't big enough for the two of us. And I have to feed her."

A few weeks ago, I'd ordered a king-sized mattress for the Emily Dickinson loft but I had to send it back and order a queen because it was too tall for the low door frame leading up to the third floor.

I said, "The boat I was staying in was damaged by the hurricane. I'm willing to pay for my room and board. Or you can deduct it from my bill."

"Of course you can stay without paying a cent. You can even stay in the Edith Wharton if you want?"

"Oh no. Not with my cat. The queen bed is supposed to be delivered on Monday. Thank you. Shouldn't you clear it with your uncle first?"

She said, "He won't mind," then she went inside.

* * *

Next to my Jeep was Randall's Fiat. I walked around to the front passenger door and opened it. I got inside and searched the glove compartment for a registration or insurance ID and found both. I wanted to find Randall's home address. When Detective Shoner had asked Brenna if Randall had filled out any kind of registration card, she'd said no. His family needed to be notified. I took a photo of each with my cell phone then put them back in the glove compartment. There was a receipt in the drink holder for a signed FedEx envelope addressed to Randall McFee from an address in Key West, Florida. I stuffed it in my pocket. Perhaps it had come from one of Randall's relatives?

When I went to the back of the Jeep to get the cat bed, I thought about Randall's senseless death. I decided to forgo bringing Jo's bed up to the loft. Tonight, I'd welcome the close comfort of my grumpy cat. Sleeping alone seemed too sad. I went inside and ran up to the third floor. I fed Jo, but instead of her inhaling her food, she took her own sweet time to finish. Then I went down to the F. Scott Fitzgerald suite—Randall McFee's suite.

In the Fitzgerald sitting room, I walked over to the desk and looked at the 1920s-era Cartier sterling picture frame with a photo I'd copied of F. Scott Fitzgerald from his Princeton days. His blue eyes, blond hair, and Nordic good looks reminded me of Jordan's husband, Hal, the man who would put *The Heiress and the Light* into print form for the Fitzgerald Family Trust's publisher. Next to the photo were a vintage Montblanc pen—Fitzgerald's favorite—and an old Remington strike typewriter. Fitzgerald might have used a similar model when typing his manuscript *The Heiress and the Light*. Would a handwritten version show up someday? It had only taken eighty-plus years for the typed manuscript to appear.

Franklin had told me Randall McFee was chosen as the authenticator of *The Heiress and the Light* based on his stellar reputation. The last manuscript he'd authenticated was an Ernest Hemingway, now published as the novella *Before the Scourge*. The scourge was a woman, and even though the novella bordered on the masochistic side, it had jumped to number one on the bestseller list. It was possible some authors didn't want their unfinished works published. I hoped no one ever published my sophomoric college journal cataloging my dismal attempts at finding love in Manhattan after moving from Detroit.

I looked at the bookcase where earlier I'd noticed the missing books. There didn't appear to be any more missing.

Detective Shoner had said Randall's death was an act of nature, but I couldn't help but feel something was off. Randall had been found near Scrimshaw House. What was he doing that far from the Bibliophile in the middle of a hurricane? Then I remembered I'd been traipsing around in the storm like a fool. It could have been me on that stretcher.

I riffled through Randall's drawers, looking for information on his next of kin, but found nothing. Then I got down on all fours to look under the desk for something that might have fallen. All I found was a white Apple laptop charger. Where had his laptop gone?

ELEVEN

When I walked into the drawing room, Brenna told me Violet had already left for her studio and planned to stay the night in the teahouse because she couldn't bear to be so close to where they'd found Randall's body. Brenna made sure Violet took her cell phone with her.

I sat in an armchair facing the fireplace. The fireplace screen was faced in a petit point tapestry depicting a woman dressed in a hat and cape looking out at the harbor where a whale had been harpooned. The line leading from the harpoon was tethered to a whaling ship. The detail was amazing—there were even small silk threads of red for blood from where the whale had been speared. The mantel held an assortment of nautical-themed Staffordshire figurines and scrimshaw carvings. Over the fireplace was an oil painting showing a tall ship caught on rough seas, the sky dark and ominous with zigzags of lightning highlighting a

Moby-Dick-sized sperm whale. The name on the ship was *Manifest Destiny*, Captain Isaiah Hollingsworth's ship.

With a shaky hand, Brenna poured me a cup of tea. Unlike Violet, she offered honey. I took the dainty Royal Aynsley floral teacup and saucer from her and placed it on the cherrywood serving cart to cool.

Brenna sat on the fainting couch. "I want to go ahead with our tea in the greenhouse tomorrow at three. Make it a small gathering in memory of Randall. I talked to my uncle and he seems all for it."

"I think that's a fantastic idea to have a memorial tea."

"I've never believed in ghosts. But I'm sure when the public finds out where Randall's body was found, it will be all over the papers. And we haven't even opened yet."

"There was a hurricane. Surely people won't blame the inn. How well did you know Randall?"

"He's been Uncle Franklin's guest since he authenticated *The Heiress and the Light* manuscript. I don't think many people know this, but Randall and I went out on a few dates. He was such a gentleman, prim and proper when he was working but knew how to whoop it up in his off time. I can't believe he's gone. I didn't see a future for us, but I did count him as a close friend."

I'd seen Brenna talking alone with Randall on more than one occasion. He'd been about fifteen years older than her. Maybe a replacement father figure for Ollie? I couldn't blame her. It was hard to picture prim and proper Brenna whooping it up. Then I remembered the ghastly tattoo on her wrist. "Did Randall have any family?"

She fingered the jade beads at her neck. "I'm not sure. He never talked about anyone. And, as I told Detective Shoner, he hadn't filled out a registration card. No one has.

Randall, Jordan, Hal, and Allan aren't paying guests." She took a sip of tea. "They're just my uncle's book people."

After I finished my tea, I went to the mantel to investigate a small locked wooden box with a glass top. Inside was the miniature self-portrait on whale bone of Sarah Hollingsworth that Violet had told me about in the teahouse. Sarah was a natural beauty. Her glossy chestnut ringlets were held back in blue ribbons at either side of her pear-shaped face, her skin appeared translucent, her eyes the color of the sky, open and innocent with youth. Sarah's pink rosebud lips looked ready to speak. *What did you want to say, Sarah?*

I faced Brenna. "I hate to bring this up now, but I think some of the books in the guest suites are missing. The Melville and Wharton, to be exact. It might be a good idea to get the insured list from First Fidelity Mutual."

She gave me a strange look, like I'd overstepped my bounds. It wouldn't have been the first time. Catterina came into the room and sat patiently at Brenna's feet. Brenna unfolded a white linen dinner napkin that had been on the sofa's arm and placed it next to her. Catterina jumped up and sat staring at me. What impeccable manners. I needed to take a page from Brenna's playbook and apply it to Jo.

Brenna said, "It would have to be on the QT. We haven't even officially opened yet. Plus, I don't want to worry Uncle Franklin. He has a bad heart. He thinks of books like they're his children."

"I already mentioned it to Elle. And one other thing—I hate to bring it up—but I have a list of all the money I'd laid out for my Cottages by the Sea work and I'd really appreciate reimbursement. I've been giving my bills to Franklin but was told you take care of the finances."

Franklin had apparently been standing in the hall out-side the room. He stepped inside. The hair above his ears came to perfect points and his spectacles were off-kilter. "Brenna, write Ms. Barrett a check immediately. I've for-warded every receipt Ms. Barrett's given me. Why hasn't she been paid?"

Brenna's face pinked. "I, uh, I've just been busy." She turned to me. "I'll write out a check now and slip it under your door." Her cell phone rang and she put the phone up to her ear. After a few seconds, she covered the bottom of the phone and asked, "Meg, do you mind taking Uncle Franklin to the cabin? I'll bring him some food in a half hour."

"Of course." I went over to Franklin and took his elbow. He blinked a few times, apparently the aftermath of the sleeping pill Brenna had given him. He let me lead him out the back entrance, and we walked a short distance to the cabin.

He said, "It's time for my bee's knees."

"It sure is. I'll even join you." I needed something stron-ger than tea. "Do you have the fixings in the cabin?"

"Of course, Ms. Barrett."

I'd never been inside the cabin or his book vault. From what I'd learned from the original blueprints framed in the keeping room, the cabin had started out as a homestead for a pilgrim family who'd come to Sag Harbor. Later, the cabin became the servants' quarters and, after that, the kitchen for the Hollingsworths' federal-style eighteenth-century main house, later turned Victorian.

The exterior of the pre-revolutionary-war cabin was built as a simple "colonial half house." It was painted white with a low-pitched roof and a three-bay side entrance and was one of the last surviving examples of early colonial architecture in Sag Harbor.

When we walked inside, I almost had to duck under the doorway. I was five foot seven; how did Brenna's six-foot frame manage in the low-ceilinged room? The smell of pipe tobacco permeated the wide wood-planked walls, floors, and ceiling. There was a primitive hearth and brick fireplace.

Franklin took a seat in one of two wing chairs in front of the hearth. The décor in the cabin was minimalist. The layout reminded me of my old rental in Montauk, but I'd managed to fill mine with items that made it feel cozy. There was one large main room which included a galley kitchen. A step-back cupboard, a small desk, a table with two ladder-back chairs, and a pair of wing chairs were the only furniture in the room. The kitchen area had a wood-paneled refrigerator and microwave. There was a small vintage gas range that looked like a potbellied stove with copper trim. Violet and Franklin took most of their meals at the Bibliophile. Or Brenna hand-delivered them to the cabin.

I said, "I hoped to see some of Violet's work in here."

"Violet's sculptures are commissioned or sold in the gallery in town."

"Brenna told me the Steinbeck bust was going in the suite at the Bibliophile."

"We'll see. I told her we might not have room."

Talking about statues and writers reminded me of the life-sized statue of Henry Thoreau at Walden Pond in Massachusetts. Franklin and Violet's cabin was similar to Thoreau's—not as small as Thoreau's ten-by-fifteen-foot cabin, but the furnishings were similar. In Thoreau's cabin, there were three chairs at his table, not two. At Walden, a card on the wall above the three chairs had a quote from Thoreau: "One for solitude, two for friendship, three for society."

Franklin directed me to the bottom of the primitive step-back cupboard for the fixings to make our bee's knees. I'd helped Brenna make them on more than one occasion.

When I brought the cocktail over to Franklin, he was fast asleep. His snore alternated between a kettle's whistle and a piggy's snort. His pink lips opened and closed, their depth of color contrasted with his chalky face. I took an antique coverlet from the adjoining wing chair, folded it, and used it as a pillow for his drooping head.

My father's detecting genes kicked in and I took advantage of Franklin's loud snoring to check out the rest of the cabin. There was a small bathroom with a pedestal sink, a claw-foot bathtub, and even a large shower. It looked like they'd converted one of the bedrooms into a bathroom. When the cabin was the main house's kitchen, the bathroom would have been an outhouse.

When I walked into Franklin and Violet's bedroom, there was still no glimpse of Violet's presence. How many nights did she spend at the teahouse, and did Franklin ever stay with her on the mattress on the floor? The bedroom was filled with books, floor to short ceiling, some even stacked in the tiny fireplace. A small closet was mostly filled with Franklin's clothes.

I looked out the small back window. Catterina was torturing a mole. Maybe she wasn't the sweet, perfect cat everyone made her out to be. Jo would never torture a mole. She'd probably run for the hills if she saw one.

There was a door in the bedroom that led to a covered annex going to the old smokehouse, which Franklin had converted into a room-sized safe. The one-room structure held Franklin's rare books, including the F. Scott Fitzgerald manuscript. Over the past few months, all my hints about being invited inside had been ignored. Maybe I just didn't fulfill Franklin's snobby bibliophilic standards.

I put my hand on the doorknob and turned. A shrill alarm went off. I covered my ears to keep my hearing aids from popping out.

Franklin scurried into the bedroom and slid open a wooden panel. He punched in a code, and when the alarm quieted he said, "What are you doing in the bedroom, Ms. Barrett?"

"Ummm. I heard a cat crying. It's Catterina. I was going to let her in."

Franklin readjusted his spectacles and walked to the window.

I prayed Catterina would still be there.

"There's no access to the outdoors through the passageway to my book vault. Plus, Catterina has never cared about coming inside the cabin before."

"Well, she was crying for something." I pointed out the top of the glass door leading to the covered annex connecting the cabin with the book vault. "Is that where you keep the Fitzgerald?"

"Yes, it is. Let's finish our cocktail and you can be on your way."

We sipped our bee's knees. I let Franklin talk about Randall McFee and all the times they'd shared discussing *The Heiress and the Light*. Franklin drained his glass and asked for another. Brenna gave him a one-drink maximum, plus she'd given him a sleeping pill earlier. I ignored his request and got him talking about his best book or manuscript purchase. He told me about the time he'd flown all the way to London with Jordan Innes then back again the same day, to snag a letter written by Nathaniel Hawthorne to his former classmate at Bowdoin College, Henry Wadsworth Longfellow. The letter had found its way into some English earl's collection. Now it was safely ensconced in Franklin's book vault. It wasn't polite to ask how much he'd paid for the letter, but I had a good imagination. It felt like Franklin and I were kindred spirits. I understood better than anyone what it was like to be on the lookout for that perfect item. I'd never flown across the Atlantic for an antique, but if I had Franklin's money, I'd do it in a heartbeat.

After I rinsed out our cocktail glasses and put them back in the cupboard, I had to ask Franklin if he'd thought about cancelling the book fair's opening-night party because of Randall.

"He would be the first to say we should go on with the party and the show, Ms. Barrett. He was very proud of his work authenticating *The Heiress and the Light*. My niece is putting together a small memorial for him tomorrow afternoon. I think he would have liked that, being surrounded by books for his final send-off."

Carrying a tray of food, Brenna walked into the cabin. She placed the tray next to Franklin's chair. "What have you and Meg been up to? Do I smell gin and honey?"

"We each had a cocktail. But only one. Right, Franklin?"

"Only one. But I wouldn't mind another," he said.

"I'm sure you wouldn't. First, eat your dinner. Then we'll talk."

Franklin seemed in good hands, so I said good-bye and headed to the inn.

When I went up the stairs to the back veranda, Ken stepped out of the door. "There is cold cucumber soup, avocado BLTs, and pear Charlotte on the sideboard. Brenna didn't serve a hot dinner tonight because of what happened. Also, there's some iced tea in the silver urn."

"Thank you. This is so tragic."

"Yes, I'd thought we got off easy with the hurricane. Apparently not."

"Your sister must be traumatized from finding Randall's body."

"It was quite a shock."

"Did your group check the area around Scrimshaw House last night?"

Ken gave me an indecipherable look, but his tone said everything. "Yes. We did."

"I didn't mean anything. Just wondering."

He stood a little straighter and stuck out his goateed chin. "I hope you aren't inferring we did a shoddy job of searching." He turned and strode toward the stables, slamming the gates together after he passed through.

CHAPTER

TWELVE

The dining room table had been set for a formal dinner, with blue-and-white transferware bone china displaying a tall ship at sea and sterling monogrammed *H* silverware on a starched white linen tablecloth. In the center of the table, a huge blue-and-white Chinese ginger jar held a bouquet of white roses and lime-green hydrangeas. There were two silver candelabras on each end of the long table and individual crystal salt cellars for each guest. I counted the place settings. Brenna or Ken had included Randall McFee—wishful thinking, sadly gone awry.

I stole a tray from under a sterling tea set on the sideboard. On it, I put my avocado BLT, cucumber soup, a generous bowl of pear Charlotte, and a glass of iced tea. This was the second time Brenna had made pear Charlotte, which consisted of honey syrup–soaked lady fingers layered with poached pears and whipped cream. It was so good the first time I'd had it that I had Brenna copy the recipe from one of her vintage cookbooks to pass on to my father.

I took my tray out to the front veranda and sat on one of three wicker sofas. Hollingsworth Avenue was quiet. The Bibliophile B & B was the largest house on the street. The other homes were meticulously taken care of, most painted gleaming white in the Greek Revival style. If it wasn't for the occasional car passing by to remind me, I felt like I was back in the nineteenth century. Scrimshaw House was also a Greek Revival from the nineteenth century, Sarah Hollingsworth's century. I didn't want to think of Sarah, because she reminded me of Widow's Point and Randall's death.

I ate my cold but delicious food quickly and stood. Out of habit, earlier, I'd put my cell phone in the basket outside the dining salon. I went inside and retrieved it. There were two phones in the basket. Mine and someone else's. The second phone's battery was dead. I put it back in the basket. Could it be Randall McFee's? In the morning, I'd ask Brenna who it belonged to.

After I brought my tray and dishes to the kitchen, I went out the back door. The Hollingsworth property was so vast, I'd never been to the boathouse. I was ready to head in the direction of the harbor to look for it when Allan Wolfstrum came toward me from the parking lot.

He sauntered up to me with his usual swagger. "Franklin called me. I can't believe McFee ended up at the bottom of Widow's Point."

"A tragedy. I'll always wonder if we could have saved him. Maybe we should have looked a little harder."

He wore the same clothes from the softball game. At least he wasn't wearing his jacket, and his shirt sleeves were rolled up. "We scoured that area pretty good." There was a white ring on the skin around his collarbone. Instead of a farmer's tan, he had an ascot tan.

I said, "I was just going to try to find the boathouse before it got dark."

He looked at me and tilted his head, like a dog sometimes did when you asked it a question. "Why the boathouse?"

"I miss being in toe-dipping distance of the water. I need a fix. Water calms me."

Allan bowed. "Let me show you the way, fair maiden."

"I'm sure you're exhausted after the softball game. And there's food at the buffet table in the dining salon. Don't you want to change into shorts and a T-shirt?"

"Blasphemy. Allan Edgar Wolfstrum in shorts and a T-shirt. I have an image to uphold. No. No. I'm fine. It will be my pleasure to show you my boathouse."

His boathouse?

He took my elbow and steered me onto a path in front of the rear iron gates. We followed a lane covered in wood chips that sloped downhill. When Ollie had cut down his trees to build the castle, Byron rescued them and had them ground into mulch for use in his landscape projects. I bet this road was one of those projects.

When the lane got narrower and steeper, I looked to my right and saw the double chimneys of Scrimshaw House. There was a small cemetery to my left. The tilted, moss-covered headstones with tall overgrown grass looked like teeth jutting out from a giant's beard.

I stepped off the lane and Allan followed.

"Yes, it's the Hollingsworth burial ground, dating back to the early seventeen hundreds. But you won't find our resident ghost here."

"Why not?"

"No one knows. There's a headstone for Captain Isaiah, but not for Sarah. There's even a headstone next to his with nothing chiseled onto it."

I said, "Maybe they didn't find her body."

"Then why would there be a headstone for Captain Isaiah? His body wasn't recovered, in fact, his whole ship, *Manifest Destiny*, was never seen again."

I said, "Maybe it was just a case of nineteenth-century chauvinism and superstition. The mighty captain deserved a proper burial, the suicidal, ghostly wife, not so much."

The sun was getting lower in the sky, and I didn't feel like spending time among the tombstones in the dusk. I hurried back to the lane and Allan followed. As we walked, the harbor and the roof of the boathouse came into view.

I said, "You know a lot about the Hollingsworths."

"Franklin and I've known each other since Princeton. An unlikely pair."

"Why is that?"

"I was a poor outgoing townie and he an introverted rich boy. He went to boarding school. I went to public school. I got a scholarship and we met in Princeton's library. We both reached for the same book on Poe. The rest was history."

"Was Franklin a writer like yourself?"

"No, Franklin was always a bibliophile. He had a bad relationship with his father, who wanted him to go into the family business. His father owned a large brokerage house on Wall Street. When his father died, Franklin and Oliver sold the company and split the inheritance down the middle. Oliver—I mean, Ollie—spent most of his half on the castle and his horses. I bet you can guess what Franklin spent his on."

"Let me see. Books, more books, and then some books. Did I say books?"

He laughed. "At least his books, and now *The Heiress and the Light,* have value and always will. He and Violet have no children, so his entire book collection will go to the Princeton University Library when he passes."

"Doesn't he think of Brenna as a daughter? They seem closer than she and Ollie."

"True. But she only cares about cooking and cookbooks. And Violet only cares about her art."

At the bottom of the incline, the lane forked into a boat launch on the left and to the right, there were steps leading down to a white shingled boathouse. A snowy white egret on toothpick legs stood on a pylon next to a docked one- or possibly two-man sailboat with an unusual shape. Most of its seating area was below the waterline. On its side, it read RAIDER. The sailboat reminded me of Cole.

Allan said, "Here's the boathouse."

I went to the window and looked in. "It's magical."

Allan reached into his pocket and took out a key, then slid open the white double barn-style doors. "Come inside."

I stepped in.

"Welcome to my writing lair."

"Based on your novels and your beach house, Moon-raker, I thought you were more into James Bond sixties and seventies décor."

"Moonraker now belongs to my ex-wife, Nicole. That and everything else. Like she really needs the money after her last film. I built Moonraker in Southampton to maintain my American James Bond stereotype." He went to the window that faced the harbor and looked out. "How's that sunset for inspiration?"

I stood next to him. "Wow. Fantastic." Then I turned around. "And so is the boathouse."

The white room had open rafters. Resting on three beams was an upside-down canoe. There was a pair of oars hanging on the wall, a desk with a white laptop on top, and a small gate leg table in the closed position painted a chalky white. Allan went over to the desk, put the laptop in its case, and turned. "Can I get you some refreshment? No bee's knees, but I do have an open bottle of Wolffer Estate rosé?"

"Sure. Why not?"

He removed two paper cups from a stack on top of a dorm-sized refrigerator. Then he opened the fridge, took out the wine, and poured us each a cup. When he brought me my cup, he tapped his against it. "Cheers."

I tapped back. "Cheers." Then I sat on a wooden swing hanging from chains secured to a beam and sipped my wine. "The boathouse reminds me of my grandfather's in Traverse City, Michigan. Boathouses make the best forts when you're a kid."

He chuckled. "They make the best hideouts when you're an adult." He took a drink, emptying the cup in one swallow. On the wall behind Allan's head was a vintage ten-foot sign in the shape of a canoe. Painted on the sign were stenciled letters saying CANOE RENTAL. I looked to my right and saw a wood-burning stove and a folded cot with a mattress.

Allan must have noticed my gaze. "After Franklin's parents passed away, he let me use the boathouse to write. There's even a small bathroom and outdoor shower. It's been a great place to escape to, especially after I lost my muse."

"Your muse?"

"Nicole."

I remembered his little temper tantrum with the actress at the ball field.

"Brenna, Franklin, and Violet know I stay here from time to time. Ollie doesn't. We don't get along. I think Ollie's jealous of my friendship with Franklin. There's a ten-year age difference between them. They were never close."

"Brenna and Ollie don't seem too close."

"You're right on that one. Ollie married young to defy his father. The marriage lasted a year. I don't think he even knew he had a daughter until she showed up at Franklin's doorstep. Apparently, Franklin had been in communication with Brenna before she came to Sag Harbor. I think the only person around here who really likes Ollie is Ollie."

"Were you friends with Randall McFee?"

"No. Never shared but two words with the guy. He seemed nice enough. A little too quiet for me. But then that's what made Franklin and me a good pair in college. I'd reel in the women and he'd quietly recite a moving passage from one of the classics. That's how he met Violet. I think it was Wilkie Collins's *The Woman in White* that sealed that deal."

"One of my favorite mysteries."

He took a seat on a bentwood rocker. "Soon it will be dark, but we have about ten minutes. Pink sky at night, sailor's delight. I love working here. I owe Franklin my career."

"Which do you prefer, here or the Poe suite?"

"You did a great job with the suite."

"Franklin told me you were a big Poe fan. That you were related to Poe in some way and that I'd better do the room right."

"Sounds like Franklin. I'm not related to Poe, but I was named after him and there is a story. In the mid-eighteen hundreds, Edgar Allan Poe moved to a white farmhouse cottage in the Bronx. Back then the cottage had a view of the Long Island Sound, and it's where Poe penned "Annabel Lee" and "The Bells." My great-great-grandmother was Edgar Allan Poe's neighbor. She helped nurse Poe's wife, Virginia, before her death. Poe didn't have much money, so he repaid my great-great-grandmother by writing her a poem. He titled it "Florence's Song." Unfortunately, the poem was lost in a fire. The story has become folklore, my father even taking it as far as naming me Allan Edgar Wolfstrum."

I got up and threw my cup in a trash can that stood next to a tall, glass-enclosed medical cabinet filled with oddities.

Allan stepped next to me. "You want to see my collection?"

"Sure."

He opened the cabinet and took out what looked like a green olive made out of wax. "It's a camera." He put it back on the shelf and took out a watch with a black band. He pulled out the stem and the watch face opened, exposing a tiny blade. "These are all props from movies based on my novels—a little cheesy, but they have meaning to me. Do you have any use for a signet ring that hides cyanide? Or"—he grabbed a pair of goggles—"night goggles that turn into a heat-seeking missile?"

I laughed. "What fun. All we need is Bond's Q."

"In my books the Q character is called Tinker. I could be biased, but I think Tinker comes up with much better gadgets than Q."

The sun set and the boathouse darkened. Allan took down a kerosene lantern hanging from a hook and turned a knob to expose more wick, then lit it with a butane torch.

"We'd better get back. Remember, we have to pass the old cemetery in the dark."

I said, "I'm not afraid of the dead. It's the living I'm more worried about." I looked up at the ceiling, where a huge iron hook dangled from a rope so thick, it would hold an ocean liner safely to its dock. The hook would have been the perfect prop in a slasher movie.

"So cynical for someone so young." He bent his head back. "That's an old whale blubber hook. I use it for a hoist for my sailboat when I store it in the winter."

Allan Wolfstrum had certainly made himself at home at the Hollingsworths'. Lucky man.

We walked back to the Bibliophile single file, Allan holding the lantern in front of him. He left me at the inn's back door because he wanted to check on Franklin and see how he was holding up about Randall's death.

I went straight up to the loft, undressed, and got into my nightshirt. True to her word, Brenna had slid a check under the door, written on the Bibliophile Bed & Breakfast's account. Jo was stretched out on the bed. I gingerly sat next to her and reached for my cell phone on the candle stand.

Elle picked up on the first ring. "I'm so glad you called. Why is it everywhere you go things like this happen?"

"Things like this? If you'll remember correctly, last time the murder took place at your great-uncle's."

"Why would you bring up murder? I'm talking about a tragic accident. There's no murder."

"Did you contact FFM about the missing books?"

"Yes. I'm going to stop by and get the list in the morning. Unless Franklin is cancelling the twenties party because of Randall's accident?"

"Is everyone sure it was an accident?"

"I was with Arthur when he got the call from the coroner. He only had a gash at the back of his head where he hit the rock and some bruising from the fall."

"You and the detective are becoming quite close?"

"Just like you and Byron Hughes. What about Cole? You don't seem the ménage à trois type."

"Stop! Of course I'm not." Like her, I changed the subject. "Franklin told me the party in honor of the book fair will go on. And they're having a small memorial tomorrow afternoon in the greenhouse for Randall. You're invited."

"I wouldn't miss it."

"Is FFM allowing you to inventory all the goodies in Franklin's book vault?

"No. We can only do a search of the guest suites, not the building Franklin turned into a vault. FFM is sending armed guards to escort Franklin and the manuscript to the party Saturday night. They'll put *The Heiress and the Light* in a display case similar to those used in museums."

"Bulletproof, I hope."

"Meg!"

"I'll come by in the morning and we can go to First Fidelity Mutual together. I need to pick up my dress for the party."

"I have the perfect jewelry picked out for you. And Maurice promised to give us a quick lesson on how to do the Castle Walk."

Castle Walk?

After I hung up, I went to my suitcase and got out my former neighbor Patrick Seaton's new book, *Montauk Moors*, and brought it back to bed. It was a glossy coffee table book filled with photographs he'd taken in Montauk.

Under each photo, Patrick had added a few lines of original prose. Georgia, my friend and the owner of The Old Man and the Sea Books in Montauk, told me Patrick Seaton had started his career writing bestselling corporate thrillers. After the death of his wife and child, he wrote a literary novel, *The Sting of the Sea*. Even though *The Sting of Sea* was written as fiction, I'd found many insights into my reclusive neighbor who routinely strolled the shoreline at night and left poetry in the sand. Last spring he'd come out with the book *Tales of a Dead Shore—A Biography of Tortured Poets*. I loved classical poets and had my own collection of nineteenth-century gilt-and-cloth poetry books.

I opened *Montauk Moors* and saw the book was self-published by a small Hamptons press. There was also a notation that all the proceeds from the book would be donated to MADD, Mothers Against Drunk Driving. Patrick's wife and child had died in a car accident—alcohol must have been involved.

I turned to page one. The first photograph was a night shot with a panoramic view of the shoreline. At the top of a cliff was a small cottage that had a single light on. Below the photo it read:

> Moonlight brightens the dull edges,
> Where dark sand meets darker sea.

The cottage in the photo was the rental I'd lived in for two years. It was comforting to know I might have been inside when Patrick Seaton had taken the photograph. I missed the ocean and my Montauk Moors. I thought of Emily Brontë's words from *Wuthering Heights*, "Heathcliff, make the world stop right here. Make everything stop and stand still and never move again. Make the moors never change and you and I never change."

Before turning out the light, Jo allowed me to rub her fat belly. She seemed cognizant of the sadness in the air. She closed her eye, then nuzzled closer.

I woke from a dream I couldn't remember. Both Randall McFee and a ghostly Sarah Hollingsworth were in it. The alarm clock said one A.M. I'd only been asleep for an hour. Jo snored softly beside me. I edged out of bed and padded over to the door leading up to the cupola. I opened the door and went up the narrow flight of stairs. At the top, I turned the key in the lock, opened the door, and walked into the moonlight.

Everything was silent without my hearing aids. Sometimes I did my best thinking without them.

I leaned against the railing and looked toward Main Street. A cool breeze from the harbor caressed my cheeks. The yachts, sailboats, and cabin cruisers docked at the wharf at the end of town gently bobbed. Under the streetlamps, a small group congregated outside the Bay Street Theater. During the summer season, the Bay Street had stellar, big-name actors cast in their productions. The lights outside the theater went off. The group moved on, walking arm in arm, like a bunch of drunken sailors. One of the men looked familiar. I was almost positive it was the Bibliophiles' concierge and butler, Ken Lerner.

I followed the circular deck on my sixty-foot-high perch until I faced south. Headlights stabbed the darkness. A gray 1933 Bentley convertible, Allan Wolfstrum's signature James Bond car, pulled into the driveway of the Bibliophile. The car wasn't the Aston Martin DB5 usually associated with James Bond. Allan had explained on our walk back from the boathouse that his Bentley was a replica of the car in the Ian Fleming novels, not the big screen.

Allan parked in the lot. A sensor lamplight clicked on and I watched him get out, then he unfolded the Bentley's canvas top and locked it in place, all the while talking on his cell phone. He made his way to the back porch, then he stopped and turned. He went to Randall McFee's car and got in. The car's interior light didn't go on, so I couldn't see what he was up to. When Allan got out of the Fiat, he looked up, like he knew I was hiding behind the balustrade. He'd told me Randall and he barely talked. Then why had he gone into Randall's car? I followed the circular deck until I faced the rear of the Victorian. Beyond the trees, near the harbor, I saw blinking white lights inside Scrimshaw House.

Before Sarah's ghost could whisk me away in Dickensian flight up to the moonlit sky, I hurried down the staircase and jumped back in bed with Jo.

CHAPTER THIRTEEN

Friday morning the sky was dark and brooding, an homage to Randall McFee's passing. Jo was on her best behavior and sat next to her food bowl without a single meow. I fed and played with her using an old feather duster from which I'd tied a string to her favorite tiger catnip toy. I felt lucky to come away with only one scratch that drew blood. Then I went down to the second floor and showered.

When I walked into the hallway from the bathroom, all the doors to the suites were closed. There was no sense exploring until Elle received the insured book list from FFM. I went back to the loft and grabbed my purse and cell phone. Usually, when I went out, I left the Cooking Channel on the TV, Jo's favorite. The only television in the Bibliophile B & B was in the lounge. Luckily, there was a tree full of birds outside the window to keep her occupied. My friend Georgia planned to be back from Maine on

Monday and promised to take Jo until we moved into my
cottage. I wasn't sure I wanted to let her go.

The dining parlor was empty when I walked in. I filled
a large *H*-monogrammed linen napkin with honey pecan
crumb cakes and placed it in the duffel bag on top of the
shoebox holding my shoes for tomorrow's gala. Then I
grabbed a to-go cup of coffee and snuck out before anyone
saw me.

Instead of continuing on to the Jeep, I felt drawn to
Widow's Point and the site of Randall's fall. I never slowed
down at traffic accidents to look at the gore, but I needed
to reassure myself there was no way we could have missed
him when we searched the grounds on the night of the
hurricane.

After I dropped my bag with my shoes in the Jeep, I
passed through the iron gates behind the inn and took a
path adjacent to the one that led to the teahouse. There
were pine trees and wildflowers lining the dirt trail that
led to Scrimshaw House. A few rogue honeybees and mon-
arch butterflies flitted from bloom to bloom. I approached
an overgrown area that, at one time, must have been an
expansive lawn that looked out toward the harbor. I could
picture Sarah Hollingsworth picking flowers to put in a
white ironstone pitcher or hanging laundry as she searched
the horizon for a glimpse of Captain Isaiah sailing into the
harbor, or even setting up an easel to paint a landscape.
Violet told me there were a few of her miniature portraits
at the Sag Harbor Whaling Museum, along with a large
painting of a child in a white dress holding a flower with
a snake curled at the child's feet.

Up ahead there were small downed trees and bushes
pushed against what was once a white wood railing. The

railing was now a weathered gray and there was a splintered opening where Randall's body must have fallen through. I stepped up to where the railing was intact and peered over. The sun came through the clouds and something white flapped between two rocks below.

I got out my cell phone and went to take a photo, but before I did, I zoomed in. I snapped the picture, then reviewed it, blowing it up even more. I couldn't tell if it was just litter or something more, and I wasn't dressed appropriately to climb down the steep incline to check it out. I would come back later with Elle. I'd learned from experience, when performing potentially dangerous feats, it was always good to have backup.

Before leaving the area, I went to the side of Scrimshaw House and peeked in a window scarred with cracks in a web pattern. The room on the other side of the window looked in worse shape than I expected. The walls had deteriorated, exposing moldy wood supports. There was a gaping hole in the plank flooring that opened to a subterranean cellar. No furniture to speak of, except for a spinning wheel missing its wheel.

I looked up at the two-story house. Once white, but now sooty gray with splintered molding and a wraparound porch that sagged every few feet like the track of an old roller coaster.

I went to the front of the house, which faced the harbor, and I could see why it was condemned. It was inches away from toppling off the cliff into the harbor. I knew of a company that salvaged old homes slated for demolition. A lot of what remained of Scrimshaw House could be recycled: the crown molding, porch balustrades, wood floors, windows, doorknobs, and light fixtures, to name a few. It would be a shame to let the house fall into the bay come the next hurricane. I snapped a few pictures with my phone, then I headed back to the inn.

On the path back, I avoided picking the wild Queen Anne's lace because it was poisonous to cats. But I picked another wildflower whose stalks were four feet tall and ended in delicate white clusters of flowers.

Near the turnoff to the Bibliophile, there was an area encircled with boxwood hedges. I went through the small opening. Eight rectangular raised beds were filled with flowers, herbs, and clover. At the rear of the area were stacks of pine boxes. On the top of each stack was a copper roof.

I'd found the inn's apiary. I didn't see one bee. A small wooden shed stood to my right, where I assumed the honey was processed. There didn't seem to be any evidence of the hurricane. Not a single branch inside the apiary, or outside the perimeter.

"What are you doing?"

I turned.

Kortney Lerner's wide mouth was twisted in a snarl. She and Ken were twins, but I didn't see much similarity, except in their pale coloring and wide mouths.

"Just looking around. We haven't officially met. I'm Meg Barrett. I'm staying at the inn."

"I know who you are. I'd appreciate it if you'd leave the apiary. My bees don't like strangers."

"I've never seen an apiary before. This one looks so organized and tranquil. Where are the bees?" I'd learned you could make more friends with honey than vinegar—especially if that someone was a beekeeper and had pride in her job.

However, Kortney seemed immune to flattery. She said through clenched teeth, "They were disturbed yesterday."

She must have meant because of the police and paramedics. "I'm an herb lover. I have my own garden in Montauk."

"Well, isn't that just swell."

"Were you taking care of the bees on the night of the hurricane? I saw you in your beekeeper's suit."

"I checked on the apiary. But I wasn't wearing my beekeeper's suit."

"Did you design this area or did Byron Hughes?"

Kortney gave me a look I'd only seen on cartoon characters.

"No! 'Lord' Byron had nothing to do with this area. Leave before I sic a hive on you."

Whoa, did I touch a nerve.

As I walked out, she called after me, "Did you know bees that feed on rhododendrons and azaleas produce poison honey?" When I didn't answer, she added, "And that white snakeroot you're clutching, even the deer won't touch. Enjoy."

She stormed into the shed and slammed the door so hard the building shook.

I dropped the flowers and continued on to the parking lot.

A few minutes later, I arrived at Mabel and Elle's Curiosities. I could have walked the distance from Hollingsworth Avenue to Sage Street, but I wanted to pick up my dress for tomorrow's kickoff cocktail party for the Antiquarian Book Fair, along with a few knick-knacks from the shop for the Emily Dickinson loft.

Elle answered the back door to her half shop, half home-sweet-home. She wore a filmy peignoir set, straight out of a Doris Day movie, or something my mother's vintage Barbie might have worn.

I looked around for Detective Shoner's Lexus. Thankfully, the parking lot was empty.

Elle held open the door and I stepped inside. "Aren't you a little early? We don't have to go to FFM until ten." She grabbed my coffee and chugged it down.

"Um. I needed that."

"Come to the kitchen. I brewed some Blue Kilimanjaro that'll blow smoke out of your ears."

"Perfect." I grabbed an aquamarine ink bottle next to the old-fashioned brass cash register and followed her up the stairs. "Put this on my tab."

"It's yours."

"In that case, I'll share Brenna's home-baked crumb cakes with you."

Elle's shop was on the first floor; her living quarters and kitchen were on the second floor. Her bedroom was on the third level—a charming garret with a balcony/widow's walk with a view of the harbor.

The second floor was surprisingly minimalist compared to the packed antiques/vintage shop below. Everything was in light shades of white or cream. Elle had a knack for mixing vintage, modern, and antique by sticking to clean lines and grouping like items in small vignettes and, at the same time, leaving lots of space on her shelves and tables.

We went through the open door to Elle's closet.

She said, "It feels surreal picking out clothing for the party when Randall McFee lies in the morgue."

"I feel the same way. But Franklin isn't canceling the party. There's been so much press and he's worked so hard on getting the first annual Sag Harbor Antiquarian Book and Ephemera Fair off the ground. We owe it to him to show up with painted smiles on our faces."

"What I think is sad is there's no one we can contact about Randall's death."

I showed Elle the photo I'd taken of Randall's car registration and insurance ID card. The address on both was the same. He lived in Brooklyn.

Elle said, "Jordan's bookstore is in Brooklyn. Maybe she could call and ask a neighbor to check out Randall's address? Text me the pictures and I'll forward them to Arthur."

"And he can send a cop car. I also found a FedEx receipt for a small package that came from Key West, Florida. I plan to search on the Internet and see if there are any McFees down there."

"Sounds like a plan. I'm not going to ask why you were going through Randall's car. That's something you should leave to the police."

"Pshaw."

"You do believe Randall's death was accidental, don't you? I know the police ruled it one."

"Pshaw," I repeated.

Elle's closet housed her vintage clothing, accessories, and jewelry. The closet/room was on the opposite spectrum of minimalism. Luckily, she had a wardrobe organizer, Maurice. He was also her assistant and top (only) salesperson.

Elle's collection was amazing, thanks mostly to Great-Aunt Mabel. On three of the four walls there were two levels of floor-to-ceiling rods holding vintage clothing. Each rod corresponded to the decade the clothing came from, starting with the 1920s. In the center of the room was a huge antique wooden dental cabinet filled with a fantastic collection of costume jewelry, three-quarters of which were rhinestone brooches worn in classic films, gifted to Great-Aunt Mabel from the famous costume designer Edith Head. Also in the center of the room were a mid-century dressing table, a floor-length three-sided mirror, two vintage dress forms, and a crystal chandelier. The wall with the door leading to the hallway was filled with framed original Edith Head watercolor sketches of costumes she'd designed for such movies as *Breakfast at Tiffany's*, *Sabrina*, *Roman Holiday*, *To Catch a Thief*, *The Birds*, *Notorious*, *Rear Window*, and *All About Eve*.

Maurice, also a huge Edith Head buff, could list each movie title she'd worked on verbatim. I only remembered the ones that were my favorites.

Elle told me that Edith Head had told her Great-Aunt Mabel that when she applied for the job as costume designer at Paramount, she'd presented them with a portfolio of sketches she'd stolen from someone else. Back then, a girl had to do what a girl had to do in male-dominated Hollywood. Later she went on to win eight Oscars.

I pulled out the chair from under the dressing table so I could watch Elle in action. The dress I was going to wear tomorrow was in the Deco/Nouveau section.

Elle grabbed a high-reach garment hook from the corner of the room and hooked the hanger holding my dress. She resembled a carnie retrieving a stuffed animal for a winner at the state fair. She slipped the dress over one of the dress forms. "I just hung the dress this morning. Never hang a heavily beaded vintage dress. Always store them flat." She pointed to the other wall where there were floor to ceiling shelves stacked with horizontal garment bags.

I reached into the bag with my shoes and brought them out.

Elle clapped her hands. "A perfect match."

"My mom's. She wore these to the Detroit PD's masquerade ball. She went as a1920s flapper in my great-great-grandmother's dress."

"Awesome. Do you have a photo of her at the ball?"

"I'm sure my dad does." My father had recently remarried. I wondered if all the pictures he'd had of my mother were still on display? Or had his new bride, Sheila, talked him into removing them?

Elle took her hook and brought down a dress from the same section as mine. "What do you think of my dress?"

She stroked the shoulders of the dress like it was a prized pet.

"That's not the one you originally picked out?"

"This is dress option number four. I still haven't decided. It might be a little racy."

It was a little on the daring side but unbelievably gorgeous. The background was a nude color, in a fabric like pantyhose. On top were translucent, pearlized sequins, hand sewn in all the right places. The hem was short, but there was beaded fringe that hit below the knee.

I said, "Too racy for the Hamptons? You're kidding, right? Nothing's too racy for a Gatsby-era party."

"These are bibliophiles. They don't care about fashion, just books."

"Not true. I think you'll be surprised tomorrow night at all the celebs who are coming. And even more surprised on Sunday at the Antiquarian Book Fair. What old-time movie is your dress from?"

"How'd you know? Not an Edith Head movie. I bought it online. It was a must buy. A dress worn by Greta Garbo in *The Flesh and the Devil*."

"A must buy? I'm not going to ask how much it went for." Elle's great-aunt had left her very wealthy. Elle's shop was just for fun, not for income. And her work with FFM was also because she loved touching all the rarities insured by elite Hamptons homeowners. Elle was quietly one of Long Island's top philanthropists. She donated money to local causes and also allowed her rare vintage clothing and one-of-a-kind costume jewelry to be used in charity fashion shows.

Elle said, "I also bought a gold floor-length gown I'm dying to wear. Betty Grable wore it in *Tin Pan Alley*. I snagged it years ago at Debbie Reynolds's last auction of her MGM collection. But it's the wrong era for the party." She went to the '40s section, hooked the dress, and danced it in front of me.

"It looks more like something Marilyn Monroe might have worn in *Some Like It Hot*."

"The fabric is like liquid gold." She ran her hand over the bodice. "Decisions, decisions."

"You know what you need in this room? A conveyor belt system like they have at the dry cleaners. All you'd have to do is push a button."

Elle smiled. "Wow. You're right!" The wheels spun on the conveyor belt in her noggin. "You're teasing. Right? Maybe I won't hand you these."

She walked over and dangled a small glassine bag over my head. I snatched the bag from her hand and looked inside. It was filled with four jewelry boxes. I reached inside to open the top box.

"Stop. I want you to wait and open them after you have your dress and shoes on. I had a nightmare last night about the Cleopatra snake bracelet Maurice picked out for you. It opened its jaw and hissed at me."

"Snake?" I immediately thought of Violet's ravensnake.

"Oops, I let the cat—I mean snake—out of the bag. Well, you still have three other surprises to wear tomorrow in the other boxes. I looked up 'snake' in my dream dictionary. They can mean positive or negative energy. The negative is easy. The snake can symbolize a ruthless, evil, or a callous person in my life. Or as a positive, a snake can mean transformation and change, as in a snake shedding its skin. It all depends on how I felt when I remembered my dream."

"Sounds pretty esoteric to me. So how did you feel when you woke up?"

She changed the subject. "How are you wearing your hair tomorrow?"

"Professor Henry Higgins—I mean Maurice—showed me how to do a chignon. Your short bob is perfect for a twenties party. You need two curls on either cheek."

"Like Violet's? I wouldn't be surprised if Franklin arranged Violet's hairdressing appointment so she would mesh with the Gatsby theme."

"F. Scott Fitzgerald wrote a cute short story, 'Bernice Bobs Her Hair.' Maybe Violet read it and wanted to get her husband's attention. Byron told me Violet can't compete with Franklin's love of books and reading."

"Do Franklin and Violet know about the missing books?"

"I don't think so. No one was around when I left the inn this morning." I told her about the cell phone I'd found in the basket outside the dining salon. I'd noticed it was still there in the morning on my way out of the Bibliophile.

"Well if it's Randall's phone, that would be amazing. We could access all his contacts. Come to the carriage house. I want to show you my latest purchases from the Bridgehampton Antique Show, then we'll head over to FFM to get the inventory list."

As we walked down the steps to the shop level, I said, "I'm curious about what's missing in Franklin's collection."

"I hope your Steinbeck book is safe."

"I just saw it. Maybe I'll make more than what Jordan said."

"Maybe Franklin will hand you a million-dollar book when you finish the Emily Dickinson loft?"

"I'd be happy with payment for services rendered. The good news is, I found out Brenna takes care of the finances. I've been putting them in Franklin's mail slot next to the concierge desk. I have the check with me. I'll deposit it when we go into town."

"See. Nothing to worry about."

CHAPTER

⤞❦⤝

FOURTEEN

When we went outside of Mabel and Elle's Curiosities, I put my dress—packed in tissue in a garment bag—my shoes, and the bag of jewelry for the party in the backseat of the Jeep and locked it. Then we went inside the carriage house and Elle showed me her finds, one of which included something for my garden: an old iron wagon wheel. I'd been on the lookout for one ever since I saw online a clever way to section off your herbs by laying the wheel flat on the ground and planting one herb in each pie-shaped section.

After the appropriate oohing and ahhing over Elle's treasures, we got into her turquoise pickup and headed to First Fidelity Mutual.

Sag Harbor's Main Street was packed with tourists and there wasn't a single parking spot.

Elle pulled to the curb. "Do you mind parking the truck in the municipal lot? I don't want to be late."

She got out and I got in the driver's seat. I loved driving her truck. Yep, my Wrangler's days were numbered.

After I parked, I stopped into a branch of my bank and deposited the check from the Bibliophile. Then I killed time by doing one of my favorite things: window-shopping.

The confections behind the plate glass display window of Chocolat were drool-worthy. The small shop was a near perfect replica of the one in the movie of the same name. Chocolat had robin's egg–blue walls, antique wood and glass showcases, and French tiled floors. The only thing missing was Johnny Depp.

Next to the French-inspired Chocolat was the Italian-inspired Leonetti's Cheese Shop. Like Chocolat, the gourmet shop maintained its old-world charm, melding perfectly with Sag Harbor's Americana feel. I walked in and sampled a creamy goat cheese with herbs and a hard cheese with truffles.

I walked out of Leonetti's and saw Elle standing in front of First Fidelity Mutual. She noticed me and waved.

When I reached her, she said, "You wouldn't believe how many pages. The good news is, the insured books are arranged by author." Elle looked up from the list when someone laid on the horn to get the traffic moving. "Keep your cool, buddy! This isn't Manhattan."

She handed it to me and I perused all the wonderful titles.

Elle nudged me. "Hey, isn't that Ken Lerner going into Yanio's Used Books?"

I looked across the street. Behind the plate glass window was the Bibliophile's concierge/butler talking to a sales clerk.

I said, "With all the books at the inn, I can't imagine what he needs at a bookstore."

"Ken's a big-time Sag Harbor historian, and Kortney told me he's also a playwright. I don't think it's unusual for a book lover to go into a bookstore, no matter how many books they own. It's like saying you and I shouldn't stop at a garage sale because we already have so much inventory."

I said, "Truer words were never spoken. You and Kortney have talked before? Today's the first time she talked to me. And it didn't go well."

"She's a little rough around the edges, but she sure makes the best Hollingsworth Honey products in her apiary. I sell some of her candles and beeswax furniture polish in my shop."

"If that's the case, I'll give her a second chance." I believed in second chances. Big time.

I handed Elle the insurance list for the books, she put it back in its manila envelope, and we started walking toward the lot where I'd parked Elle's pickup.

She said, "Speaking of sales, the Presbyterian church is having a white elephant sale this morning. Should we check it out or is it too disrespectful to Randall McFee's memory?"

"I'm sure they won't release the body for a few days. Plus, we can't find anyone to release it to."

She said, "Remember, Maurice wants to show us the Castle Walk, although I don't know if anyone will be in the mood for dancing."

"Well, it can't hurt to learn it. Maybe I'll teach Byron and we can be like that couple they show in a Fred Astaire movie: the crowd on the dance floor parts and the spotlight shines on the couple in the middle, hoofing it like pros."

"It's possible. You're a great dancer."

"I wouldn't go that far."

As we walked to where I'd parked Elle's pickup, we passed Sag Art. The gallery had two large showcase windows on each side of the door. Displayed in the windows was a single sculpture of a lifelike bust.

I grabbed Elle's arm. "Let's go inside. I think those sculptures in the windows are Violet Hollingsworth's."

The interior of the gallery had stark white walls and floorboards.

A woman wearing a caftan and Birkenstocks greeted us. "Welcome. Feel free to look around." She went to a white chair-rail ledge and picked up a small brass bell tied with a red string. She shook it. "Ring the bell if you need assistance. We like to leave our patrons alone while they soak in all the art."

When she went into the backroom, I said to Elle, "*All* the art? There's only four pieces."

I couldn't help but stare at the floor-to-ceiling white canvases on both of the side walls. From a distance, the canvases looked blank. When I got closer, I saw that someone had painted an entire fishing village in an area smaller than a postage stamp on one and on the other was a teensy lighthouse scene. Had the artist had a side job of painting rice kernels at street fairs?

I joined Elle at one of the picture windows. The sculpture we'd seen from outside was on a lazy Susan.

Elle had spun it around so it faced her. "You were right. It is Violet's." She pointed to the placard that read: E. L. DOCTOROW, BY VIOLET HOLLINGSWORTH. "How did you know?"

I told her about the John Steinbeck bust Violet was working on.

"Doctorow was a resident of Sag Harbor. Before he passed away, he was very involved in the community."

"What a loss. When I was reading about Poe, I read that E. L. Doctorow, the *Ragtime* author, had also been named after Edgar Allan Poe—Edgar Doctorow."

"Just like Allan Edgar Wolfstrum."

We walked to the other window.

This time I spun the lazy Susan. I spun it too fast and the giant female head teetered. I grabbed it before it hit the floor. Luckily, it was a million times lighter than it looked.

Elle stood behind me, blocking the view from the back of the gallery, in case the owner came out wondering why bells weren't ringing.

Too late. I heard, "Oh my goodness, please don't touch the art." The gallery owner bolted to my side and helped me center the piece on the turntable.

"It's so much lighter than it looks," I said.

The huge head was titled: SARAH HOLLINGSWORTH. Sarah the ghost.

Instead of being angry of my mishandling of Sarah, the gallery owner went on to instruct Elle and me on the process Violet used to make her humongous heads, using words like "score" and "slip" and "garrote." I'd watched Violet the afternoon of the hurricane slicing off the top of John Steinbeck's head. The gallery owner even went into detail about how hot the kiln needed to be for the first firing, then its glaze firing. All I could think of was the unsettling dream I'd had about Randall being baked alive in Violet's kiln.

Elle dropped me at my Jeep because she decided to go to the white elephant sale alone. She handed me the inventory list. "You might as well start with the F. Scott Fitzgerald suite before getting ready for the memorial."

After she drove down the alley-sized street, I took my car key from my bag and walked toward my Jeep. Then I stopped short.

The passenger side window was shattered.

I looked inside. The dress for tomorrow night's party was gone.

CHAPTER

⤶⤶⤶

FIFTEEN

As I went up the steps to the veranda of Elle's shop, Maurice stepped out, holding the OPEN sign. He said with his posh Londoner's accent, "What's wrong, Eliza Doolittle? You look like someone stole your last shilling."

"You're close. Someone broke into my Jeep and took my dress for the twenties party. Luckily, my mother's shoes and the jewelry Elle loaned me were left behind."

I brought him over to the Jeep and he put his hands on his hips and sighed. "What canker blossom would do such a thing?"

"Canker blossom?"

"A Shakespearean insult. I think it's time you got a new automobile. One with an alarm system. You have too much class to be driving this eyesore."

"Well. Thanks for the compliment, but what should I do?"

"Poor Cinderella. Well, there's more where that frock

came from. Come inside and I'll pick out something for you."

"Remember how hard it was to come up with this one. I'm three inches taller than Elle."

"Don't worry. Professor Higgins will find you something worthy of your date with Mr. Hughes at the 'castle.'"

"Not you too. Does everyone think Byron's out of my league?"

"Not out of your league, just in a league of his own." Maurice winked.

"Ugh. Here we go again."

Maurice grabbed me by the arm, turned the OPEN sign to CLOSED, and led me up to Elle's dressing room. We chose a simpler version of my turquoise dress, and I got a crash-course lesson on how to do the Castle Walk.

I arrived at the Bibliophile B & B in time to grab lunch. I stepped into the front vestibule and took the hallway to the left of the staircase. As I passed the stained-glass French doors to the morning room, Franklin and Allan were in a heated discussion. Allan was waving his arms and Franklin was waving his pipe; loose tobacco flew into the air and rained on the carpet.

When the inn officially opened, Brenna said the morning room would be a place where Ken could set up his concierge services. Franklin and Allan stood in front of a tiger maple mail sorter Brenna said had come from an old, demolished nineteenth-century hotel in town. It had square cubbies filled with Hamptons tourist and recreational brochures and menus from local eateries. A stack of free *Dave's Hamptons* newspapers filled one large cubby and there were mail slots for Franklin and Brenna. Nothing for Violet.

I walked past, then doubled back and hugged the wall until I was in lip-reading distance. I peered in. Allan was asking for a small loan, and Franklin was telling him it wasn't a good time. Allan put his arm around Franklin's shoulders and said something I couldn't make out. Franklin looked at Allan and smiled. Allan would get his loan. I scurried down to the dining salon. Before going in, I reached inside the basket and took out the mystery cell phone then dropped mine inside.

Brenna sat alone at the long mahogany table. "Don't let my uncle see you with a cell phone." Her plate of food looked untouched.

I walked over to the ornate marble-topped sideboard, placed a large wedge of quiche on a china plate, and added a small helping of mixed-green salad, knowing all the greens were organic and came from the inn's kitchen garden. After slathering honey butter on a freshly baked roll, I joined her at the table. "The phone's not mine. It's been in the basket for a couple of days. I was wondering if it might belong to Randall McFee?"

"Can I see?"

I handed it to her.

"I hope it is Randall's." Her voice cracked. "Now we can access his contacts and find his family."

"My phone's a different brand. This one's battery is dead. Maybe Randall's charger is still in the Fitzgerald suite?"

Brenna pushed her plate toward the center of the table and all six feet of her stood. "You might be right. I'll go up now and see. Don't forget to try the key-lime-pie-stuffed strawberries." She nodded her head toward the end of the Victorian server. "They were Randall's favorites."

As she headed to the door, I called out, "Did you tell your uncle and aunt about the missing books?"

She placed her large hand on the door frame and turned to look back at me. "I had to. FFM called my uncle to make sure he was on board after Elle called them. He didn't take it too well. I have all my keys to the locked bookcases, but my uncle's are missing."

"I have the key to the bookcases in the Fitzgerald suite. It was in the keyhole when I noticed the missing books."

She gave me a look that bordered on accusatory. "Well, don't you think you should have told me this earlier? Where's the key?"

I'd never had anything but warmth from her. That wasn't the case right now. "I'm sorry. I assumed Franklin gave Randall the key so he could read the books in the case at his leisure."

"You don't know my uncle very well if you think that. I'm barely allowed to touch them. And before I do, I must wear gloves while Uncle looks on."

"Randall was trusted with handling a five-million-dollar manuscript, so I didn't think it was a stretch."

Her shoulders loosened. "I suppose you're right."

"Elle gave me the list of the insured books in the inn so I can get started. I told her I'd start with the F. Scott Fitzgerald suite. If you want, as soon as I finish this delicious quiche, I can take the phone up with me to look for a charger, then turn it over to the police."

"It's actually a tart. Pancetta, leek, and goat cheese. I'll look for the charger. Finish your meal. Remember, we're meeting at three in the greenhouse for the memorial. I've invited the staff, and even Ollie, at my uncle's insistence.

It's not exactly the way we intended to christen our first high tea at the B & B. Is it?"

"No, it isn't. But it's the right thing to do."

I'd helped Brenna with the interior renovation of the old greenhouse. And I had to say, it had turned out to be one of my favorite projects.

When I finished eating, I brought my dishes to the kitchen. Besides the author suites, the kitchen was one of the best rooms in the Bibliophile. It was less formal than the rest of the house and reminded me of the "downstairs" in a PBS series. The kitchen had a stone floor and a huge restaurant-sized stove disguised to look antique. The back-splash behind the sink had its original blue-and-white delft tiles. Against the brick wall was a large white plate rack with slots that held thirty-two antique transferware dinner plates. Copper pots hung from blacksmith's hooks on the beamed ceiling, along with herbs that were drying. Instead of a center island, there was a huge wood chopping block.

I placed my plate in the double sink. On the counter was a cookbook in a protective Plexiglas stand. The cookbook was opened to page 115 and displayed a recipe for honey twists. I could almost taste them.

Keeping my finger between the pages to mark Brenna's spot, I took the cookbook out of its stand and flipped to the front of the green cloth–covered book. It was titled *The American Woman's Cookbook*, published for the Culinary Arts Institute with a copyright date of 1939.

Ken Lerner entered from the keeping room. "What are you doing?"

"Salivating over a recipe Brenna's about to make, or has already made."

He held a tray in his hand with a barely eaten piece of goat cheese tart. On a napkin next to the plate was a pile of loose pipe tobacco.

I put the cookbook back in its stand. Ken barely acknowledged my presence and dumped the contents of the plate into the bin under the sink.

I said, "It looks like Franklin doesn't have much of an appetite. I can't blame him."

No comment from Ken.

"Elle told me you're a Sag Harbor historical expert. We saw you in town at Yanio's. I know they have a nice local history section."

Ken placed Franklin's plate in the wood-faced restaurant-sized dishwasher and then scraped off a single crumb from my plate in an exaggerated motion, even adding a sigh. "Yes. I was there. What about it?"

He walked to where I stood. For a minute, I imagined a ref in a black-and-white striped shirt grabbing each of our arms and raising them in the air until the bell sounded.

Instead, Ken stepped back, like I had a communicable disease. However, he was still in spitting distance. "My sister said you were disturbing the bees. She is very protective of her hives and would appreciate it if you'd stay away from the apiary." Then he walked past me and went into the dining salon.

I had a feeling I was officially on the Lerner twins' doo-doo list. But why?

I left the kitchen through a door next to the pantry and peeked in. The butler's pantry was the size of the living room in my cottage. Instead of placing a table in the kitchen, Brenna had put a long, narrow farm table in the center of the room. There were four rows of built-in shelves that followed both sides of the pantry. The left-side shelving held sixty-four-ounce vintage blue-green mason jars filled with flour, sugar, and grains as well as boxed and canned goods. The entire right-side shelving held Brenna's amazing cookbook collection, some of the volumes dating back to the Civil War.

Instead of going back inside the dining salon, where Ken had clomped off to, I entered the Early American keeping room. It was the only room in the Bibliophile that hadn't been touched. The room was bare, much like Franklin and Violet's cabin. The exact way you might have found it in the late eighteenth century. For some reason, it reminded me of the fable "Hansel and Gretel." Inside the brick walk-in fireplace was a huge black witch's cauldron hanging from a dangerous-looking hook. There were dark wood beams across the room's low ceiling. The wooden bench looked less comfortable than a church pew, and on a rough-hewn shelf was a line of pewter chargers and dome-top tankards. A pine dry sink, a wood spice cupboard, two rocking chairs, and a braided rug were the only other items in the room.

I walked up to the north-facing wall to study a framed quill-and-ink map on parchment paper that showed an 1846 rendering of the Hollingsworths' twenty-acre plot of land. The year coincided with the decline of the whaling industry in Sag Harbor. Ezekiel and Captain Isaiah Hollingsworth's homes were labeled. They stood like proud sentries overlooking Sag Harbor Cove. A forest of trees was their backdrop. The family cemetery and Widow's Point were also on the map. Widow's Point was listed as Bay Point. It earned its name after Sarah, Captain Isaiah's wife, threw herself into the harbor.

I left the keeping room and stepped through another entrance to the dining salon. *Phew!* No Ken Lerner.

Hal Innes stood at the sideboard, holding a plate of food. His other hand held a crystal pitcher from which he poured iced tea into a cut-glass goblet.

"Wait until you taste the tart." I went next to him and took an empty glass. I added lemon wedges and a few sprigs of mint.

Hal filled my glass with tea.

I took a sip. "Thank you. Brenna makes the best iced tea."

"Brenna makes the best everything. I'm trying to lay off carbs, which is near impossible around here." He smiled and took a fork and a cloth napkin off the silver tray. Then he went to the table and sat.

I took a seat across from him. "How's Jordan doing? Is she all set for the book fair?"

"She's amazing. The most organized person I know." He took a forkful of the tart.

"It's so tragic about Randall. I'm sure the two of you spent a lot of time talking about *The Heiress and the Light* manuscript?"

"Not as much time as I wanted to. Every time we made plans to meet, he canceled. Something was definitely on his mind. And the one time we met in his room, he went flying out the door after Brenna handed him an envelope. That was Tuesday. The last time I saw him."

"So how does one go about transposing a manuscript into a published book?"

"It depends on the manuscript. It might sound easy to just transpose the words to a document but, in this case, there are numerous scribbled notes and editing marks, making it quite challenging to put into one cohesive piece of work without losing the author's voice."

"It must feel like quite an accomplishment to put a long-lost novel by someone as famous as F. Scott Fitzgerald into book form."

"I've been a scholar of Fitzgerald's works for years. I'm working on his biography in my spare time. But, as Jordan will tell you, it's definitely on the back burner."

"I'm sure people must have told you that you look like F. Scott Fitzgerald."

Hal blushed and busied himself with his napkin.

I stood and took my glass off the table. "I better get going. I have a few things to do before the memorial. I'll see you later."

"Yes. Three o'clock. Right?"

"Yes."

I checked on Jo, retrieved the key for the bookcases in the F. Scott Fitzgerald suite, and grabbed the packet with the list of insured books.

When I walked into the Fitzgerald bedroom, the regency nightstand had been pulled away from the wall. Brenna must have found Randall's cell phone charger. Which meant the phone belonged to him.

I sat on the geometric Art Deco rug and began inventorying the books inside the polished walnut bookcases. They were early editions written by F. Scott Fitzgerald and his contemporaries: Ernest Hemingway, William Faulkner, and other American authors who wrote in the mid-1920s to the mid-1930s. I pulled out the copy of Fitzgerald's *The Last Tycoon*. He'd written the unfinished manuscript at the end of his life and it had been published posthumously. It was based on Fitzgerald's frustrating experience as a Hollywood screenwriter.

"My niece told me you had the key to the bookcase. What have you found missing?" Franklin stood under the door frame, an unlit pipe in his hand.

"It's hard to tell. FFM has everything listed by author. I know you've put a mixture of books relating to the times the authors lived in each suite. For instance, I don't see the copy of *The Great Gatsby*. Do you have it?"

"Why would I have it? I have a first edition in my book vault, and I'm hoping to snare a signed first edition *Gatsby* at the book fair. There are about a dozen reading copies in the greenhouse. The books in these cases are valued mostly in the five hundred dollar range. I know for sure there was a copy of *The Great Gatsby* in the bookcase on the left."

"Did you ever let anyone have the key to the bookcases?"

"No, Ms. Barrett. Brenna and I are the only ones with keys. Mine are missing." He stepped in and grabbed the handle on the Deco chrome-and-etched-crystal bar trolley to steady himself. Instead of a champagne bucket, I'd placed a huge silver-plated football trophy dated 1918. Fitzgerald had been athletic and the trophy could also hold a bottle of his favorite champagne.

I held up the key to the bookcases. "As soon as I inventory these bookcases, I'll give the key to Brenna."

"See that you do."

There was an awkward silence.

I said, "What is your favorite F. Scott Fitzgerald novel?"

"*The Heiress and the Light.*"

"I can't wait to read it."

"Well, you'll have to wait a couple years until it's published, like the rest of the world. How are you coming along with finishing the Emily Dickinson loft?"

Was Franklin insinuating I was overstaying my welcome? "Everything's coming along beautifully. I'm waiting for the queen-sized mattress to be delivered Monday. I still need to go through a few boxes we brought up when we switched the Emily Dickinson loft with this one, and I haven't finished with the items in the loft's storage cupboards."

"Anything having to do with our ghost, Sarah Hollingsworth, I'm sure my wife will want. Many of the items from the loft came from Scrimshaw House. Violet is quite obsessed with Great-Great-Aunt Sarah. She actually believes Sarah's miscarriage and subsequent suicide is the reason we couldn't have children. She thinks there's a curse on the Hollingsworths. Rubbish."

"I think having a ghost adds to the atmosphere of the Bibliophile B and B."

"Of course you do, Ms. Barrett. Do you think Sarah pushed Randall off of Widow's . . . I mean, Bay Point?" He laughed, but his face paled and he placed his hand over his heart.

"Maybe you should reconsider having books in the guest suites, even at five hundred a pop. It might be tempting to a bibliophile?"

"No, Ms. Barrett. The whole purpose of the Bibliophile B and B is for other bibliophiles to be able to soak up the ambiance of the author-inspired rooms, and what better way than with the books relating to the time period when the author lived? We are only talking about seven rooms, and we will be taking deposits on credit cards and each guest will sign a paper saying that if anything is missing it will be charged to their room."

"That's a good idea." I couldn't help but think he and Brenna might think I'd taken the books from the Fitzgerald and Wharton suites. After all, I wasn't a bibliophile or a paying guest. "Are you happy with my work, Mr. Hollingsworth?"

His gaze left my face and he glanced around the room. "Yes. Ms. Barrett, I am very happy with your work. And

I know Randall McFee loved this room. As you know, because he told you over and over again." He took a few steps backward into the hallway. He opened his mouth to say something, then closed it and shuffled away. I remembered he had heart problems and felt a prick of guilt for challenging him about my interior design prowess.

Before I changed for the memorial, I went to the greenhouse to see if I could help Brenna with the setup. Only Brenna wasn't the one setting up the greenhouse; Ken and Kortney were.

I wasn't afraid of confrontation and Elle had told me I should give Kortney another chance, so I stepped inside. "Can I help you guys with anything? I have some free time."

The twins turned at the same time and looked in my direction. They said in unison, "No."

I ignored them and took my time looking around. The late-nineteenth-century greenhouse was a reader's dream—perhaps not a top-tiered bibliophile's dream, but there was a magical quality to it. There were books, plants, and stained glass windows hanging from chains suspended from the iron beams and glass ceiling. The base of the greenhouse was built with layers of red bricks stamped with SAG BRICKWORKS.

Franklin had Brenna set up the numerous iron shelves with books he'd amassed from his lifetime of collecting, along with those that had been stored in the loft during the Victorian's renovation into the Bibliophile B & B. Some of the books came from Scrimshaw House, but because of the years of neglect, they'd lost most of their value. The subject matter of the books was vast and included every topic and genre. On the lower potting shelves, Brenna had added a few ferns and hardy indoor plants she displayed on tarnished silver tea trays I'd found at estate sales. A going-out-of-business sale at a vintage-themed yogurt shop in Riverhead had netted me eight ice cream tables and thirty-two filigree wrought-iron chairs we'd scattered around the greenhouse. Elle had contributed a chandelier hanging with hundreds of crystal prisms from her shop, which Ken had hung in the center of the greenhouse. When the inn officially opened, Brenna planned to serve high tea, scones, and finger sandwiches to the inn's guests at three every afternoon. Who would have thought the greenhouse tearoom would become the site of a memorial?

On my way out, I spied a copy of the Sherlock Holmes tale, *The Hound of the Baskervilles*. I took it off the shelf. I'd read the book so many times, I'd memorized all the good parts. My favorite movie version of the Sherlock Holmes novel was the old 1939 black-and-white film with Basil Rathbone. Every year, on May 22, Sir Arthur Conan Doyle's birthday, Maurice and his partner hosted a Holmes marathon of movies and television episodes featuring each of the different actors who portrayed Holmes over the years.

I opened the book and read Sherlock's line, "The world is full of obvious things which nobody by any chance ever observes." It seemed ironic that the theme in *The Hound of the Baskervilles* had to do with an eighteenth-century manuscript describing a family curse. Perhaps there was a curse on *The Heiress and the Light*? I took the book with me as I walked to the inn; after all, the greenhouse was a lending library.

Elle came to the Bibliophile at two, and we went over what I'd found in the Fitzgerald suite. I told her *The Great Gatsby* and *This Side of Paradise* were missing and that Franklin said he never allowed anyone, including Randall McFee, access to the bookcases. Afterward, we went up to the Dickinson loft. I changed while Elle presented Jo with a handful of her favorite fish-shaped cat treats. I told her about my run-in with Ken and how he'd defended his sister and her bees.

Elle said, "I'm surprised. He's always been so nice when I've talked to him. Wasn't he nice to you when you worked here during the last few months?"

"You're right. We always got along. After my little chat with his sister in the apiary, his whole 'tude changed."

"Did you find out if that cell phone in the basket was Randall's?"

"I gave it to Brenna. The battery was dead and she was going to look for a charger. I told her to turn it in to the police afterward."

"I'll mention it to Arthur. He had the Brooklyn police go to Randall's house after I sent him your text with Randall's address from his car's registration. They didn't find any contacts for next of kin and the neighbors didn't even know him."

"That's what happens sometimes in the city. People tend to keep to themselves."

"Hey, I almost wore my hat from *Sunset Boulevard*, you know, the one Norma Desmond wore by the pool."

"Sorry, I don't remember hats. I just remember movie sets."

"Well, it's a big black straw affair, perfect for a funeral, but I didn't want to overdo it. What do you think of this one?" She did a little pirouette, and bowed her head. "It looks fine to me. Why didn't you ask your Englishman Maurice about the proper high-tea wardrobe?"

"I would have, but after he told me about the break-in of your Jeep and the stolen dress, he had to take off to coach his soccer team."

"You mean 'football' team."

"Ah. The Brits."

The dress Maurice picked out for me hung from the folding screen.

I said, "I'm sorry about the other dress. I promise to repay you."

"Don't worry. I have plenty more where that one came from."

She put on a brave face but I knew, just like Franklin thought of books as his children, Elle thought of her vintage clothing as close relatives—they both told a story.

Elle took the list from FFM and put it in her vintage Enid Collins bag that was bedazzled with jeweled seahorses and seashells. She promised to make me a copy.

At 2:50, we headed out to the greenhouse.

The exterior of the greenhouse looked like something out of the pages of a child's fairytale. The entrance was framed in wrought-iron curlicues and filigree decoration. It glowed with frosty light in the afternoon gloom. The exterior had been left untouched, the panes of glass layered with decades of Sag Harbor weather. To me, that was part of its charm. Elle and I walked in. Someone had set up four industrial-sized fans. The building had steam heat that traveled through old pipes near the floor when the greenhouse had been used for its original purpose of growing hothouse flowers, not displaying volumes of books. There were four chairs to each of the eight ice cream tables. It was interesting to see where everyone chose to sit. In the center of the room were Franklin; his wife, Violet; and his brother, Ollie. Naturally, Brenna belonged at the table with her aunt, uncle, and father—but I had a feeling there was nothing natural about Ollie and Brenna's relationship. The only thing they seemed to share was indifference to each other. Brenna and Allan had their own table. Allan sat in front of a black laptop, typing away. I assumed he was working on his next spy novel. Elle and I took a seat at Hal and Jordan Innes's table.

The twins, Ken and Kortney, sat alone at the table farthest from the door.

In the center of each occupied table was a bone china teapot covered with a knitted tea cozy. I'd bought them at a church bazaar in Montauk. They'd been knitted by Montauk's own centenarian, Bea Nasaw. When I'd let her critique the scarf I made with alternating knit/purl rows of red yarn, she'd laughed so hard she almost lost her dentures. It was good to see she still had a sense of humor at one hundred years old. I liked to think the occasional knit/knit or purl/purl boo-boo rows made the design more avant-garde.

Also on each of the four tables was a glass tiered stand with fluted edges, stacked with finger sandwiches and scones. Cucumber over dilled cream cheese were on top. That would be my first choice. There were vintage English bone china teacups and saucers, matching creamers and sugars, and individual honey pots. Each table's tea set was in a different floral pattern and melded perfectly with the greenhouse's old world charm. Everyone waited for someone to speak, and I should have known who it would be.

Ollie stood up and I could see where Brenna had gotten her height. "Let's get on with this little tea party. I have the event planner coming in a half hour to set up for the gala.

Well, what can I say about someone I barely talked to?" He looked at Franklin. "I suppose my brother is happy Randall McFee authenticated the Fitzgerald manuscript before he croaked. Right, old sport?" He laughed that insufferable laugh of his and slapped his knee. "A little funeral humor."

Almost everyone's mouths and eyes opened wide, except Brenna's. I had a feeling she was used to her father's bad timing.

She stood, "Thank you for that warm tribute, Ollie. Maybe you should run back to your castle and . . ."

I got up with my cup of tea and went to Brenna's side. I put my hand on her arm. "I think it's important to remember that even though none of us knew Randall McFee well, he was a kind and gentle soul." I glanced over at Franklin, whose gray, wan face looked ready to crumple. "If he's looking down on us right now, I know he'd be happy that we got together to remember him. As Willa Cather once said, 'I shall not die of a cold . . . I shall die of having lived,' and from what I knew of Randall, he was passionate about his career. He was a meticulous researcher and a lover of the written word. So, let's raise our teacups and toast to a life well lived."

Violet handed Franklin his cup of tea.

He opened his palm and pushed it against the saucer like a cranky toddler. "How many times do I have to tell you? I hate tea."

Violet looked hurt and embarrassed. Ken Lerner rushed to Franklin's side with a pitcher of ice water with floating lemon slices. Ken poured water into a glass and handed it to Franklin.

Franklin stood and addressed the room, "Randall

McFee and I shared a fondness for one of F. Scott's musings which went something like this: 'That is part of the beauty of all literature. You discover that your longings are universal longings, that you're not lonely and isolated from anyone. You belong.'" Then he fell back onto his chair.

Elle raised her teacup and said, "Here's to Randall. May he rest in peace."

The crowd murmured, "To Randall."

A wren had gotten trapped inside the greenhouse. Its wings flapped against the glass-peaked ceiling. Its solo chirping became frenetic, like a needle stuck in the groove of an old record. Brenna started sobbing. My tears welled. Then came that scratchy feeling at the rear of my throat that usually predicated hysterical crying or laughter—I never knew which.

Ken, with the help of his sister—who stabbed me with her dagger stare each time she passed—cleared everything from the tables. Violet was the only one left with a pot of tea under a knitted cozy and a cup—no honey, cream, or sugar. As Ken and Kortney walked out the door, the bird flew out with them. Maybe the wren was Randall McFee, reincarnated, trying to tell us something. "Tweet, tweet. Follow the evil twins."

A few minutes later, Elle and I sat on a cement bench between the apiary and the greenhouse.

Elle said, "I should have known, when I saw my neighbor's black cat climb through a hole in my picket fence with something in its mouth, today would be a bad day. Look what happened to your dress for the party."

"Black cats don't mean bad luck. As you perpetuate the superstition, you make things very dangerous for them out there."

"I know that. I'm the biggest cat lover there is. If it wasn't for me, you wouldn't have Jo. The cat wasn't bad luck, it was what was in its mouth."

"Let me guess. A mouse?"

"No."

"I give up."

She said, "A snake, although a small one. Actually, it could've been a big worm. It did rain last night."

I gave her "the look." Between Elle's dream, Violet's tea reading, and now a cat with a snake, it was hard to not be creeped out. I heard Rod Serling's voice from *The Twilight Zone*: "For your approval . . ."

I said, in a chipper voice, "I need you to do me a favor before we go back to the inn. I want to check something out, and you can be my backup."

"That sounds dangerous."

"Just follow me."

We took the trail that led to the apiary, passing the occasional cement fountain, obelisk, or meditation bench. Byron must have had his hand in drawing up the landscaping plans for this part of Franklin's property. I had no desire to go inside the apiary, in case Kortney was inside, but Elle insisted we peek in. Inside the boxwood entrance, a swarm of bees hovered over a bed of honeysuckle like a sinister magic carpet. That was all Elle needed. We continued on.

It was almost impossible to find the trail that led to Widow's Point. Making me wonder once again: what was Randall's thinking on the day of the hurricane?

At one point, Elle yelled, "Something's got me!"

I turned and saw that her skirt had been snared by a holly bush. I called out, "Hope it's not a snake."

Her screech echoed across the harbor.

"Relax, you're caught on a thorn."

"Don't tell me to relax. I know this has something to do with Randall's accident, and I also know we're heading to Scrimshaw House."

As I untangled her, I said, "And don't forget Widow's Point and Sarah Hollingsworth's ghost."

"Ugh. You're kidding, right?"

I told her about my conversation with Violet and all the unusual sightings at the captain's house.

"Thanks," Elle said. "Now you tell me. Living in Sag Harbor, I've heard all the rumors, but if someone who's lived here for decades says there's unexplained going-ons, it feels more credible."

"I'm sure there is an explanation for everything. Including Randall's death. And I don't think a gust of wind is to blame. We're almost there."

We stepped into the clearing that led to Widow's Point. The sun had come out, but I still felt the gloom.

I grabbed her wrist. "Come to the railing. I want to show you something." When we reached the railing, I pointed down. "Look, there's a piece of paper wedged between the rocks."

Elle looked over the railing then stepped back. "It's not safe to go down there."

"Easy peasy. I'm going to climb down and get it."

"Be careful. Take this to preserve fingerprints." She handed me one of her vintage floral handkerchiefs.

"Wow. You're learning, Watson."

"I don't know if that's a good thing, Sherlock."

The trail down wasn't as treacherous as it looked. There was actually a safe path between the rocks. Slowly but surely, I made it to the shoreline. I grabbed the end of the piece of paper with Elle's handkerchief and looked at a

typed envelope addressed to Randall McFee, care of the
Bibliophile B & B, remembering the envelope I found in
his car. Were the two related? I climbed back up, not wanting to linger over the large flat stone with the dark cran-
berry stain. I thought of Randall's unmarked face on the
ambulance stretcher. He must have fallen backward off
Widow's Point. Had he been backing away from someone
and if he was suicidal, wouldn't he have jumped face-first?
And the big question: what was he doing there in the first
place?

When I got to the top of the cliff, Elle said, "How's this
for backup?" She shoved her phone in my face and I saw
911 on the screen. "All I have to do is press send."

Thanks, friend." I showed her the envelope. "The return
address is a law office in Key West. A different address
than the FedEx envelope I found in Randall's car."

Elle said, "That was disappointing."

"You never know, Watson."

Before leaving, she said, "Have fun on your date with
Byron tonight. Have you made any decisions on the course
of your love life?"

"No. Have you?"

She answered with flushed cheeks and a sly smile.

My dinner date with Byron would be a welcome distraction from the thought of Randall's tragic fall and that
stained rock.

CHAPTER

SEVENTEEN

When I entered the lounge, or the former-library-turned-lounge, I went over to the bar where Brenna was the barkeep. The inn didn't need a library because of the greenhouse and all the rooms filled with books. Brenna offered me a bee's knees.

I said, "Thanks anyway. I have dinner plans tonight. I don't want my date finding my head in a plate of spaghetti." I chose a bottle of Perrier. She poured it in a tumbler and added two wedges of lime.

The lounge had a flat-screen TV inside a huge mahogany cabinet. The polished, ornately carved bar was a recent addition to the room. Brenna told me it had been shipped on an eighteen-wheeler from a famous Art Nouveau–style Baltimore hotel bar that F. Scott Fitzgerald had frequented. Hal and Jordan sat on a tufted leather sofa holding hands. They each held a glass of rosé. Allan sat at a chess table

with a bottle of thirty-year-old Macallan scotch. I knew
the Macallan cost a pretty penny because it was my ex-
fiancé Michael's favorite. Allan's recent hardcover flop,
The Mars Project, lay on the table. He'd told me last week
he was writing the sequel, even though his publisher
wanted him to do a stand-alone book. He'd said, "A contract is a contract. If the sequel becomes a bestseller, it will
boost the sales on *The Mars Project*, no matter what the
reviews."

I'd wished him good luck with that theory.

Franklin lounged on a leather wing chair and ottoman.
His legs were covered with a beautiful crocheted afghan.
He looked fragile, the dark bags under his eyes magnified
by his thick spectacles. He didn't hold a book or his pipe,
but he did hold a bee's knees.

Just as I breathed a sigh of relief that there was no obnoxious Ollie present, I looked out the window and saw
him pull up—on a white stallion, no less. He tethered the
horse's reins to the porch railing on the side veranda.

As soon as Ollie walked into the lounge, he said to
Brenna, "Brenna, where's my well-deserved drink?"

And surprise of all surprises, Brenna handed him one.
He sat on a bar stool and his not-broken-in cowboy boots
rained dried clumps of dirt onto the parquet floor.

I immediately moved next to Violet and sat in a club
chair that faced the fireplace.

Violet held a cup of tea. I'd never seen her touch a drop
of alcohol. She wore her trademark shawl and a sheer pais-
ley multicolored tunic, like something by '60s designer
Pucci that Elle might have in her closet.

I said, "Is that your special gold leaf tea?"

She stopped rubbing her fingers together and brought

the cup below her chin. She looked in, like she didn't re-member what she was drinking. After a few minutes she said, "No. This is Tienchi flower tea." She tipped her teacup in my direction. What looked like tiny broccoli florets swam in pale green water. "It's a one-cup cure-all for a myriad of ailments. I wish Franklin would drink it. He doesn't look well."

"Well, he loves honey. I've seen him slather it on his scones and, of course, it's in his bee's knees. Isn't honey good for you?"

"I wouldn't know about honey. I know about tea. You'd have to ask Kortney."

Yes, that would be happening—about the twelfth of never.

The echoing gong of the front doorbell rang. Byron! I jumped up and went to answer it, meeting Ken in the hall-way. He turned and walked away with stiff butler posture and a slight curl to his lip.

After a quick but satisfying kiss on the lips, I led Byron into the lounge.

Brenna greeted him with a bee's knees. He took a sip and smiled.

Violet invited Byron to sit next to her and asked him what she should do about a dying orchid in her studio. I slipped out to fetch my purse.

When I got up to the loft, Jo was giving herself a bath. She looked over at me and gave a final lick to the white end of her tail.

"Don't you look fresh as a daisy, Miss Josephine."

Ever since she'd been trapped in the loft, we'd started talking to each other. I would say something, and she would think I was offering food and respond with a rattling hum.

Of course, I gave her a treat like a good Pavlovian subject.

I took my phone out of my purse and texted Elle: *Can you stick my copy of the insurance list under the driver's seat mat? The Jeep's open, as in busted window. Thks.* I pressed send.

When I came back into the lounge, Byron was standing next to Ollie, and Ollie had his arm around Byron's shoulders.

I heard, "And would you believe, old sport, I sold the horse, there and then, to a marquis for a hundred thou!"

Byron pulled away. "There you are, Meg. We better hurry or we'll lose our table."

Ollie said, "She can wait. I didn't get to the good part."

Byron turned and looked Ollie in the eyes. "No, she can't wait, old sport. Have a good evening." He grabbed my hand and we walked out of the room.

We had a delicious meal at the American Hotel, consisting of pâté de foie de canard for our appetizer and, on our waiter's suggestion, chose wild striped bass with fennel and saffron in a bouillabaisse broth for our entrée. After a few laps walking through town, we ended up at Chocolat for dessert.

We were sitting at a small table in the corner when my phone vibrated. I didn't usually take out my cell phone in a restaurant, but with all the recent disasters, I had to check. I glanced at Elle's text: *Have fun. No hanky panky unless you give me all the details.* I quickly deleted it and, once again, thought about Cole Spencer.

Byron said, "What's wrong? You don't like your frozen hot chocolate?"

"No, it's great. Tastes similar to Serendipity's in Manhattan. Have you ever been?" The movie *Serendipity* had been named after the restaurant where John Cusack and Kate Beckinsale's characters fell in love over chocolate dessert.

"Many times."

Of course he had. And I bet he ordered their *Guinness World Records* Golden Opulence Sundae, touted as the most expensive dessert in the world, for a thousand dollars. It had Tahitian vanilla ice cream, hundred-dollars-a-pound candied fruit from Paris, and the most expensive Venezuelan Chuao chocolate. There was a twenty-three-karat goldleaf edible flower on top that took eight hours to make. In all fairness, the goblet holding the Golden Opulence was Baccarat and cost three hundred dollars. Yours to keep as a souvenir. So the sundae was a bargain at seven hundred. If Violet ordered it, she could accompany it with her gold leaf tea, special ordered from Japan.

Byron said, "Here, have some of my blackout mousse." He stuck his spoon in, scooped out a bit of mousse, and brought it to my mouth. "Open the garage door. Here comes the Willy Wonka chocolate express."

I opened my mouth and started laughing. Before I could swallow the mousse, not-so-frozen hot chocolate sprayed out my nose. Talk about embarrassing. I laughed even harder.

Thankfully, after handing me a napkin, Byron joined in. Not in the chocolate snorting—in the laughter.

After a trip to the ladies' room, I asked him about

Kortney Lerner and the delicate matter of why she wasn't in charge of landscaping the Hollingsworth's property and he was.

"Originally, Kortney started out as Ollie's assistant, but, according to Ollie, she fell in love with him, and he had to reassign her. She'd taken over the apiary after her mother, who was Franklin and Ollie's housekeeper, died. So, Ollie talked Franklin into giving her the title of groundskeeper. Even if in name only. I've been in charge of the plans and landscaping for Franklin and she does the upkeep on Ollie's property and the area inside the apiary. And she . . ." He hesitated and took another spoonful of mousse.

"She what?" I asked.

"Never mind. I just feel sorry for her. She can be very needy at times."

"I also feel sorry for her. Especially if what you say is true, and she was in love with Ollie. Yuck."

"Yuck is right."

I told Byron about the furniture Ollie tried to steal from the Edith Wharton suite.

"That doesn't surprise me. There are rumors at the polo field that he is a big-time gambler and a big-time loser."

Later, when Byron walked me up the sweeping front veranda of the Bibliophile, I felt like I was in an old-fashioned television show—Aunt Bee peering out from behind the lace curtains to make sure nothing untoward was going on. It was a good thing someone had fixed the railing that had been damaged in the storm because Byron grabbed me, bent me backward, then planted a kiss that would keep me satiated until he came by tomorrow night to take me to the twenties gala cocktail party. Then he hopped into his Maserati—Fonzie-style, without opening the door—and drove away.

I put my hand on the door handle to go inside the inn, then remembered the insurance list waiting under the mat in my Jeep and turned around. Stopping at the bottom of the veranda steps, I admired the view of the harbor on a moonlit night. It wasn't the ocean, but it would do. The air was cool and an owl hooted in the near distance. I hurried to the parking lot, gravel crunching under my feet. I opened the driver's door, bent down, and grabbed the insurance envelope under the mat.

Then I heard more crunching on gravel. I shot up and turned.

Kortney Lerner was ten inches away.

I looked at her. "You frightened me."

"You should be frightened," she answered. Moonlight glinted off her eyeteeth, then she turned and walked toward the back gates, her utility boots crunch crunch crunching, while the owl hoot hoot hooted.

I clutched the insurance documents to my chest and ran up the front steps to the inn.

CHAPTER

EIGHTEEN

The first thing I did Saturday morning was feed Jo. Her sedentary lifestyle, and the numerous cat treats Elle and I kept giving her to keep her sated, caused what was once a simple potbelly to resemble a nine-month womb ready to unload sextuplets. I'd have to remember to ask Brenna for a full roll of paper towels for Jo to tear apart—Jo's favorite between-meals activity and pacifier. All I had to do was sprinkle a little catnip inside the cardboard tube and she'd be as high as a kite for hours, wrestling her demons.

The second thing I planned to do was drop off my Jeep to get the window repaired. I would bring my laptop and walk to Sag Coffee while I waited. I wanted to search the Internet for possible relatives with the last name of McFee in Key West. Brenna had told me last night that she'd charged Randall's phone, and had left numerous messages for an entry he'd assigned the name "Sis." Then she'd given the phone to the Desk Sergeant at the Sag Harbor Police precinct.

The last thing I planned to do before I had to get ready for the cocktail party was start to inventory the inn's books. I came up with a brilliant idea. I'd take photos of the bookcases by room with my cell phone, then check them off the alphabetical list from FFM with a notation of what was missing. I wouldn't even need Brenna's keys. I could do all the cross-referencing in the Emily Dickinson loft and spend some quality time with Jo.

When I passed the dining salon on my way out, there wasn't the usual breakfast spread on the sideboard. No Brenna. No Violet, Franklin, or Ollie. No Allan, Jordan, or Hal. And no obnoxious twins.

I stepped out the front door. The veranda was so large, there were three complete sets of wicker furniture with soft cushions. Ken brought the cushions out every morning and took them in every night. The polyurethaned pale gray floorboards were covered with sisal rugs. Iron plant stands held lush ferns. If I squinted my eyes toward the harbor, I was back in the 1800s—the metal masts on the sailboats in the harbor turned to wood, and a billionaire's yacht morphed into a whaling ship set for Honduras. The sky was dark, but the air was cooler than it had been in the past couple of days. If the rain held off, it would be a perfect evening for the gala.

I made my way to the parking lot. Whereas the inn was deserted, the same couldn't be said for the grounds. Ken Lerner stood by the open back gates. A large white truck passed through. The side of the truck read: HAUPPAUGE PARTY printed above MORE FUN FOR LESS MONEY. It was surprising that over-the-top Ollie would rent party supplies from a discounter. The Hamptons had a plethora of top suppliers worthy of the opening. The 1920s gala to celebrate the first annual Sag Harbor Antiquarian Book and Ephemera Fair had been in the planning stages for months, enough time to hire a local business. Then I remembered what Byron had said about Ollie's gambling debts. Brenna told me her Uncle Franklin was financing the party. Did Franklin know Ollie was cutting corners on his dime? Behind the truck was a line of unmarked white vans. Ken glanced my way and I waved. As expected, he didn't wave back. What had I ever done to him or his twin?

A few minutes later, I dropped the Jeep off to get the passenger window repaired. I could tell the glass technician was wondering why I'd sink more money into the old Wrangler. I was beginning to see that our days were numbered.

At Sag Coffee, I ordered the house blend with cream, no sugar, and was lucky enough to score a table in the corner. I really wanted a frothy caramel concoction topped with fresh whipped cream, but if a new car was in my future, I needed to start pinching pennies.

I opened my laptop and went surfing. Virtually. I played an online video game that had me fighting sharks and avoiding wipeouts while I rode my rad surfboard. For every wipeout, there were instructions on what I'd done wrong. I was learning to surf—cerebrally. Now all I had to do was sign up for actual lessons at Ditch Plains Beach in Montauk. Surfing was on my bucket list. But so was knitting. I didn't think I was allowed to cross that one off yet.

When I looked at the online version of all the local Hamptons and Long Island papers, I didn't see any mention of Randall McFee. I did see lots of hype about tonight's party at Ollie's castle. There was even a picture of Ollie standing in front of his ugly mansion next to a woman who looked familiar. I magnified the photo to 150 percent and almost fell off my chair. Tara Gayle—crackpot, thief, and Cole's ex-girlfriend—stood next to Ollie. She looked better than the last time I'd seen her in Montauk, when she'd been in a hairnet, washing dishes at her grandfather Mickey's restaurant. Or before that, in an orange jumpsuit, picking up litter from the side of Montauk Highway. I read the caption under the photo: *Ollie Hollingsworth, host of the first annual Sag Harbor Antiquarian Book and Ephemera Fair's kick-off gala, with Tara Gayle, owner of Champagne and Caviar Event Planning, Inc.*

"Say what!" The patrons in Sag Coffee looked my way. "All good," I said. Though it wasn't. I couldn't believe felon Tara Gayle was in charge of the 1920s-themed party. Now I understood the reason for the discount party rental truck. Last October, Tara had tried to compete with my Cottages by the Sea interior design firm by poaching would-be clients in Montauk. That didn't work out, so she'd decided to become an event planner? Tara's former shop in Bridge-hampton, Champagne and Caviar Antiques, had been forced to close down for legal reasons. Tara's aesthetic was a perfect match to Ollie's over-the-top medieval-castle style. Finally, a man who deserved Tara's attention—they were a match made in hell.

I put the name "McFee" into the search on my laptop, along with "Key West," and only came up with one result. I didn't find a relative of his, but I did find a small news article written about Ernest Hemingway.

> One of Ernest Hemingway's heirs is questioning the validity of their ancestor's newly published book, *Before the Scourge*. A local district court must agree,

because they ordered all the bookstores selling the just-released novel to pull them off the shelves until a jury can decide if the manuscript was indeed written by Hemingway or by a plagiarist.

Randall McFee's name was mentioned as the authenticator of Hemingway's long-lost novel. Could that have been what was in the FedEx envelope? Court papers calling him to testify? I still had the envelope I'd found on the rocks in a plastic bag in my purse. I took out the envelope and read the return address. The lawyer's name was the same as the Hemingway heirs' lawyer in the article.

I wrote down the name of the judge and made a mental note to ask my father to look into it. My father had some free time now that he was retired, in between cooking and volunteering at the youth center. Maybe Randall had thrown himself off Widow's Point because of the controversy over the Hemingway possibly being a fake. I called Doc to see if he could pass on any intel about Randall McFee's body. I got a recording of the Beach Boys' "Surfin' Safari" with Doc saying in a chipper voice that he was out hitting the waves. I left a message about the autopsy, knowing I was chancing a stern talking-to from my father's best friend. But no one could read an autopsy report better than a retired Detroit PD medical examiner.

As I waited for the call that my Jeep was ready, I went to Cole's website and found photos of him and Tripod on their latest journey to deliver a gorgeous vintage sailing yacht and former America's Cup winner, to an island near Saint Thomas. In the photo, Tripod wore a captain's hat— tipped at a jaunty angle. Tripod looked more endearing than ever, and his master wasn't bad either. Late Thursday night, Cole had called to check on me, and his yacht, wondering why I hadn't called him to say I was safe. Luckily, we'd had a bad connection. I'd quickly apologized and white-lied, saying we were all fine. An understatement if there ever was one. Sully had assured me he'd take care of everything at the East End Yacht Club. "No worries," he'd said.

Sully was right. Cole's damaged yacht was repairable—Randall McFee's death, irreparable.

CHAPTER

NINETEEN

When I got back to the Bibliophile, all the usual suspects were in the lounge. It was three hours too early to get ready for the party but, obviously, it wasn't too early for cocktails. As F. Scott Fitzgerald once said, "Here's to alcohol, the rose-colored glasses of life." I was tempted to go inside, where I saw Brenna had set up a raw bar on ice: oysters on the half shell, littleneck clams, crab claws, and, of course, local lobster, but when I saw Kortney sitting next to Violet on the sofa, I vetoed the idea. Plus, I wanted to hit the Louisa May Alcott suite to take pictures of the bookcases in case Brenna planned to use the room to get ready for the party.

I went up and said hi to Jo, grabbed the insurance list, and went down to the second floor. The Louisa May Alcott suite was next to the Herman Melville suite. Not that the authors had ever hung out together, but I wondered what they would have thought of each other if they had. Herman Melville was born in 1819 and died in 1891. Louisa May

Alcott was born in 1832 and died in 1888. It also made it easy for me to switch decorative items between rooms because the authors lived around the same time period.

I walked into the Alcott suite. Through the bedroom doorway, I saw the imprint of Brenna's long body on the simple ecru coverlet on top of the bed. I'd hired my go-to construction team, Duke and Duke Junior, to build a half-moon wooden desktop on a pedestal between two lace-curtained windows. The desk was similar to the one Louisa May Alcott's father had made for her at Orchard House, in Concord, Massachusetts. The same desk where she'd penned *Little Women*. I had placed a framed photo of Louisa on top. It showed her looking off into space with a pen in hand, sitting at her davenport desk. She'd bought the more ornate second desk with the money she made from her stories, but she kept both desks in her room at Concord as long as she lived. Also on the half-moon desk was a simple vase that Brenna kept filled with a single yellow rose from the Bibliophile's kitchen garden, a cloth-and-gilt version of *Little Men*, and a silver-plated inkstand with a glass inkwell that had a perch for a brass-tipped pen. I'd taken a pen from my collection. Sometimes I had to sacrifice a few of my treasures to make clients happy.

In the sitting room was a Fraktur-decorated chest that stored extra guest blankets. In Louisa May Alcott's time, the trunk would have held costumes for her and her sisters' "theatricals." Above the two locked bookcases were a pair of framed, hand-tinted lithographs of snowy owls on a tree limb. I'd found them at Elle's shop. The owls reminded me of the oil painting Alcott had in her bedroom in Concord that her sister May had painted. May Alcott had been a skilled artist, and her influence could be seen throughout the Alcott house when Elle and I had visited. Louisa never married, but when her sister May died, she took on the responsibility of her children.

Also in the sitting room was a pair of upholstered chairs in front of the fireplace with a small tea cart between them. I'd found an unusual item at a nearby estate sale that I'd placed near the hearth: a Victorian foot warmer. It consisted of a punched-tin box with a wooden frame that would be filled with either a heated brick or coal. The top of the warmer, where you placed your feet, was usually covered in fabric, or a piece of needlework. Perfect to rest your feet to keep them toasty while you read in front of the fire on a cold Sag Harbor night. The tea cart was topped with two red-and-white Coalport transferware cups and saucers in a similar pattern to what Louisa's mother, also named May, owned. Ever since my tea reading with Violet, I'd had a habit of looking inside teacups for prophetic tea leaves. Thankfully, these were empty.

I turned off the flash on my camera and took a dozen shots of the books behind the glass. Most of the books in the Alcott suite were those written by the author, along with volumes by Ralph Waldo Emerson and Henry Thoreau. Emerson and Thoreau had been friends with Louisa's father, Bronson Alcott. Louisa and her father spent many days in philosophical transcendentalist conversations with both men.

The mahogany mantel clock with a painted-on-glass harbor scene chimed four. I took a few more photos, then scurried down to the John Steinbeck suite.

For some reason, when I walked in, my Steinbeck book, *The Winter of Our Discontent*, came to mind. It was loosely based on Shakespeare's tragedy *Richard III*:

"Now is the winter of our discontent
Made glorious summer by this sun of York;
And all the clouds that lour'd upon our house
In the deep bosom of the ocean buried."

These last few days were turning into a Shakespearean tragedy.

Steinbeck had lived in Sag Harbor during the last years of his life, from 1955 to 1968. Before Elle and I worked on the suite, we'd trespassed on Steinbeck's modest homestead overlooking Noyac Bay in Sag Harbor. Steinbeck had called it "my little fishing place a mile out of town."

Elle and I had been like two clumsy ninjas snapping photos and drooling over the sunset through the windows of Steinbeck's six-sided writing studio. The hut was perched on a bluff overlooking Upper Sag Harbor Cove, surrounded by windows with only room for a desk and a canvas folding chair. The tiny writing studio was the same place Steinbeck had penned *The Winter of Our Discontent*. Over the door, Steinbeck had printed "Joyous Garde." A huge fan of the King Arthur tales, I'd found out later Joyous Garde referred to Lancelot's castle. Our biggest surprise was the huge stone unicorn in the middle of Steinbeck's vast lawn. Elle and I rubbed his horn for good luck and then sat on the dock where Steinbeck had once sat, soaking in all the charged particles of creativity that floated in the air.

That was until a caretaker, carrying a big stick, ran us off the property.

The price you had to pay for design inspiration.

I admired Steinbeck even more after I read an article on him in *Dave's Hamptons* about what Steinbeck had written to an old friend after moving to Sag Harbor in 1955: "It's a whaling town or was and we have a small boat and lots of oak trees and the phone never rings. We run there whenever we need a rest—no neighbors, and fish and clams and crabs and mussels right at the door step." That's how I thought of my cottage in Montauk, decades later.

As Franklin had requested, I'd made the Steinbeck suite a manly suite. I glanced around the outer room to the suite and felt Steinbeck would have appreciated my design ethic. It wasn't easy to balance a mid-century vibe in a Victorian mansion. My favorite thing in the room was a Hans Wegner "teddy bear" or "papa bear" chair. It was in the Danish style from the early fifties and had black wool upholstery on teak. When I sat in it, it felt like huge bear paws were reaching out to hug me from behind. Everything in the room was worn and lived in, including the typewriter on the desk. Next to the chair, I'd filled a revolving bookcase with well-worn copies of Steinbeck's work along with his contemporaries'. Unlike the books behind the two glass-front bookcases, the books in the revolving bookcase had little value, because I'd liberated them from the greenhouse. All were meant to be read, spines cracked, and pages fingerprinted with chocolate. I had no idea where I'd put Violet's bust of Steinbeck. Violet and Franklin could figure that one out.

I looked at the vintage Big Ben clock on the shelf and realized I'd have to hurry and get ready for the party. I was excited to dress up and play a Gatsby guest for the evening. I was even more excited because Byron was my date. And when the evening ended, we still had something to look forward to: tomorrow's first annual Sag Harbor Antiquarian Book and Ephemera Fair.

CHAPTER

TWENTY

I waited on the veranda steps for Byron to pick me up for the party. It wasn't raining. But the air was so humid, it might as well have been. After only fifteen tries, I'd managed to put my hair in the chignon Maurice suggested. The jewelry Elle and Maurice had picked out had an Egyptian Art Deco feel. Everything was gorgeous, but I felt they suited the more flashy stolen dress, not the simpler one Maurice and I had chosen as a replacement. After I'd put the beaded headband on, I looked in the mirror. When I was younger and first started wearing hearing aids, I wouldn't have been caught dead with my hair up. Now, I barely remembered they were there.

The snake on the coiled arm bracelet had ruby eyes and a pavé rhinestone body. Instead of fear, the snake instilled confidence and power—like Cleopatra herself. The beaded headband originally came with a brooch depicting the profile of Hermes wearing a winged rhinestone helmet. The messenger-of-the-gods piece was too flashy to keep on the headband. So I took it off and pinned it to the sash hanging below hip level on my dress. Long, dangling rhinestone ball earrings added to the Gatsby look. The last piece of jewelry had been a cocktail ring the size of my hand in the shape of a scarab with wings. I'd left it behind.

Byron's Range Rover passed through the front gates.

I went down to the bottom step and took my roaring twenties pose.

A sleek white limo came through the front gates and stopped at the path leading to the front of the inn. Byron turned the corner. He walked toward me, holding a single white lily. He wasn't a young Robert Redford or a Leonardo DiCaprio in his three-piece white suit—he was something all his own. I wished I could run inside and check the book he'd given me to see the meaning behind a lily. Then I remembered *The Illuminated Language of Flowers* was back at my cottage. Byron smiled his signature smile and, just as I leapt off the step to run into his arms, someone dressed in red came barreling up behind him.

Looking more beautiful than was humanly possible was Allan Wolfstrum's ex-wife, Nicole.

"Byron, Byron. Wait up."

I had to give him credit—he seemed surprised by her appearance. But I gave him a demerit when I saw him give her the same smile he'd just given me.

He said, "Nic."

I went to where the two were standing. "We'd better get moving. It's going to pour." Then I slipped my arm through Byron's.

He took a step, then stopped and looked at the flower in his hand. "This is for you."

I went to give him a kiss on the cheek but missed and ended up giving him a kiss on the nose. My deep red lipstick marked the spot. I didn't wipe it away.

Nicole took advantage of Byron's now free hand and slipped her arm through his. "I hope you don't mind hopping in my limo? My date broke his tibia and I had to come stag. I'll be the talk of the tabloids if I show up alone." Her red beaded-and-sequined dress made noises against her shapely body as she walked. A large ostrich feather was tucked in her sequined headband, and instead of it being over-the-top, it completed her outfit perfectly. The diamonds she coyly fingered at her neck were undoubtedly real.

All I could think was *Uggh!* as Nicole led us to her limo and the three of us got in.

As we approached Hollingsworth Castle, there were signs of newbie party planner Tara Gayle's influence. Two dingy-looking party tents stood next to each other. Both sagged in the middle. If the rain started as forecasted, the tents would probably collapse on the partygoers. There were tiki torches lining the pathway, one of which was dangerously close to a tent. Byron told the limo driver to stop and he got out. He went to the torch, uprooted it, and placed it a safe distance away. Nicole and I didn't have much to say as we waited for him to return. What were you supposed to say to the popular girl? *That's swell you and Biff were named Homecoming Queen and King. Heard you just bought your own private jet. Or, sorry you lost to that twelve-year-old at the People's Choice Awards.*

Byron hopped in the limo. "Miss me?"

We said in unison, "Yes!"

A few hundred feet before the main entrance to the

castle, the limo let us out at the admission table. I knew the tickets to the gala were pricey because I'd bought one, even though Franklin told me I didn't need to. Twenty-five percent of ticket sales would go to SAIL—Franklin's pet project—Save America's Invaluable Libraries. The rest of the money went to Ollie for party expenses.

I gave a young girl wearing a nose ring my invitation. Even though she'd tried to cover it with makeup, I saw the outline of a scorpion tattoo on her hand. The tattoo reminded me of Brenna's and I thought again of how unBrenna-like her skull tattoo was.

Tara's hired staff wore large men's T-shirts with a crude drawing of a champagne glass overflowing with odd-shaped black eggs that looked more like whale excrement than caviar. Below was *Champagne and Caviar Party Planners—www.champandcav.com*.

The girl checked me off the list, then handed me three tickets, two for drinks and one for a one-time pass through the food tent. She went on to explain there was no need for a ticket for the hors d'oeuvres served inside the castle.

Byron went through the same procedure. But when megastar actress Nicole Wolfstrum came up, the girl ripped off about twenty drink and food tickets and told Nicole there wasn't any need for her to show her invitation.

When we arrived at the open Noah's Ark doors to the castle, the dancing had already begun. Everyone was flipping up their heels to the Charleston, beads swingin' and toes tappin'. Luckily, as soon as we stepped inside, Nicole was waylaid by a few fans asking for autographs. A little tacky to do at a Hamptons event. Everyone was supposed to pretend hanging with celebs was a normal occurrence— even if they wanted to pee their pants in excitement.

Putting my arm through Byron's, I nudged him forward. The renaissance-style banquet hall rose two levels. Twenty feet high on the far wall was a narrow balcony with a heavily carved wooden railing. It ran the length of the room below. I pictured a Montague cursing out a Capulet—or vice versa.

The banquet hall floor had six-foot-by-six-foot black-and-white tiles in a chessboard pattern. There were numerous machine-made tapestries and a banner with some kind of family crest incorporating a lion. Shields and dangerous-looking crossed swords and hatchets—ready for a beheading—covered the walls. Naturally, flanking the perimeter of the hall were a half dozen knights in armor holding lances.

Byron was immediately stopped by one of his female clients. I grabbed two gin and tonics from a roving waiter and handed one to Byron. The waiter didn't leave. Did he want a tip? Then I remembered to fork over two tickets. I was surprised Ollie wasn't serving bee's knees or a similar drink from the 1920s. I excused myself to Byron when I spotted Elle and Maurice in the corner, near a jazz band. I plowed my way toward them, weaving in and out of all the black-tied and white-tied tuxedoed males and fringed, feathered, and sequined females. In the center of the dance floor, I passed a random, four-foot-tall marble pedestal.

Elle and Maurice greeted me with hugs.

The acoustics in the hall were loud and echoey.

"Meg, you look stunning," Elle said as I read her lips.

"I was just going to say the same to you."

Elle wore a fuchsia beaded-and-sequined short dress with a low-waisted matching belt. Of course, it wasn't one of the four choices she'd told me she had narrowed it down to. She'd probably called this morning and had it flown in from Paris. Instead of a headband, she had on a sequined cloche hat. It was perfect for her short dark hair. Both her and Maurice held plastic champagne flutes. Another Hamptons no-no—plastic—for ecological and snooty reasons.

I cupped my hand around Elle's ear and said, "This jazz trio seems too small for the size of the banquet hall. The room necessitates a full orchestra. No doubt, it was Tara Gayle's idea to cut corners."

She said, "I can't believe that loser is now a party planner. What's next? Mayor of Montauk?"

"Blasphemy! Do they allow mayors to have criminal records?"

Behind the trio was a two-story cement fireplace mantel straight from the Middle Ages. It had a hearth big enough to roast a boar, or a human.

The musicians stopped playing, and piped music filled the room. I was going to ask Elle where Franklin and Violet were, when a trumpet blared. One of those long-necked trumpets used in medieval pageants to announce royalty.

The music stopped and the crowd on the dance floor parted to let the procession make their way toward the marble pedestal in the center of the room. Franklin held a crystal box. He was dressed in a top hat and tails, complete with black-and-white spats. Violet wore violet. Her sash on her beaded dress and headband held peacock feathers. The sequins changed colors—blue, green, and violet—as she stepped under the huge wagon wheel chandelier suspended from buttressed beams. Behind them were Ollie, Brenna, and two gangster-attired men with open jackets exposing shoulder holsters. FFM insurance guards. The guns probably weren't part of their costumes.

Ollie was dressed in a black-and-red tuxedo with tall black boots and a black sequined top hat. He resembled a circus ringmaster—all he needed was a whip. Brenna wore a turban with a jeweled pin in the center and a fringed green dress with a low, sweeping back.

Franklin gingerly placed the crystal box on top of the pedestal. He looked down at it like an anxious father checking on a preemie in an incubator. Franklin hadn't given birth—F. Scott Fitzgerald had. Then one of the guards covered the manuscript with a white satin cloth. Ollie nudged Franklin aside, and Brenna pulled him back. She whispered something in her father's ear. If I had to guess, it would have been something along the lines of, "This is your brother's moment in the spotlight, not yours." Ollie stomped away. Thankfully he went to the other side of the room. Apparently, we would all have to wait for the unveiling of *The Heiress and the Light*.

Doc and Sully arrived. They made quite a distinguished pair, although Doc looked like he was ready to hit a twenties golf course at Carl Fisher's Montauk Manor. He wore a cap, long argyle socks, and below-the-knee pants. Sully was a replica of his great-grandfather, Carl Fisher's yacht captain. Sully wore white pants with a stiff crease, an emblemed navy blazer, and a nautical hat. When they reached Elle, Maurice, and me, Sully said, "I saw the guest of honor in the center of the room."

"You mean Franklin Hollingsworth?" I asked.

"No. *The Heiress and the Light*."

I looked across the room. Ollie was sitting on his pompous

rear end in a gothic throne-type chair on a dais and Tara was feeding him a burnt potato-puff straight from a bulk-shopping food warehouse. Ollie and Tara were going to score big-time on the proceeds from the party. I wasn't an event planner, but with this many people and only twenty-five percent going to charity, one of them was going to come out in the black. If any of the celebs and rare-book collectors had known ahead of time about the party's tacky décor and cuisine, they probably wouldn't have come. And even though I wasn't opposed to Tara and Ollie having a flop on their hands, I wanted Franklin to raise tons of money for Save America's Invaluable Libraries.

I looked again at Tara. Something seemed familiar about her. I excused myself and made my way to the other side of the room. As I got closer, I realized what it was.

Tara was wearing the dress that had been stolen from my Jeep!

I hadn't recognized it at first because she had a shapelier figure than I. The fabric between the turquoise sequins was stretched and showed a fair amount of skin. I charged up the dais and stabbed my finger on her chest.

"What are you doing wearing my dress?"

Tara took a sip of champagne from a *glass* flute. She looked down her nose at me. "Get a load of this poser, Ollie. What are you doing here? Surely, you weren't on the guest list?"

Ollie said, "What's this about a dress? Here you go again, accusing innocent people of stealing."

Tara put her hand on Ollie's shoulder. "I bought this dress and I don't need to explain anything. Although, I can see why you'd want to wear my dress instead of that simple, boring schmatta you have on."

I wished I was holding a champagne glass so I could douse her with it. Instead, I charged back to Elle to tell her about the dress. Detective Shoner had joined her, Maurice, Doc, and Sully. The jazz trio started up and I had to shout, "Arrest Tara Gayle. She's wearing Elle's dress that she loaned me. The one stolen from my Jeep!"

The band stopped playing and a group of guests moved toward us.

Maurice took me aside. "Meg, don't make a scene. Remember, this is for charity. Let Tara win the battle, not the fight. Right, Detective?"

Detective Shoner said, "What's this about a dress? Someone copied your dress? Not grounds for arrest."

I said, "Oh, yes, it is. And you, Detective Arthur Shoner, of all people, know what Tara is capable of."

Elle took my hand. "Maurice is right. Don't worry. I'll press charges after the party. You filed a police report, right?"

I gulped. "I, uh, planned to. I only filed an insurance claim for the window." I looked at the crowd gathering and felt guilty about my childish temper tantrum. I'd played right into Tara's hands. Having Ollie as a witness caused the Barrett blotches to crawl higher up from my navel to my cheeks. As a distraction, I pulled Doc to the side and asked him if he'd received my voice mail about Randall's autopsy report.

He hadn't. He put his phone to his ear, listened, then returned it to his pocket. "Megan Elizabeth Barrett! What are you getting involved in now?"

I had no problem hearing Doc over the music and the crowd.

Before Doc could continue his tirade, I grabbed Maurice's arm. "Let's do the Castle Walk."

Maurice led me to the center of the dance floor. We Castle Walked ourselves into and out of the crowd like pros.

He said, "Have you ever seen so many spatterdashes in your life?"

"Huh?"

"You mean, 'Pardon,' not 'huh.' Don't you, Miss Doolittle? 'Spatterdashes' is the original word for spats. Before gangsters wore them as fashionable footwear statements in the twenties, they kept socks and ankles from being spattered with rain and mud."

"Well, aren't you a walking fashion encyclopedia, Professor? They probably wore them to keep the blood off their cuffs after one of their St. Valentine's Day-type massacres."

Then my suave English dance partner stepped on my toes.

"OUCH!"

"Oops. Sorry about that. You've taken to the Castle Walk a lot faster than Elle. I'd better pay attention. I think the dance's inventors, Vernon and Irene Castle, would have been very disappointed in me."

"Do you know them?"

"A little before my time. The Castles were the first professional dance pair to perform in street clothes, not costumes. And in the second decade of the twentieth century, this dance was thought to be very naughty by American standards, because you faced your partner."

Before I could comment, he guided me toward the pedestal holding the F. Scott Fitzgerald manuscript. As the dance called for, I flipped up one of my heels. My other heel stepped down on something slimy. I went flailing backward. Luckily, Hal Innes stopped my descent.

Jordan grabbed my elbow. "Whoa, Nellie, Meg. You guys were doing great until the wiener."

"Weiner?" I looked at my right shoe. Half of a pig in a blanket, smothered in ketchup, clung to the heel of my mother's dancing shoes.

CHAPTER

❦

TWENTY-ONE

I found Byron in the food tent with Allan Wolfstrum and Nicole. Nicole was three sheets to the wind. No, make that four. It looked like she'd cashed in her handful of drink tickets. She was holding onto both Byron's and Allan's arms, occasionally bending at the knees and kicking her right leg in the air.

"Hey. I found you," I said to Byron.

Nicole slurred, "Hidey-Ho, blondie. Sorry to have borrowed your man. He saved me from near death by ice." She giggled.

I looked at Byron.

He said, "That ridiculous ice sculpture of F. Scott Fitzgerald slid off its pedestal and almost stabbed her with its nose."

Nicole's mouth was smeared clown-style with red lipstick. I grabbed a napkin off the table and dabbed around her perfect, pouty lips.

"You're so sweet. Isn't she sweet, Byron?" Nicole looked around. "Byron, where are you? Byron? Where'd you go?"

Byron came up to us with a folding chair. He opened it and Nicole plopped down.

"You're so sweet. Isn't he sweet, Allan?" She added a belch. Only Nicole Wolfstrum could belch prettily. Her short dress had inched up, exposing a red sequined garter belt.

Allan said, "Yes, Nicole. Everyone is sweet. Now, let's get you out of here before the press puts you on Page Six." He whispered to us, "I'm going to take her back to the Bibliophile before things get out of hand."

Byron and I watched Allan half carry, half drag Nicole to her limo. I was amazed at the amount of tenderness Allan showed his ex-wife, especially after seeing him so angry with her at the Artists & Writers Charity Softball Game.

On our way back inside the castle, I overheard an A-list actor say, "I just swallowed part of a toothpick. Stay away from those pigs in a blanket."

I seconded that statement.

We returned to the castle just in time for Franklin's official unveiling of the long-lost *The Heiress and the Light*. Elle, Detective Shoner, Maurice, Hal, Jordan, Doc, and Sully were front and center next to Franklin, Violet, and Brenna. I hadn't seen the Lerner twins all evening.

I watched Ollie step down from the dais, leaving Tara standing next to his throne like a lady-in-waiting. Didn't she have party things to attend to?

Ollie reached Franklin's side. He had a small microphone attached to his lapel. "Ladies and gentlemen, now is the time we have all been waiting for. My brother, Franklin

Hollingsworth, will read the first chapter of Fitzgerald's novel *The Heiress and the Light*." He slapped his brother on the back. "It only cost you five million dollars. Right, old sport? I figure that's about seventy dollars a word. So, everyone, listen up. Stay and get your money's worth."

Ole Ollie seemed jealous of his brother, or jealous of the money spent on the manuscript. It would have gone a long way toward paying off his gambling debts. Ollie transferred the microphone to Franklin's lapel and stepped back. Franklin removed the satin cloth, exposing the clear box. The two guards from FFM moved closer to Franklin. One of them gave Franklin what looked like a television remote control, then shielded him while Franklin punched in the code that opened the box.

When the guards moved away, Franklin, wearing white gloves, flipped up the top. "Thank you, Ollie. Before I read the first chapter from *The Heiress and the Light,* I want to thank the Fitzgerald Family Trust and their publisher"—he looked at Hal Innes—"for giving everyone a sneak peek into what I think will be the novel of the century. I hope when everyone attends the first annual Sag Harbor Antiquarian Book and Ephemera Fair tomorrow, they will also delight in the chance to buy a rare book or item that will give them as much pleasure as this novel has given me."

The crowd applauded.

Franklin reached into the box and picked up the entire manuscript of typed pages tied with a string. Then he placed the bundle on top of the box. Franklin's security detail put their hands inside their suitcoats and glanced furtively around the room.

Franklin untied the string.

The crowd oohed.

He picked up the first page and read:

"'He stood watching her, the strong beating of his heart in tune to the tumult of the waves breaking the shore. She was here. She was everywhere. Her pull so strong, she called to him like a siren. He would brave the crashing of his heart against the rocks, for just one chance.

"'Would she ever feel the same stirrings and emptiness and fullness and bursting of emotion he felt when just the scent of her name floated toward him on the breeze?

"'But he was just a beachcomber, a man who talked to gulls. He'd first seen her from his shack, wandering the barren dunes. How could she not feel him as she passed by, her scarf trailing in the wind, the Atlantic's majesty eclipsed by her halcyon beauty?

"'At night he watched her on the veranda. The lights inside the big, rambling house a soft backdrop to her beauty. She was restless. He wanted to calm her.

"'She was his lighthouse, a beacon, bright and new. Without her, he was a ship without an anchor, a pirate with nothing to plunder.

"'The foghorn called too late. The mist creeped, slithered over the sand, then covered the house and erased the light.

"'"Who goes there?" a voice called from the darkness.'"

When Franklin reached for the second page, he hesitated. Then he stooped down and let out a sound so guttural and raw it echoed and bounced off the walls and coffered ceiling. The crowd opened their mouths. Franklin ripped off his gloves and picked up the entire manuscript. He paged through it in a frenzy. When he got to the middle of the stack, he started whipping pages to the floor.

Byron grabbed my hand and squeezed.

"It's gone. It's gone," Franklin muttered over and over again as he clutched at his chest.

And if that wasn't enough, someone tapped me on the shoulder.

I looked to see who it was.

Cole Spenser stood there with a major frown on his face. His cerulean eyes seemed to glow as they zeroed in on Byron and my clasped hands. He turned, strode through the crowd, and I lost him in a sea of feathers.

I didn't follow—though my damn heart told me to. Then my damn head said, "Stop. Think this through."

CHAPTER

TWENTY-TWO

The Heiress and the Light, with the exception of the first page, had been replaced with a photocopy. Franklin and Violet were immediately ushered out of the castle, accompanied by two security guards. As they passed us, Violet said, "Where's Allan? I think my husband could use a friend right now."

I looked at Byron. "He had to take Nicole back to the Bibliophile. She wasn't feeling well."

Violet snapped, "Well, neither does my husband. If you see Allan, tell him to come to the cabin."

The security detail from FFM called in more recruits and, with the help of Detective Shoner, every female guest's bag was checked, every male frisked. How they thought a two-hundred-page manuscript could fit inside a women's evening bag or a man's vest pocket was beyond me. Elle was convinced someone had pulled a David Copperfield. Detective Shoner had to move the pedestal below the box that held the fake manuscript to show her there wasn't a trap door in the floor.

Elle left with Doc, Sully, and Maurice. Detective Shoner and the team from FFM followed them out the door. They planned to search the book vault. It was obvious to me the switching of the manuscript must have happened in the book vault. After I'd tripped the alarm in the cabin, Franklin had come running in to disarm it. Who else knew the code? Violet? Ollie? Brenna? Jordan? Hal? Allan? Ken? Kortney? And last but not least, Randall McFee?

Nicole's limo was gone, so Byron and I decided to walk back to the Bibliophile. As we exited the castle, Allan Wolfstrum ran up to us. "What's happened? Why is everyone leaving?"

I started to explain, but Byron cut in. "How's Nicole?"

Allan clenched his jaw piranha-style and said, "My wife is sleeping comfortably in the Edith Wharton suite."

He didn't say *ex*-wife. Allan and Byron looked ready for a Mexican standoff.

I said, "We'd better get going. It's starting to drizzle."

Allan got into his car and left, not bothering to offer us a lift back to the inn.

As we watched Allan's Bentley pull away, Byron said, "What's his problem?"

I looked at his face, "He sees you as competition for Nicole."

Byron didn't comment, he just took off his tuxedo jacket and held it over my head to shield me from the rain.

We started our walk back to the Bibliophile. Luckily, my mother's T-strap shoes had a low heel and were quite comfortable. The torches had been extinguished and the outdoor tents were gone, but there were about fifty black garbage bags lining the road. I held tight to Byron's elbow as we walked down the gravel lane.

About halfway down the path, we heard loud voices ahead. Ollie's and Brenna's. They had stopped about a hundred feet ahead of us.

Ollie said, "Do as I say, Daughter. I don't think you want your uncle to find out what you were up to before you came to his doorstep, all sweet and niece-like."

Brenna took off for the inn like a giraffe with her long-legged strides. Ollie followed, but at a slower pace.

I stopped. "What was that about? Let's give them a little time. Who needs more drama?"

Byron turned to me. "Yes. Let's stop. So I can do this."

When I peeked from under his suit coat, he took advantage and kissed me.

All I could think about was Cole. *Lucy, you've got some splainin' to do.*

When we got to the gates, after *many* stops, there were flashing lights coming from the Bibliophile's parking lot. I assumed in response to the stolen manuscript.

I was wrong.

My grandmother Barrett liked to say, "Every cloud has a silver lining." When we passed through the gates—there wasn't much silver up ahead, not even rusted tin. Instead, another ambulance. Another body. Only this one, thank God, was breathing.

And it belonged to Nicole Wolfstrum.

We hurried to Allan and Brenna just as they loaded Nicole into the ambulance. She was delirious and kept retching into a plastic bowl held by one of the attendants.

I asked, "What happened?"

Allan said, "Hal came back from the castle, found her

passed out on the floor, and called nine-one-one. It must be alcohol poisoning."

Byron hurried to the ambulance and climbed inside. Brenna came closer to me and shared her umbrella. I saw Byron take Nicole's hand and I read his lips, "Hang in there, Nic. You're going to be just fine."

Allan didn't need to read Byron's lips. Instead, he rushed to the ambulance and pushed Byron aside. "She's my wife. I'm going with her."

Violet came out on the side veranda. "Come inside for tea. Franklin is still in the book vault. Where's Allan?"

Brenna said, "He's in the ambulance with Nicole. We'll be right there." Then she said to me, "I'm so worried about Uncle Franklin and his heart, and now Nicole Wolfstrum. How much more can we take?"

Byron joined Brenna and me as the ambulance backed out of the parking lot.

The headlights from the ambulance shone on my Jeep. A single yellow arrow with red tail-feathers was sticking out of each flat tire.

What the . . . ?

CHAPTER

⚜

TWENTY-THREE

Byron left right after the ambulance. I wouldn't have been surprised if he'd planned to follow Nicole to Southampton Hospital. After I'd checked on Jo and changed, I went down to the second-floor bathroom. I removed my scarlet lipstick, took out the forty-plus bobby pins stabbing my scalp, and tiptoed down to the Edith Wharton suite. It was only ten in the evening, but it felt like two in the morning.

I walked into the sitting room, then went to the bedroom. I'd never seen such carnage. If an elephant dropped by looking for a hidden peanut, it couldn't have done more damage. The bed sheets were stripped from the bed. An assortment of broken pottery and glass littered the floor, and there were trails of vomit scoring the Aubusson rug. Nicole's dress was draped over the gilt desk chair, the ostrich feather from her headband broken into tiny pieces.

"It's a good thing I heard groaning through the open

door and went to check it out." Hal Innes stood in the middle of the sitting room. He held a sheaf of papers.

I said, "It looks like a scene from *The Exorcist*."

"When I came in earlier, Ms. Wolfstrum was passed out on the floor. I got her on the bed and made sure she had a pulse. When she was lucid, I told her I was calling an ambulance. She told me not to, it might leak to the press. But when Ms. Wolfstrum's lips turned blue, I dialed nine-one-one."

"Well, it's a good thing you did. What did the paramedics do?"

"They treated her for possible drug and alcohol overdose. Gave her a shot of naloxone to see if it was an opiate overdose, but it had no effect."

"I saw her at the party. She was pretty looped, but I didn't think it was that bad."

Hal walked into the bedroom and went to Nicole's red dress and picked it up. There was a gaping hole in the chest area that looked like it had been torn apart by a lion's talons.

He said, "This is too depressing. I was ordered down to the lounge and told to bring my copy of *The Heiress and the Light* to prove it wasn't the one that replaced the real deal at the party."

I looked at the pages. "Have you gotten very far in your transcription?"

"Not at all. I don't plan on doing anything until I'm back in Brooklyn in my office with my computer and research materials. I brought this with me so I can visit some of the areas mentioned in the novel and get more of a feel of the setting, including Montauk Point Lighthouse and the surrounding area."

"Well, any time you want to stop by my place in Montauk, feel free. I'm right on the beach."

"That would be great. Fitzgerald calls Montauk 'the end of the world.' Maybe after the book fair's over. Is Tuesday any good?"

"Sounds good." Both Doc and Sully had read the manuscript. Did they have any idea how privileged they were?

Hal followed me as we went down the grand staircase. He held open the door to the lounge and I walked in. Inside, roles were reversed: Brenna was holding a cup of tea and Violet was behind the bar.

Violet looked at us. "I thought you were Allan with news of his ex." She held a bottle of Macallan.

Franklin, who'd been sitting at a window overlooking the bay, got up. "Is that it?"

Hal walked over to Franklin. "Yes."

Franklin grabbed the manuscript and riffled through the pages. Disappointment showed on his chalky face. He pushed the bundle into Hal's chest and slumped back into his chair.

Jordan looked at Violet. "I don't think a bee's knees would hurt your husband."

I took a chair in the corner. I was overwhelmed by everything and simply wanted to observe. Not easy when there were so many things going on: the missing manuscript, Cole's appearance, my flat tires (Tara?), and Nicole leaving in an ambulance. And, of course, Randall McFee's death. Instead of the curse of the Baskervilles, these few days were shaping up to be more of the curse of the Hollingsworths. With that thought, Ken Lerner entered the room dressed in shorts and a T-shirt.

Ken went over to Franklin. "I just heard about the

manuscript. One of the foals has an infection and won't eat. What can I do?"

Franklin looked at him, his eyes moist behind his round spectacles. "You can find my manuscript."

I had to ask, "Is anything else missing from your book vault?"

Both Ken and Franklin looked at me like I had three heads.

Franklin said, "We'll find out soon enough, Ms. Barrett. As soon as FFM finishes inventorying it."

Violet came from behind the bar and handed her husband a tumbler filled to the brim with bee's knees. I was reminded of the Edith Wharton suite and the aftermath of Nicole Wolfstrum's alcohol-fueled bender.

Franklin took the glass and chugged it down, not bothering to thank his wife. Violet went to the teapot on the table by the window overlooking the parking lot and poured herself a cup. She performed her tea ritual. She seemed to notice my stare and our gazes locked. I'm sure we were both thinking the same thing—i.e. ravensnake.

No one offered me a drink, so I went behind the bar and removed a bottle of ginger ale from the small refrigerator under the counter. I wished it was a Vernors—the magic potion my mother gave me as a child when I had an upset stomach. I poured it into a glass and threw the empty bottle into the recycling bin. It nestled on top of a sea of Hollingsworth Honey jars.

Brenna set her teacup down. "Meg, I just told everyone I heard from Randall McFee's sister. She's going to claim his body and have the funeral in Pennsylvania. It's thanks to you we found her number in his phone."

"Oh, Brenna, that's wonderful news." I came from

behind the bar just as Detective Shoner and Pete Wagner, the CEO of First Fidelity Mutual Insurance, entered the lounge. Pete and I had a good relationship because of some investigative work Elle and I had performed in the past.

Franklin looked up expectantly, but when he saw Pete's face, his crumpled.

Detective Shoner said, "I'm sorry, Mr. Hollingsworth. We weren't able to figure out where the original manuscript went."

Pete went to Franklin's chair and kneeled down. "The good thing is, everything else is accounted for. When's the last time you actually looked through *The Heiress and the Light*?"

Franklin murmured, "Last week. I read the first chapter out loud in practice for tonight."

Pete stood and removed a piece of paper from his inside jacket pocket. He unfolded it, then folded it back up. "There was only one time the alarm was triggered, this past Thursday evening. But you disarmed it right away."

Franklin looked at me. "Ms. Barrett set it off."

Violet's teacup clattered on top of its saucer. "She what?"

"All I did was try to open a door to let Catterina in." I looked to Franklin for help.

Instead, he said, "It was a little suspicious. She fixed me a drink. The next thing I know I'm woken from the sound of the alarm going off."

"Suspicious? I just explained what happened." I stood next to Detective Shoner. "But he came in right away and disarmed it."

Ken said, "Did you happen to see him punch in the code?"

I turned. My frustration had been building for a while. "Mind your own damn business. No, I didn't see what the code was. What would I do with a five-million-dollar manuscript? You're the one sneaking into Yanio's Used Bookshop. What do you need with a bookstore when you work here? And what about the missing books from the inn? Are you fencing them to Yanio's?"

Ken took a step toward me.

"OK, everyone calm down," Pete said. "I'll make a note about the alarm going off. In the meantime, I need to know the names of everyone Mr. Hollingsworth granted access to the book vault."

Franklin said, "The only person besides Violet, Brenna, and Ollie, was Randall McFee. No one but I know the access code."

I think we all had our mouths open on that one. What if Randall switched the manuscript with a photocopy when he'd been inside the vault, then fell to his death before he could fence it or do whatever else he wanted with it?

We all thought it, but Detective Shoner said it. "I want to search Randall McFee's room." He turned to Brenna, "Has any housekeeping been done since the day of the hurricane?"

"Uh, no. Not really. Though, Ms. Barrett was in there a few times inventorying books."

When did I become Ms. Barrett, not Meg?

Before she could continue and make me appear even more guilty, I looked at Pete. "Pete, you know about the missing books. I was only helping Elle."

Pete said, "Let's do as the detective said. My team will turn the room upside down. Did this Randall fellow have a car?"

Detective Shoner said, "We just had it towed to a lot

behind the Sag Harbor station. I'll call and have them get on it."

The merry group disbanded. I slunk out the side door and sat on a wicker settee on the front veranda. The rain had stopped, but the humidity pushed down on me like all the innuendos I'd weathered inside. I'd never been considered a suspect before.

Not a good feeling. All I could think of was: *Daddy* . . .

On the morning of the book fair, instead of excitement and anticipation, foreboding and dread swept over me. Doc had left a voice mail message about his part in Cole's appearance at the party. He was complicit in telling Cole about the damages to the *Malabar X* because the repairs were almost completed and Sully had a question about replacing some of the teak molding below deck. Doc had also mentioned I'd be at the gala, but he had no idea Cole planned on flying in to surprise me. I also learned from Doc that Cole had taken an early flight back to Saint Thomas first thing this morning. I suppose, if I went to surprise him and witnessed him holding hands with another woman at a party, I might have done the same. Doc hadn't known about my relationship with Byron because, if I'd told him, he'd have a dossier on my doorstep listing Byron's past transgressions. I wasn't hiding Byron from him, but as far as Doc was concerned, Byron was just my landscape architect. Doc had also informed me he was having a hard time getting a copy of Randall McFee's autopsy report and wanted to know why I needed it.

The dining salon was empty, as I knew it would be. The show must go on—as in the first annual Sag Harbor Antiquarian Book and Ephemera Fair. After last night's confrontation about me setting off the alarm to the book vault, I was ready to move into Elle's place if I had to. Monday was the delivery of the bed for the Emily Dickinson loft. After a little fluffing and finessing, I was out of here.

I went to the Empire marble-top server, poured a cup of coffee, and took it up with me to the Emily Dickinson loft. I didn't have much of an appetite. On the second floor, Randall McFee's door was closed. I naturally turned the handle. Locked. Ken came out of the Edith Wharton suite carrying a bucket filled with cleaning supplies. I ignored him and continued up to my suite, happy he was given the dirty job.

Elle had texted that she'd talked to Detective Shoner. They hadn't found anything in Randall's room or car. The fair didn't start until ten, so I planned to finish going through the items that had been stored under the eaves in the loft.

Jo was missing when I walked into the Emily Dickinson loft. I ran to the door that led up to the cupola. It was closed. I turned the key in the lock, just in case. Jo was one mighty smart feline, and I wouldn't have put it past her to open it with a swipe of her meaty paw. She was easily tall enough to reach the door handle.

I heard a scuffling sound coming from under the eaves, in the exact location where I planned to inventory. If Jo was afraid of mice, I was surprised she'd go inside.

I called out, "Treats."

Jo head-butted the cupboard door open and I saw a glowing orb.

"Well. Aren't you a not-so-fraidy cat."

She charged out for her treat, gobbled it, then ran back into the cupboard. I crouched and followed her through the double doors, feeling like Alice going down the rabbit hole. I couldn't imagine what Jo found so interesting. I used my cell phone as a flashlight and scanned the interior of the storage space. Jo went to the left, where a child's Victorian rocking horse lay on its side. Jo sniffed and kneaded its mane. No doubt, it was made from real horsehair.

I went to the right. At one point, I was able to stand in a slouched position. Thankfully, there weren't any mice or their droppings. Next to me were two flat-topped trunks, one humpback trunk, and a stack of leather "valises." Elle's word, not mine.

Three dozen sneezes later, I'd managed to drag out all the trunks and suitcases. I'd already taken a shower, but it looked like I'd have to take another. When Jo emerged behind me, she graciously allowed me to take away the cobwebs sticking to her whiskers.

Excited about what I might find, I sat cross-legged on the hand-hooked rug, designed with clusters of crimson blossoms. Trunk number one was disappointing. It was packed with yards of calico cotton—the fabric heirloom quilts were made of. Unfortunately, there were more holes than fabric.

Trunk number two was a gold mine. It was filled with twenty brightly illustrated paper-on-wood children's games. All were marked *McLoughlin Bros. New York* and were dated between 1886 and 1889. The skill level of the games was simple. There were chutes-and-ladders-type board games, lotto, anagrams, and card games: old maid, Peter Coddle, and snap. The larger, exquisitely illustrated paper-on-wood board games featured anamorphic cats, dogs, monkeys, and frogs dressed in Victorian clothing. Most of the earlier games had spinners on wood because dice had been considered instruments of the devil by early Victorians.

When I was small, the wood-and-glass general store display case in my mother's shop, Past Perfect, held an assortment of colorful paper-on-wood McLoughlin games and Bliss dollhouses. The wood dollhouses were also covered in brightly-colored chromolithographed paper. My mother taught me that chromolithography was the late–nineteenth century printing process in which crayon or wax was drawn on limestone, leaving one section free for the colored ink. It was a time-consuming process because it called for a separate printing surface for each color, but was quicker than hand tinting each children's game or book. She'd also told me that, even though the Victorian games were at an elementary skill level, they were played in the parlor by the whole family, usually on Sunday evenings. Maybe that was where she got the idea for Sunday game night. Only we'd play poker, euchre, and Michigan rummy. My father always won at poker, Mom at Michigan rummy, and me at euchre. I swiped a nostalgic tear and continued on to the humpback trunk.

The humpback trunk was filled with clothing. The style of clothing seemed more mid-nineteenth century. The canvas fold-down partition that separated the bottom of the trunk from the top had the initials *S. H.*, cementing my suspicion that the trunk belonged to Sarah Hollingsworth.

Inside were delicate christening gowns and bonnets trimmed in fine lace, meant to be worn by both male and female infants. The women's dresses required corsets and most of the fabric was in muted brown wool or navy silk. Wrapped in muslin were two beaded handbags sewn with delicate pearlized beads that shimmered in hues similar to peacocks' feathers. I was sure Violet would want them—especially knowing her obsession with Sarah, the resident ghost. At the bottom of the trunk was a black-haired china-head doll with an open mouth and teeth, dressed in a home-spun dress that covered a body filled with straw. I could picture a child clutching the doll as she bounced up and down on the seat of a covered wagon heading west for the frontier.

I searched the trunk's pockets and fabric lining for letters or a diary. Weren't humpback trunks the perfect place to find such correspondence? Apparently not.

The last suitcase or valise held something that might get me out of hot water with Franklin—a book: *Alice's Adventures in Wonderland*, by Lewis Carroll, illustrated by John Tenniel, and dated 1869. I could tell by the date it was a rare volume. I'd pass it on to Franklin. Maybe he'd start to believe I wasn't a thief.

Jo nuzzled my shoulder.

"What's up, Miss Josephine? If you're nuzzling, that means you want something."

She ambled over to the now-closed cupboard door, sat in front of it, and meowed. I didn't have time for her games, I had to get to the book fair. I'd promised Jordan and Hal that I would cover their booth when they went to lunch.

Jo mewed.

"I know what you want, your buddy the rocking horse."

I opened the cupboard, shooed her away, and dragged out the rocking horse. The amount of dust on the primitive carved horse looked undisturbed for a century and a half. I set the rocking horse upright in the center of the floor, its curved runner warped with age. It teetered more than tottered. Jo was thrilled and clawed and swiped at its long tail. After I lured her away, and used an entire roll of paper towels and half a bottle of cleaner Brenna had given me yesterday when I told her I was tackling the cupboard space, the rocking horse glowed. Then I went downstairs for my second shower of the day.

When I walked back into the loft, Jo was innocently lying on the bed licking her paws. What wasn't so innocent was the rocking horse that lay decapitated on the floral rug. "Oh, Jo. What did you do? It looks like a scene from *The Godfather.*"

She glanced over, and I swore she shrugged her shoulders.

I moved the horse's body to its upright position and picked up the head. The horse's mane was whorled and tangled, explained by Jo's beheading of it. I centered the head over the body and patted it down. It was as good as new—or as good as "old." Then the darn thing fell over again. The head hit the carpet, and two things rolled out from the hollow cavity inside the horse's body: something wrapped in a lace handkerchief tied with a blue ribbon and a small leather-bound diary.

Another Nancy Drew fantasy fulfilled: *The Clue in the Diary.*

I untied the ribbon. Nestled inside the handkerchief was a miniature oval portrait of a young man. He had fair hair and instead of wearing a scowl, like the portrait in the morning room of Captain Isaiah, he smiled. His smile reached his sea-green eyes. I thought I knew who had painted the miniature: Sarah Hollingsworth. I laid the mini portrait on top of the handkerchief and opened the brown leather diary. On the first page, written in quill and ink with a flowery hand, was the signature, Sarah Ann Hollingsworth.

Next, I did what any normal nosey person would do. I went to the last entry. It was dated August 1845.

When I was done reading, my mouth opened wide. It seemed that innocent Sarah Hollingsworth hadn't been a dutiful, loving wife after all. Sarah had been in love with her husband's first mate. And if I wasn't reading into things, which I didn't think I was, then Sarah had thrown herself off Widow's Point after she miscarried, because someone named Seth had perished at sea on the *Manifest Destiny* along with her "cantankerous, domineering" spouse, Captain Isaiah. And the kicker was, the baby was Seth's, not her thirty-year-older "ancient iceberg" husband's.

I could only imagine Sarah's state of mind when she miscarried after finding out her lover and the father of her child was lost at sea—no wonder she haunted Scrimshaw House after her suicide. Did Ezekiel Hollingsworth, Captain Isaiah's brother, find out Sarah had an affair with Seth and that was why she didn't have a headstone with her name on it in the family cemetery?

I placed the miniature picture of Seth on the lace handkerchief, tied it up with the blue ribbon, and put it back inside the rocking horse. The diary I would give to Violet, the connoisseur of all things Sarah.

On the way to the book fair, I stopped at the police station to file a report on the vandalism done to my Jeep. AAA had managed to plug up three of my tires after they removed the arrows, but one tire had to be replaced with my donut spare.

I pulled up to the white-columned Neoclassical Revival facade of the Jacob Johnson Memorial Library. A banner on the lawn announced the first annual Sag Harbor Antiquarian Book and Ephemera Fair. There wasn't parking, so I ended up having to park an equal distance from the book fair as if I'd walked from the Bibliophile.

I grabbed *Alice's Adventures in Wonderland* and Sarah's diary before getting out of the car, planning to give the *Alice* to Franklin and the diary to Violet. Hopefully get into both their good graces.

I climbed the granite steps and stepped into the grand marble foyer. A security guard stood at the door and greeted me. His job was to check that all purchases leaving the book fair were accompanied by receipts. I showed him *Alice's Adventures in Wonderland* and Sarah's diary. He wrote out two receipts, proving I'd brought them into the book fair with me.

At a long table covered with bibliophile-related advertising flyers, I handed over my twenty bucks and got my hand stamped. I grabbed a numbered map denoting the book dealers' locations and followed the crowd to the end of foyer, then down three steps.

I'd been to many book shows in the past, but when I walked into the huge room, the first annual Sag Harbor Antiquarian Book and Ephemera Fair was like no other. Each dealer's space had been cordoned off into small, cozy rooms. Every room had a desk where the dealer sat, a wing chair or loveseat, sometimes both, all surrounded by book-filled cases. The booths were filled with antique and vintage items for sale, all relating to books: desk accessories, bookends, reading lamps, and bookrests. The bookcases were exquisite, in all styles: Classical, modern, Nouveau, Deco, Arts and Crafts, and mid-century; depending on the dealer and what era of books and paper items they were selling.

Franklin had done a magnificent job. The only glitch I could see was that I doubted there'd be any bargains. On the other side of the coin, the clientele seemed wealthy enough to purchase a signed, first edition of *The Winter of Our Discontent*. If Jordan sold my Steinbeck, I'd use the money to buy a new car—or truck.

Of course, the other major glitch was the *Heiress and the Light* theft. Brenna had told me her uncle had only agreed to show the Fitzgerald manuscript at the fair's kickoff cocktail party because it would be under his control the entire time.

Rebecca Crandle sat in a booth reminiscent of Sherlock Holmes' study. There was even a replica deerstalker hat and pipe on the small mahogany table. Rebecca and her mother, Sylvie, were former Montauk clients. And because of her and her mother's recent fame at the top of the *New York Times* Best Sellers list under the pseudonym S. R. Crandle, *Coastal Home* had included the interiors I'd designed of their cottages in the center pages of the July issue. Not too shabby to have Cottages by the Sea mentioned in the special Hamptons issue.

Rebecca got up from the wing chair. She had corkscrew shoulder-length auburn hair and deep blue eyes. Her face always looked flushed, like she was in a constant state of excitement—which she usually was. Rebecca was definitely a glass-half-full type of person. She'd loved the job I'd done decorating her cottage in Montauk.

She bounced over. "Meg. It's so great to see you. It's been too long."

"I've been working on the décor in the author suites at the Bibliophile B & B for the past few months. Come by and I'll give you a tour. I'm sure you'll appreciate the Edgar Allan Poe suite."

"It's a deal."

"Where's your mom?"

"Shopping, of course. She's already snagged a first edition nineteen sixty-three P. D. James *A Mind to Murder*, the second in the Adam Dalgliesh series. We have a friendly competition going on."

"I've seen yours and your mother's collections. What possible mystery novels could you be missing?" The mother-daughter mystery-writing team were also major bibliophiles. They collected first edition mystery and detective novels.

"I'm on the lookout for Hammett's *The Maltese Falcon* and *The Thin Man* and Mom has a list yay long." She extended her arms. "I read about the theft of the unpublished F. Scott Fitzgerald manuscript in *Dave's Hamptons.* I assume you were at the party last night?"

"Yes. It was quite a night. How come you and mom didn't come?"

"We had a book signing at The Mysterious Bookshop in Manhattan or we would have been there with bells on. We love costume parties."

Rebecca showed me a first edition Agatha Christie she was thinking of buying. I was reminded that inside my handbag was *Alice's Adventures in Wonderland* and Sarah Hollingsworth's diary. I asked Rebecca if she'd seen Franklin and she pointed him out.

"Mr. Hollingsworth hasn't left the chair by the bay window since I've been here. Everyone's going up to congratulate him on the success of the book fair. You can tell he's devastated by what happened last night."

"Thanks. I'll be covering the Carpe Librum booth in fifteen minutes. Stop by and . . ."

A portly man wearing a mustard-colored Mister Rogers cardigan pushed a book into Rebecca's hand. It was protected in plastic and the front of the dust jacket had a black-and-white silhouette of Nick Charles. The dealer talked in a low voice, like he was selling something on the black market. "I couldn't help but overhear you're looking for a copy of *The Thin Man.* This is a fine first edition with the original dust jacket, inscribed by Hammett. Today, only seventeen thou."

Rebecca handed it back to him. "Give me your card and I'll think about it."

When he scurried to get his card, she winked at me.

"I think we'll have to sell a few thousand more books before we upgrade to signed first editions."

I smiled, happy at the thought of my signed Steinbeck. I left Rebecca conversing with the mystery bookseller and continued down the aisle. It ran the length of a basketball court. Flanked on either side were numbered booths corresponding to the map I was given when I walked in. Jordan's booth was all the way at the end, on the right.

When I reached the Carpe Librum booth, Jordan was in negotiations with a thirteen-year-old who wanted a first edition *Harry Potter and the Sorcerer's Stone.* His ex-supermodel mommy talked on her cell phone to someone called Soledad, who needed to get Maximilian up from his nap so he could make his scheduled playdate with Frederick and to not forget his swimsuit and water wings.

Jordan said to the boy, "How about eight hundred? My final price."

The kid tried to keep a straight face, but I saw the gleam of his braces through his half smile. "Sold." He didn't even have to ask Mommy for permission. He handed Jordan his phone so she could scan and debit his account.

I left the booth, saying I'd be back in two minutes, and went over to the windows in front of which Franklin and Violet were sitting.

"Hey, you two. The book fair looks like a huge success. You must be so proud."

Franklin barely glanced at me. His round spectacles needed a cleaning and, for the first time, he wasn't holding a book.

"We are," Violet said, then turned to Franklin. "I'm going to get you something to eat. Do you want coffee or water?"

"I told you, I'm not hungry. Leave me alone. Stop clucking for two damn minutes." Then like an angry child he turned his body away from her in a pout.

I reached inside my bag and brought out the Alice book and the diary. "Look what I found in the loft." I handed Violet the diary. "It's Sarah Hollingsworth's. I think you'll be surprised at the last entry."

"And, Franklin, look at this *Alice's Adventures in Wonderland*. It's an early edition, possibly a first." I passed it to him.

He pushed it back at me. "Not now, Ms. Barrett. Enough of your games."

My games?

Violet looked at him and shook her head.

"Okay, then. I'll bring it back to the inn and leave it in the cabin."

"Don't you dare come near the cabin, Ms. Barrett. At least until *The Heiress and the Light* is returned. Now, shoo."

There went that plan for my salvation.

I was rescued from further embarrassment by the arrival of Allan Wolfstrum, complete with an ascot and a pair of jodhpurs. He grabbed Franklin's arm. "Come on, buddy. You have to check out this steal of the century at Floyd Faber's booth, an Edgar Allan Poe collection that will rock your world."

Franklin stood.

Violet said, "He needs to eat something. He hasn't eaten since last night."

Allan reached his hand into his pocket and pulled something partially out. Violet didn't see, but I did. It was a silver flask. "Don't worry. I'll make it my mission to get him feeling right as rain."

I asked Allan, "How's Nicole?"

Violet took her husband's other arm.

He shook it off. "One coddler at a time."

Allan offered his arm and Violet happily took it. As they walked away, Allan looked over his shoulder. "Not good."

How much had Nicole drank for her to be that sick? For all I knew, she could be a diabetic or an alcoholic. You never really knew people from their public personas.

CHAPTER TWENTY-SIX

I went back to Jordan and Hal's booth. Their area had a vintage, industrial-chic Brooklyn feel. The center of the space had two Eames chairs facing each other. Between the chairs was a rotating bookcase similar to the one I'd put in the Steinbeck suite. The small area had four antique wooden library carts on caster wheels, all filled with books in plastic protective wrappers. There were open gray metal shelves on the side walls. Two huge pull-down schoolroom maps backed the open bookcases. A glass-fronted floor-to-ceiling bookcase covered the back wall. Inside the locked bookcase I spied my book, *The Winter of Our Discontent.*

On top of the scarred pine desk, Jordan had placed a plaque on an easel that read: IN A GOOD BOOKROOM YOU FEEL IN SOME MYSTERIOUS WAY THAT YOU ARE ABSORBING THE WISDOM CONTAINED IN ALL THE BOOKS THROUGH YOUR SKIN, WITHOUT EVEN OPENING THEM.—MARK TWAIN.

Jordan came up to me and gave me a hug, her full expressive mouth always upturned at its corners. "Thank you. I'm starving and I seem to have lost my husband. It wouldn't be the first time a book held him captive."

"Scoot, then. Anything I should know?"

"Not really. If someone wants to haggle over a price, just put their item on hold in the locked bookcase. Here's the key. And guess what? The head of Southampton College is interested in your Steinbeck. My fingers are crossed."

"Fabulous. Oh, before you go, I want to show you something I found in the Emily Dickinson loft." I pulled out *Alice's Adventures in Wonderland* and handed it to her.

She carefully thumbed through it. "This is the first American edition from Lee and Shepard, dated eighteen sixty-nine. Illustrated by John Tenniel. The fore edge is lightly bumped and there's light foxing and rubbing and minor wear to the extremities. But all in all, an amazing copy. Charles Lutwidge Dodgson aka Lewis Carroll wrote it for Alice Liddell, the frequent star of his photography."

"Yowza. You sure know your stuff. What do you think it's worth?"

"I'd guess in the thousand-dollar range. Now, if you had a nineteen sixty-nine copy of *Alice's Adventures in Wonderland*, illustrated and signed by Salvador Dali, it would be worth twenty thousand."

"No wonder Franklin wasn't that excited. I was hoping it was worth a lot more."

"I doubt he's thrilled by much of anything at this point. Even the book fair. I feel partially to blame. He had a choice of displaying *The Heiress and the Light* at the Grolier Club or the cocktail party. I thought the manuscript's debut should be in the Hamptons, where it had been found."

"Grolier Club?"

She straightened a row of books as she talked. "The Grolier Club is the oldest ongoing literary society in the United States, and expects its members to debut their special acquisitions in their Manhattan clubhouse before they show to the public."

"I'm sure he doesn't blame you."

"Well, he's barely shared two words with me or Hal since last night."

After Jordan showed me around the booth, she went to scout out her husband so they could have lunch. She left me with her cell phone number so I could text her if needed and instructed me that I should let the browsers browse. She wasn't a fan of the hard sell. And neither was I. I sat behind the desk, opened the drawer, and saw a pair of white gloves. When I'd helped Elle inventory the Seacliff estate in East Hampton, I'd had the privilege of handling rare books. The main rules were: hold with two hands in the middle of the book, never at the top, and for dusting, use a soft natural-bristle paintbrush. I followed these same rules for my gilt-lettered and cloth late-nineteenth-century books, valued at only around fifty dollars each. The only thing I didn't do was wear cotton gloves to protect the oil from my fingers from transferring to the page. My books were meant to be touched. I loved the thought that someone, over a hundred years ago, had turned the same page as I.

I glanced at the booth across the aisle. It had the most unwelcoming interior. There wasn't a place to sit—no rug, bookends, or lamps. Taped to the glass of the only two bookcases were handwritten signs I could see clearly from where I sat: DO NOT TOUCH. VIOLATORS WILL BE PROSECUTED TO THE FULLEST EXTENT OF THE LAW. "Please" wasn't part of the reed-thin, greasy-haired bookdealer's vernacular. When someone stepped into his booth, his head bobbed on his birdlike neck and his long nose went to work sniffing out prospective buyers like a pig searching for truffles. No one stayed in his booth longer than two seconds—with one exception: Ken Lerner. I held up the book *The Sun Also Rises* by Ernest Hemingway, shielding my face while I observed Ken. He shook hands with the dealer. Then the dealer removed a small package wrapped in brown Kraft paper from his inside jacket pocket. Ken took it and scurried out of the booth. No money was exchanged, unless what was in the brown paper was a stack of cash. I wished I could follow him, but I couldn't abandon Carpe Librum's booth. Although, I almost did when I saw his twin Kortney. Her frizzy bleached hair bopped along with a life of its own as she turned the corner. She grabbed her brother's arm and pulled him into an alcove. Kortney seemed pleased with herself. The same way Jo looked when she got away with one of her cat-ate-the-canary exploits.

A half-hour later, Jordan and Hal came back to the booth, holding hands. Each held a bag and both swore they'd gotten the deal of the century. Jordan was happy I'd sold two first edition novels without lowering the price. And I was happy because the man wanting my Steinbeck had stopped by to say he was definitely buying it and would return at four to pick it up.

I wandered around the fair, happy to see that almost every booth was packed with attendees. I shouldn't have been surprised at all the celebrities, but I was. I counted sixteen A-listers, all dressed-down and in pursuit of that perfect book or piece of ephemera. I glanced at my watch. Elle promised to be at the fair around two. It was one thirty.

I'd covered most of the fair but had saved two of the most promising booths for when Elle arrived.

I was killing time in a booth across the aisle from where I'd first seen Rebecca Crandle, and picked up a pair of vintage brass Scottie bookends. They were sculpted by animal artist Marguerite Kirmse, the same artist who'd illustrated *Lassie Come Home*. They would be perfect for one of my former Cottages by the Sea clients, who just happened to own a real pair of Scotties. I was just about to ask the price of the bookends when I heard familiar voices coming from behind the booth. One of them was super irritating—Ollie Hollingsworth's. I put the bookends down on the credenza and moved to the back wall. I reached into my purse and turned up the volume on my hearing aids.

Ollie said, "We will stop soon. Pretend that we hate each other."

Then I heard a female voice say, "I do hate you."

Followed by Ollie's obnoxious laugh.

I was pretty sure the other voice belonged to Brenna.

The booth owner asked, "Can I help you with something?"

I grabbed a book off the shelf to my left. "I've been looking all over for this one."

Five minutes later I was the proud owner of *The Art and Science of Embalming*.

Elle didn't show up until three because the book fair had brought in added customers to Mabel and Elle's Curiosities. We spent the rest of the afternoon perusing the booths. I found a vintage book on landscaping, dated 1928. Elle bought a twenties lithographed poster featuring Carl G. Fisher's Montauk. The poster read: 125 MILES OUT IN

THE COOL ATLANTIC! MONTAUK BEACH ON THE SLEN-
DER TIP OF LONG ISLAND, N.Y. THE GATEWAY TO MON-
TAUK AND ALL LONG ISLAND SEASHORE RESORTS. Depicted
on the poster was Montauk Manor—"A Hotel of Distinction." Below the picture of Montauk Manor there were men
and women dressed in colorful twenties clothing. A fisher-
man, golfer, polo player, tennis player, archeress, bathing
beauty, yachtsman, and aviator. Montauk Point Lighthouse
stood sentry in the background. After Elle paid, the book
dealer hurried us along so he could sell a distinguished
gentleman with a walking stick an asylum log book with
Mary Lincoln's name on one of the pages. Only twelve
thousand dollars.

In the next booth, I talked Elle out of buying the eleven-
course dinner menu from the day the *Titanic* sank for
$70,000. It had come from one of the survivors in lifeboat
one. Too macabre for my taste. It would make me think of
the fifteen hundred people who hadn't survived, but Elle
said it would remind her of the lucky seven hundred that
did. In the same booth there was a book titled *The Wreck
of the Titan, or Futility*. It was about a fictional ship named
Titan, the largest ship ever built, said to be unsinkable. In
the book, the *Titan* hits an iceberg in April and sinks. Only
half of the passengers survived because there was a short-
age of lifeboats. The fictional book was written by Morgan
Robertson fourteen years before the actual *Titanic* set sail.
Talk about prophetic. The 1898 first edition had a seven-
thousand-dollar price tag.

Elle and I stayed until after the book fair ended to help
Jordan and Hal pack up. It was the least I could do after
being handed a check from Jordan for *The Winter of Our
Discontent*. I couldn't wait to go shopping for new wheels.

I'd take Doc with me. He was an automobile aficionado—Motor City born and bred.

Jordan and Hal said they'd meet us at the Bibliophile B & B after they oversaw their furniture being loaded into a truck bound for Brooklyn. Elle waited for me at the library's entrance while I went to the restroom.

A security guard gave me directions to the ladies' room. I followed a hallway behind the partition of the first booth I'd gone into at the start of the fair.

I turned the corner, looked down at the floor, and screamed.

Sprawled on the floor was Franklin Hollingsworth. Franklin's unblinking gaze behind his round spectacles looked up at me. I crouched next to him, feeling for a pulse I'd never find.

In Franklin's arms was a copy of *The Great Gatsby*; the celestial blue eyes on the dust jacket also stared up at me. My mind went to the billboard depicted in *The Great Gatsby* films, of the huge eyes behind wire-rimmed spectacles advertising optometrist Dr. T. J. Eckleburg.

The same omnipresent eyes thought by many to be Fitzgerald's symbolism for God.

God couldn't help Franklin now.

No one could.

"I'm telling you, I did not steal this book. Don't you have bigger things to deal with?"

Elle and I were trying to leave the library. After I'd found Franklin's body, I'd called 911, and we'd stayed with Franklin until the ambulance came. It had pulled away silently, with no need for a siren.

Now, besides the security guards and janitor, we were the only ones in the library.

The guard said, "Then where is your receipt? You have one for this book." He held up the landscaping book.

I dug in my purse for the receipt I'd received when I walked into the book fair. My hands shook so badly, I couldn't find it.

Elle grabbed my purse and did her own search. "I can't believe how much stuff you have in here." She handed the guard her business card. "I tell you what: keep the book for now." She grabbed the landscaping book and receipt, and we went out the door before the guard could protest.

I was so weary, I nearly stumbled down the library steps.

Elle said, "Where are you parked?"

"Far away."

"Come with me. I'm right over here. I think we'd better get back to the Bibliophile. Arthur will be there to break the news. I texted him."

"You've been calling him by his first name."

Elle gave me a weak smile. "Not in public. Just between you and me. Okay?"

"Of course. I can't believe Franklin is dead. I know he had a bad heart and there has been so much going on."

"People always say, 'At least he didn't suffer' or 'He died doing what he loved.' I'm not so sure there's any good way to die."

"He was holding *The Great Gatsby*. Too bad it couldn't have been *The Heiress and the Light*." I remembered Franklin's eyes. His open eyes.

Elle said, "Thankfully his death was from natural causes, not murder."

When we walked into the drawing room of the Bibliophile B & B, Detective Shoner was on his way out. Elle pulled him into the front vestibule. I followed.

She asked, "How did they take it?"

"As you'd expect." He took a hankie out of his jacket and wiped at his brow. "I think the niece took it the hardest. And I was surprised how torn up his brother was. He doesn't seem the type to show his emotions on his sleeve."

I said, "That's for sure. When will you have word on how he died?"

"A day or so. There's nothing suspicious. His wife said he's been on medication for his heart for years. Listen, I have to go. There's a protest scheduled in Montauk concerning a proposal by the Army Corps of Engineers. A lot of surfers and locals think the proposed sandbagging will ruin the ocean shoreline. Unfortunately, at the last protest, we had to make a few arrests." He touched the top of Elle's upturned nose with his pointer finger. "I'll talk to you later. Try to stay out of trouble."

"It's Meg who's always in trouble. Thanks for coming, Detective."

As he walked away, I said to Elle, "Meg's always in trouble. Nice."

We walked into the drawing room.

Everyone in the room stood when we entered. Brenna, Ollie, Hal, Jordan, Allan, Ken, and Kortney. It felt like they were waiting for me to say, "April Fools! Franklin was just playing possum."

Brenna ran over and took my hands. "Oh, Meg, this is so tragic. What happened? Was it an accident? What was my uncle doing there all alone?" She looked over at Violet.

Violet put down her teacup. "He wanted to stay until the last dealer left. He perked up at the end of the book fair after he purchased a signed *Gatsby*. Although, I think another reason he perked up was because someone gave him a few swigs from their flask." Violet gave Allan a chastising look.

"Everyone needs a pick-me-up now and then." He held a tumbler of scotch.

Ollie stood. "Well, Ms. Barrett, spill. I want to know the

details. I also want to know why you stayed so late at the fair. Did you try CPR? Chest compressions? Did my brother speak or have any last words?"

I stepped back like I'd been slapped. Jordan led me to the fainting couch. I wished I could faint, but that wasn't my style when it came to Ollie Hollingsworth.

Even knowing everyone was bereft and on edge, I said to Ollie, "No, Mr. Hollingsworth. I didn't try any life-saving techniques, because it was too late."

Ollie walked over and leaned down. "Answer my question about what were you doing there so late. I just got a text from one of the security guards that you tried to leave with a rare book you didn't have a receipt for. Were you trying to steal it, Ms. Barrett? Perhaps you thought with all the commotion you could walk out scot-free. Priceless, seeing you've accused me of stealing and even my party planner of stealing your dress."

Little Elle came to my rescue and pushed him aside and sat next to me.

Brenna shouted, "Stop!"

Ollie looked at his daughter, then retreated to one of the wing chairs in front of the fireplace. On his way, he grabbed Allan's bottle of Macallan. "You don't mind do you, old sport?" He didn't wait for an answer as he sat and swigged from the bottle.

Hal said, "I know you're upset, Ollie, but Meg and Elle stayed to help Jordan and me. She was invaluable today."

Ollie didn't answer, just took another swig of scotch.

Violet walked to the tea cart and poured tea into her cup. She turned and looked like she wanted to ask me something, then changed her mind. "I'm going up to the Edith Wharton suite. I can't bear going into the cabin alone."

Brenna jumped up. "Here, let me take you, Aunty."

Violet said, "I can manage on my own. I'd like some toast and jam brought up. I don't care for any dinner. Save everything for tomorrow's meal." Then she exited the room.

It was the first time I'd seen Violet take an assertive role.

Brenna sat on the loveseat. "I don't think it's hit her yet. It hasn't hit me."

The whole time, Ken and Kortney sat mute. They were seated at the mahogany game table topped with a chessboard and ivory nautical-inspired game pieces. It was Sunday evening. Game night.

Brenna said, "Ken, please bring Aunt Violet her toast and a fresh pot of tea."

Ken stood and Kortney followed. I had the strangest feeling Kortney was trying to hold back a grin. Was she happy I'd got a talking-to by Ollie—or was it something else?

An hour later, my father said, "Put Jo on speaker."

I tapped the cat on the rear end and she opened her eye.

"How's my big girl? Has your mother been treating you well? Plenty of omega-3 fatty acids, I hope?"

Jo stretched and moved closer to the phone. Then she gave it a little nuzzle.

"How do you do that? I think she's smiling."

"We bonded last time I was there."

"You bond every time you're here. It might have to do with the gourmet seafood dinner you prepare for the spoiled brat."

"I'm not usually a cat lover, but Jo's not an average cat."

"No. Nothing about Jo is average, including her appetite. I can't wait to get her out of here. I feel bad she's been cooped up for so long."

"From your description, the Emily Dickinson loft sounds wonderful. But I understand, after everything you've just told me, why you'd want to leave."

"It still seems surreal."

"I don't have much to tell you yet on Randall McFee and his connection to the Hemingway fraud case. I have a call into the judge on the case. And there's nothing on Mr. Hollingsworth's missing Fitzgerald manuscript. Are you sure he died of natural causes?"

"Pretty sure on that one. He had a bad heart. Took meds. And what would be the point of killing him now that he's five million dollars poorer?"

"Well, I'd look into it. Just in case. I, and Deep Throat from the movie *All The President's Men* say, 'follow the money' when you're dealing with items this valuable."

"True."

"I'll call you tomorrow for your big day."

"Thanks, Dad. Love you."

"Love you too. Bye."

TWENTY-EIGHT

Monday morning I was up and in the bathroom by eight. After my shower, I felt a little better than I had last night. All night, I'd kept jerking awake with the vision of Franklin's unblinking bug eyes behind his round spectacles.

I opened the bathroom door and banged my funny bone on the door frame. My blow-dryer slipped from my hand and landed on the big toe of my right foot. "Mother of . . ."

Brenna ran over. "Are you okay?"

I hopped up and down on my left foot. "Fine. Sorry to scare you."

"You can leave all your toiletries in the bathroom. You're the only one who uses it."

"Thanks." I reached down and picked up the blow-dryer and put it in the cabinet under the sink. Brenna held a feather duster in her hand, and I followed her to the Edgar Allan Poe suite. The timing wasn't great, but I said, "I got a call from my bank that the check you gave me bounced.

When you have a chance, can you look into it? It's just that I have some bills to pay, including the queen bed that's supposed to arrive today for the Emily Dickinson loft."

I wasn't wearing my hearing aids, so I didn't realize Violet was behind me until I felt her breath on my neck.

She walked up to Brenna. "What's this about a bounced check?"

Violet didn't look well. The circles under her eyes matched her name. And her hand shook when she reached for the wall to steady herself.

Brenna must have noticed. "Nothing, Aunty. Must be some kind of mistake on Ms. Barrett's part. Go back to the Edith Wharton suite. I'll have Ken bring your breakfast."

Violet swayed. I took her arm and led her back to the Edith Wharton suite.

I was reminded of the aftermath of Nicole Wolfstrum's drunken night at the cocktail party. It didn't seem possible the party was only two days ago. And the hurricane only five days ago.

The Edith Wharton suite looked back in order, but the Aubusson rug was missing—no doubt sent out to be professionally cleaned.

I led Violet to the Rococo Revival rosewood chaise lounge in front of the oriel window and covered her with a knitted throw.

"Can you please hand me Sarah's diary?"

I took it off the bed and gave it to her. "Did you read the last entry?"

At first she ignored me as she looked out at Hollingsworth Avenue. "You never really know a person, do you?"

"Maybe if you read all of the diary you'll learn why Sarah fell in love with her husband's first mate. She called

Captain Isaiah 'cantankerous and domineering.' What if he didn't deserve her loyalty? Maybe he was abusive? As you said, 'You never really know a person.'" Violet ignored me and opened the diary, so I exited the bedroom.

As I was leaving the suite, Violet called out something I couldn't hear without my hearing aids. I went back inside the bedroom.

"Tell Brenna to bring me some tea from the teahouse. Second glass jar on the left."

"Will do."

What happened to the word "please"? Grief, I assumed.

I left the suite and went down the hallway to the Poe suite. I deserved a better answer from Brenna about the bounced check, and I needed to tell her about Violet's tea demand.

I'd naturally designed the Poe suite to be on the dark, macabre side. But it still had a cozy feel because I'd made it look like a fiction writer's room, not a gory scene from one of his stories. There was little influence of Allan Wolfstrum's presence. On the desk were rolled sheets of paper tied with string. I wanted the desk purposely messy, like the father of the modern detective story's mind. "I became insane, with long intervals of horrible sanity." The chair I'd placed at the desk was in the American Empire style, similar to what Poe might have used when he'd worked as a literary critic at a newspaper in Richmond, Virginia. On an inkstand were ink bottles, pens, a box of sharps—the term used for the pen's metal tips—and an ink blotter. I chose not to copy the décor at the Edgar Allan Poe Cottage in the Bronx. I would let his fans take a trip and experience it for themselves.

Brenna was fluffing the pillows on the bed. She knew I was standing there but didn't acknowledge me.

I said, "I'm sorry, but I'd like to know what you want me to do about the check. Resubmit?"

She shot me a look, then almost knocked over a glass cloche filled with a stuffed raven on a branch. I'd bought it at a shop in Greenport. The owner produced fake birds and small animals, then put them under glass cloches to mimic taxidermy displays popular in the nineteenth century. When you walked into the tiny shop, you felt like you were in a room at the American Museum of Natural History or Charles Darwin's study.

"I said I'd take care of it," Brenna said.

No, she hadn't. "Okay."

"I have more important things on my hands, Ms. Barrett, than checks or beds. My uncle just died. I need to make all the arrangements because my father is an imbecile. I don't want my aunt to have to deal with things. You saw her. How do you think she looked?"

"Not good." I admitted. "I'm sorry. Is there anything I can do to help?"

She sat on the bed. Tears made white rivulets through her tawny blush. "Yes. Bring my uncle back." The feather duster fell to the floor.

I reached to pick it up and felt a lump under the Persian area rug. I got down on my knees and lifted the edge of the carpet. Between the hardwood floor and the rug was the missing cannibal-head letter opener from the Herman Melville suite. I grabbed it by the head and pointed the curved blade downward as I stood. "Look what I found."

Brenna said, "What is Allan doing with that awful thing?"

"It belongs in the Melville suite."

"Knowing Allan, he was probably using it for inspiration

for one of his spy novels." She stood. "I better get to it. I need to talk to Ken about my aunt's breakfast."

"She wanted me to tell you she wants some of her tea from the teahouse. She said, 'the second container on the left.' I could fetch it for you if it helps?"

Brenna mumbled under her breath.

"I'm not wearing my hearing aids. Do you mind facing me so I can read your lips?"

"I said, that would be great. Sorry I was so snippy earlier. I just don't want my aunt to worry about anything right now, especially money." She reached into a tote filled with cleaning supplies and brought out a key ring. She flipped to a copper one, took it off the ring, and handed it to me. "Between you and me, because I'm sure it will come out later, my uncle took out a sizable loan and a second mortgage for the renovations of the Bibliophile Bed and Breakfast. He wasn't willing to sell anything from his collection, in fact, he used some of the loan money to buy *The Heiress and the Light.* Now everything will go to Princeton University, and I'm sure the inn will have to be sold for what he owed. I'm sorry. I'll find a way to get you your money. Just give me a little time."

"Of course. Does your aunt know about the loans her husband took out?"

Brenna said, "I'm sure she does." Then she walked out of the suite.

On my way out of the sitting room in the Poe suite, I saw the two glass front bookcases were packed with books. No empty spots. I was reminded of the missing *The Heiress and the Light* manuscript. Thankfully there were copies. When Poe died, he'd left behind an unfinished two-page story about a lighthouse keeper who went to an isolated seaside location. The author Joyce Carol Oates finished the story in the twentieth century. The gothic story was titled "The Fabled Lighthouse at Vina del Mar."

I followed Brenna out of the suite, into the hallway. Then stepped back inside. Something was missing from the sitting room: a five-hundred-page modern reprint of an 1850s book, *The Book of Poisons.* Elle had sold it to me to put on a lectern in the Poe suite. She'd used it in the past when she decorated her shop for All Hallows' Eve. Instead of the poison book, someone had placed an old copy of *Gray's Anatomy* on top of the wooden lectern. *Gray's* was open to a hand-tinted drawing of a red heart. A tell-tale heart?

The missing *Book of Poisons* wasn't worth much, about thirty dollars. I wouldn't mention it to Brenna. But I would ask Allan Wolfstrum why he was redecorating. The first edition of *Gray's Anatomy* was published in 1858. Poe died in 1849. Allan needed a history lesson.

When I returned to the hallway, Brenna was gone. Before going up to the loft, I took the letter opener to the Melville suite and knocked on the door, but there was no answer. I turned the door handle. Locked. I continued up to the Dickinson loft, bringing the letter opener with me. I put it in a box with things to go to the whaling museum. It had haunted my dreams for too long.

After I made sure Jo was taken care of, I put in my hearing aids and dressed for the day.

I was happy to leave the Bibliophile and head to my little end of the world. Franklin's death was something to be shared with his family and close friends. Of which I was neither. I'd scurried past the dining salon, not wanting to be called in, even though the smells coming from the sideboard tried their best. I left through the back door and headed toward the gates at the back of the property that led to the teahouse. In the parking lot, Allan was getting into his Bentley. I was sure he saw me, but he got in, shut the door, and started the engine. I trotted over and rapped on his window. The car was even more magnificent up close.

He rolled down his window and loosened his ascot. Good idea, because it was almost ninety degrees. "Meg. What's up? I'm in a hurry."

"Any news about Nicole? How is she feeling?"

"Apparently fine. I went to Southampton early this morning because she was going to be released, but your boyfriend Byron had beat me to it."

"Oh. That was nice of him."

"Just peachy," Allan said. "She wasn't released, however. They still needed to run tests. I don't think this is a simple case of alcohol poisoning. The longer she stays in the hospital, the bigger chance the press might get ahold of it."

"I hope they find out what's wrong."

"Me too. You do know Byron and Nicole had a thing, don't you?"

"Yep. Sure. I knew that."

He probably knew I was lying.

"Byron Hughes has quite a track record with the ladies of the Hamptons." He put the car in reverse. "Watch your toes." He pulled out so fast, he almost clipped the bumper on my poor Jeep.

I patted my Jeep's backend sporting the bumper sticker:

MONTAUK—THE END. "Sorry, Rocinante, your days are numbered." Rocinante was what John Steinbeck named his camper truck when he went on his travels with Charley, his French poodle, to find America in 1960. Steinbeck got the name, Rocinante, from Don Quixote's horse. Later, he wrote the book *Travels with Charley*, in his Sag Harbor writing hut, and went on to win the 1962 Nobel Prize in Literature. The twelve-thousand-dollar check from Carpe Librum for the sale of my Steinbeck would go toward a new car. Thank you, John. I'd deposit it today, before something happened to it, like with the Bibliophile's check.

I went through the open rear gates and took the path to the teahouse. I didn't have time for sightseeing and wasn't in the mood to admire Byron's landscaping. Things happened for a reason. Maybe Cole was my future. Or maybe not. I was still miffed he hadn't called or made contact. Maybe, in his mind, I was the one who owed him an explanation.

As soon as I stepped into the teahouse, I was reminded of my day and night with Violet during the hurricane. The fountain had been turned off, but something bubbled at the bottom. All the fish were alive. Not like the numerous goldfish I'd brought home from carnivals when I was child. Those goldfish would last one, maybe two hours. My mother wasn't like other moms who ran to the pet store for replacements, letting their children think the fish were eternal beings. She wanted to teach me the circle of life, like in Disney's *The Lion King*. All I learned was never to bring home goldfish. A box of candy lasted longer.

There was a container of fish food behind the pump of the fountain. I pinched a small amount into the water. Next, I went to the counter and pulled out the large glass jar filled with tea, the second one from the left. Did Violet expect me to carry the whole jar back to the inn? I searched under the cupboard for some storage bags or containers. Nothing. I even looked in the bedroom and bathroom. The only thing in the bathroom was a couple of toothbrushes and toothpaste. The bed was unmade, the sheets twisted, reminding me of the Edith Wharton suite bed the night Nicole was ill. Nicole and Byron. Meg and Byron. Meg and Cole. Meg and no one.

I went back into the main room. The kiln door was ajar. I peeked in.

Inside was the John Steinbeck head that would go to the Steinbeck suite. Violet definitely had a talent.

I grabbed the huge glass jar of tea and left the teahouse. I balanced the jar on my hip and locked the sliding door.

When I turned, Kortney was standing behind me in her beekeeper's suit.

She held the hat and veil in her arm. "Boo."

"Are you kidding me?"

"Are you kidding me?" she mimicked. "What are you doing snooping around Miss Violet's studio?"

"I'm not snooping. I was told to come here to get some tea."

"That's my brother's job."

I went down the steps. "Back off."

"Haven't you overstayed your welcome? I know Ollie thinks you have."

"Ollie didn't hire me. Franklin did."

"Well, that's a moot point now. Isn't it?"

"I don't have to answer to you." It felt like we were in grade school. I wished she had pigtails so I could pull them. I elbowed her out of the way and strode down the hill to the path that led to the inn. I waited a few minutes before I turned around. She was nowhere to be seen.

I hurried back to the Bibliophile, looking over my shoulder at every turn. What was Kortney's problem?

I brought the tea to Brenna, who was in the kitchen filling a basket of honey twists from the recipe I'd seen the other day in her vintage cookbook. She thanked me for the tea but didn't offer me a twist.

It didn't matter anyway. I planned on having breakfast in Montauk and Paddy's Pancake House never disappointed. I also needed to drop off a load of laundry at the Wash n Dri. Violet had told me they were planning the funeral for Wednesday and the viewing at the funeral home tomorrow, and I was out of clean clothing. After living on a boat, even a yacht, you learned to pack to fill small storage spaces. I'd overstayed my welcome at the Bibliophile, but I'd promised Franklin I would finish the Emily Dickinson loft, and I meant to keep my promise.

CHAPTER

❦

TWENTY-NINE

Montauk looked the same. It was crowded with vacationing families and twentysomethings who traveled by train or Hampton Jitney from Manhattan to the easternmost tip of Long Island for perfect weekend getaways. Most hotels had a three-night minimum in the summer, so Mondays were still happening days.

Monday was also my designated morning to meet Doc at Paddy's Pancake House. And, for once, Doc hadn't canceled to go surfing, and I knew why. His septuagenarian girlfriend had just gotten in last night from a bike tour in Maine. Georgia, the owner of The Old Man and The Sea Books, was on a mission to *youth*inize her younger sexagenarian boyfriend with health food, meditation, surfing, and knowledge of all things wireless.

Before going to Paddy's, I stopped at the Wash n Dri to drop off my laundry.

As soon as I walked in, Paula ran toward me and

grabbed my laundry bag. "You're overdue. Are you wearing your socks and underwear inside out?"

"Yuck. No. But I do need everything in a couple hours."

"No problem. How's the latest job going?"

"Don't ask." It had started out so wonderfully. Now I wasn't even sure the Bibliophile B & B would be opening. It had been Franklin's dream.

"Okay, I won't ask." Paula loved her job. You felt like you were doing her a favor when you dropped your laundry off. She never took a tip. Instead, she directed you to the jar for donations to the Montauk Volunteer Firefighters' Fund. Paula and her husband were both volunteer firefighters. Another thing about Paula: she was so honest, if you left a penny in your pocket, she'd return it to you.

After the Wash n Dri, I parked on Main Street and went straight to my bank to deposit Jordan's check. I knew the bank manager from the closing on my cottage and went over to him.

Greg reminded me of James Stewart from *It's a Wonderful Life*. I couldn't imagine him ever turning anyone down for a loan. If he had to, he'd probably run into the men's room for a good cry.

"Hey, Meg. Long time. What can I do for you?"

"I have a check here that's drawn on the same bank. I just want to make sure there's enough to cover it."

"Hand it over."

I sat at his desk and took a hard candy. And a free pen. And a pocket calendar for next year. As if I would ever remember to use it come January. January was the quietest month in Montauk. And one of my favorites. Give me an ocean view, a fireplace, and now a feline companion, and I was all set. Who needed Byron or Cole? I didn't. A little secret I wasn't about to share with the public: even on a thirty-degree day, if the sun was shining over the ocean and the wind was light, you could sit on your balcony in just a long-sleeved shirt.

Greg looked up from his screen and pushed his glasses higher on his nose. "Looks like no problem clearing this check. No problem at all." He even added a whistle.

I left the bank happy but confused. Jordan made it seem that she and Hal weren't doing so well with their bookstore in Brooklyn. Greg hadn't let me know the exact amount in their account, but it was probably in the millions. Greg was used to large Hampton's account holders. There was no way Jordan and Hal had stolen *The Heiress and the Light* and sold it to another collector. Then again, Jordan had her exclusive connections.

When I walked into Paddy's, a cheer sounded from the back of the restaurant. "Surprise!"

Sitting at three tables pushed together were my favorite Montaukians: Doc, the retired coroner; Georgia, the bookseller; Barb, the real-estate broker; Barb's sister-in-law, Morgana, who worked at Montauk's small East Hampton Town Police outpost; and my new friend Karen from Karen's Kreative Knitting. Also present was my best buddy, Sag Harborian Elle Warner.

How had they known it was my birthday? I hadn't told anyone. My father, of course. He must have called Doc.

Paddy and his wife came through the kitchen's swinging doorway with rolled Swedish crepes pierced with birthday candles. Elle grabbed my arm and set me at the head of the table. When the singing was done, I blew out the candles to roaring applause. Embarrassing, but heartwarming.

I'd rather celebrate at Paddy's than the top restaurant

my ex-fiancé, Michael, had taken me to in Manhattan for one of my birthdays. "The most expensive restaurant in North America," he kept saying ad nauseam. When the bill came, Michael said, "Hmm, twenty percent of eight hundred, what is that . . . ?" My father had said, "One hundred and sixty dollars." Michael replied, "Shall we make it an even grand?" Then he put down his black credit card and charged the meal to the magazine's expense account. If only I hadn't ignored my father's body language. Father knew best. The gourmet home cook who created and enjoyed only the finest meals hadn't even finished his entrée that night. Later, my father told me he'd held back about his misgivings about Michael, mainly because he knew I loved my job as managing editor of *American Home and Garden* magazine. Good guy that he was, he never mentioned a thing until I left Manhattan and Michael.

I had my usual ham-and-Swiss crepes topped with rivers of hollandaise sauce, and half of Elle's two Belgian waffles sandwiched with cannoli cream and sprinkled with dark chocolate shavings. I was tempted to ask for the last scrap of apple streusel French toast on Barb's plate, but she speared it with her fork before I had a fighting chance.

When everyone had finished their meals and we were on our coffees, Duke and Duke Junior, my go-to construction guys, rushed into Paddy's. They were dressed in twin outfits—jean shorts, work boots, and yellow Duke Construction T-shirts.

Duke Senior's massive size filled the entrance to Paddy's. He said, catching his breath and bending at the waist, "Meg, thank goodness we saw your Jeep. Something's happened at your cottage. Come quick. We need you to make an immediate decision before it's too late."

"Oh no. Tell me this is a joke?" I looked at each of my friend's faces.

They seemed as shocked as I.

Duke Junior came to the table and grabbed my elbow with his huge workman's hand. "Come on, Meg. We don't have much time."

Doc threw some money on the table and everyone filed out. Doc got in the Jeep with me and we burnt rubber. In my rearview mirror, I saw the rest of my birthday posse following closely behind.

We pulled into Surfside Drive. Luckily, there weren't any fire trucks or sirens. Duke and Duke Junior led the way to the front of my cottage. They stopped under the covered wood landing above the beach.

Duke Senior said, "We have an important question that needs an answer."

"Yes? What?"

"What kind of sealer do you want?"

Elle nudged me forward. I stood on the landing and looked down. Steps! Glorious steps! Steps that led down to my beach, my ocean, my dream come true. More applause. I looked behind me.

Doc said, "What are you waiting for?

I climbed down. Counting each step as I went. On step thirty-six, I jumped off and did a drop-and-roll. The sand got in my mouth. I'd never tasted anything better. And the smell. The briny, yet fresh ocean scent.

Everyone stayed above, giving me time to christen the beach.

I sat on a boulder and looked at the Atlantic. "Thank you. Thank you. Thank you." Then I found a piece of driftwood and left a message in the sand for my old neighbor, reclusive author Patrick Seaton. Patrick wouldn't be back until after Labor Day, but it felt good to leave a quote from Elizabeth Barrett Browning on *my* beach. Something uplifting to commemorate my birthday:

> *Light Tomorrow with today.*

I wanted to stay longer, but my posse of friends waited at the top of the steps. I'd never have to worry about going to the gym for a workout. The steps would tone me in all the right places. Or that was what I told myself when I reached the top and collapsed in Barb's ample arms.

She asked, "Happy?"

"Beyond."

"You're a mess. You have sand everywhere. You'd better go inside and take a shower."

"Huh?"

Barb took one arm and Elle took the other and led me up the front porch steps to my cottage. Elle opened the door and they pushed me under the threshold and into the main room.

I looked around. Nothing seemed different. Boxes were still stacked against the walls and there were only a few pieces of furniture—my sofa, kitchen table and chairs, desk, and bed. Then I heard a hum. There was a definite hum and the air was cool.

Doc and Morgana walked in

"Surprise!" Doc said as he flipped the light switch and there was light.

Morgana said, amid her gum-chewing, "Pretty swanky digs, Ms. Barrett."

I ran to the bathroom and turned on the faucet for the sink and the one in the shower. Water!

I went into the front room, where all the coconspirators stood. "Does this mean I'm approved? And I'm official?"

Doc said, "Yes. Even the stairs leading to the beach passed inspection. I put the paperwork on top of your desk."

"You're a doll. How'd you do it?"

"You'd have to thank Cole. He figured out why you kept getting turned down. Tara Gayle was dating someone on the zoning commission. Cole had a little chat with him and, the next thing you know, you got your stamp of approval. By the way, Cole told me to tell you Happy Birthday." Doc gave me a quizzical look but, for once, didn't push it.

I should have known Tara had been behind it—the dress-stealing budget party planner and Cole's ex. That explained things. How was I ever going to repay Cole?

Elle said, "Here. Open this pronto!" She shoved a package wrapped in brown paper tied with string into my arms.

I tore the package open, hoping it was what I thought it was. Wishes do come true. It was the 1920s poster picturing Montauk Manor that Elle had purchased at the book fair. She'd found the perfect period frame and I held it up for everyone to see.

Doc said, "Hey, that looks like Sully's and my outfits we wore to the book-fair party." He pointed to a golfer and a ship's captain. "You have to show Sully. Maybe the artist used his great-grandfather, Captain Cooper, as a model?"

Karen from Karen's Kreative Knitting gave me a vintage collapsible cloth knitting basket on a wood frame.

Inside was a complete kit to knit a beginner's throw, including yarn, instructions, a plastic case filled with gadgets I had no clue about, and a pair of circular needles, not as big as my size 50s but still on the jumbo size. The yarn was a silk/cotton blend in a creamy off-white. I looked up at her rosy face topped with sleek blonde hair cut straight across her jawline. I put on a brave face and met her topaz eyes. "Do you think I'm ready?"

Karen laughed. "Of course you are, and I'm here for you all the way."

I relaxed my shoulders.

Morgana, the Montauk police post's gal Friday, gave me a canister of pepper spray in a leather case. "Not legal for a civilian, but with your track record, Barb and I thought it was a no-brainer gift." She took a few chomps of her gum, then blew a bubble. At least it wasn't a Maltipoo; Morgana was a part-time dog breeder and a big-time pup pusher. Not that I wouldn't love a pup, but my cat was enough to handle right now and I had a feeling Jo was the jealous type.

Barb, Montauk's top Realtor, said, "My sister-in-law might be stretching things by saying I approved of her gift choice. Here. From Jack and me, on your father's advice." She handed me a large envelope.

I opened it and took out an embossed card. "Oh. Um. Thanks. Cooking lessons."

Barb looked me in the eyes, her beehive hairdo swaying slightly. "I can get a refund if you don't want to use them. Pierre Patou is the top chef at Montauk's Pondfare and he's also been on *Top Cuisine Challenge*, although he didn't get past round two because of a disastrous soufflé. He used two tablespoons of corn starch instead of flour and then went on to blame his poor sous chef."

I was going to kill my father. He was always trying to get me to learn to cook. "It's perfect! Thanks, Babs." She gave me a mamma bear hug that nearly crushed my ribs. Barb was always on a diet, but I loved her just the way she was.

Georgia and Doc gave me a combined gift. I ripped it open and found a vintage *To Kill a Mockingbird* with a pristine dust jacket.

Doc said, "Before you get excited, it's not signed, but it is a first edition."

"Book club edition, for clarification. Not first printing, first edition," Georgia said.

"I love it!" I threw open my arms and took them both in an embrace, kissing one cheek, then the next.

Duke and Duke Junior had mysteriously disappeared. They came through the doorway carrying something between them—an antique pine fireplace mantel!

Duke Senior said, "We also got approval to break through the chimney to install a fireplace in your attic bedroom. Duke Junior salvaged this from a nineteenth-century house on Navy Road. Happy birthday!"

I looked around the room—my room—and felt blessed to have such wonderful people in my life. "Wow, you guys sure know how to put the 'happy' in 'happy birthday!'"

CHAPTER

✺

THIRTY

After everyone left my cottage, I took a few minutes to soak in the JOY. I took out the plans I'd made, and re-made, regarding the interior décor of the cottage. While I'd waited for zoning approval, poor Elle had been forced to look over all my numerous revisions. The first thing I'd planned to do was install a secret bookcase that would lead from the living room to a small room on the eastern end of the house that would be my library. The room would also have a reading nook built into the shelves with a view of the Montauk Point Lighthouse. I'd gotten my design inspiration from the grand nineteenth-century estate Sandringham, only a mile up the road.

As I was locking the cottage door, Duke and Duke Junior came up the path carrying ladders and buckets of paint. They planned to complete painting the interior of the cottage by Wednesday, the day I planned to leave the Bibliophile B & B after Franklin's funeral.

When Jordan's check cleared, there'd be a nice bonus for the Dukes.

On my way out of town, I stopped at the Wash n Dri to pick up my laundry. Paula was in the back next to the front-loading industrial dryer, sitting on a beach chair reading *Dave's Hamptons*. She jumped up when she saw me.

"I was just reading about that guy who bought the Fitzgerald manuscript from cousin Sully. Sad story."

"Yes. Very sad. I didn't know you and Sully were cousins."

"Not blood-related but there is a connection there some-where. Most of the locals who were born in Montauk are related in one way or another. What's left of us after the Hamp-tons' eastern migration, that is. Let me get your laundry."

She went into the back room and came out with my cloth bag filled with folded clothes in one hand and ten items on hangers in the other. "Also, on top of the laundry, in a bag-gie, I put what was in your pockets."

"Anything good?"

"Not to my eye, but you never can tell what is valuable to someone else. No winning lottery tickets. Sorry."

I paid her and remembered to add money to the Mon-tauk Volunteer Firefighters' jar.

Route 27 had its usual summer traffic, and I traveled through Amagansett at a snail's pace. There were no traffic lights and all the cars had to stop for pedestrians crossing the street, of which there were many. I didn't mind. I wasn't looking forward to returning to the inn, especially with all the animosity toward me from Ollie, the new patriarch of the family, not to mention from Ken and Kortney. Even Brenna, who I'd thought of as a friend, had no problem throwing me under the bus when needed.

There were only two things I did look forward to: Jo, and finishing the Emily Dickinson loft.

In East Hampton, I pulled in behind a red Ferrari and parked. The car reminded me of Byron's Maserati. It also reminded me about what Allan had said about Nicole and Byron having a past. When I was in my cottage, I'd found the book Byron had given me when we first met, *The Illuminated Language of Flowers*. I looked up the meaning of the white lily he'd given me on the night of the party. Lilies represented beauty. When I thought of beauty, I thought of Nicole Wolfstrum.

The delivery truck with the bed for the Emily Dickinson loft was scheduled to arrive at three. I still had time for my favorite distraction, antiques and vintage shopping. As a celebration of my birthday, I planned to buy something special for my cottage. I'd already pilfered everything I could from Mabel and Elle's Curiosities. I got out of the Jeep and went into Grimes House Antiques.

The shop was the busiest I'd ever seen. Rita, Grimes House Antiques' owner, had exorbitant prices on her items that visiting celebs and billionaires didn't mind paying. Proof in the pudding was the red sold sign on a nineteenth-century floor-to-ceiling carved mahogany apothecary cabinet with mirror-backed shelves and a wood counter. A steal at a hundred thousand. I hated to see the cabinet go. It was original to the shop, which, at one time, had been a circa 1845 drug store.

I perused the shelves and bumped elbows with a few television stars. I limited my television watching to PBS, along with detective and mystery series with low-gore quotients. I'd seen enough gore in real life. Also, growing up with a Detroit homicide detective as your father, you were bound to overhear a few gruesome tidbits when he talked on the phone.

When I got to the back of the shop, I found it. A bamboo easel from the Arts and Crafts period. It would be perfect in the corner of my living room with an old, unframed seascape oil. What wasn't perfect was the price—twenty-eight hundred. I kept looking.

I went to the corner, near the antique paper section. I saw an old pull-down herb chart. It would be great in my kitchen, seeing as I was an herb addict. It was a little less expensive than the easel, but not by much. I was about to give up when I spied a small bookcase with its original milk paint. It was on the primitive side. Two hundred and fifty. Not bad. I pulled it out from the wall to inspect the back and bumped into a glass-enclosed cabinet. Inside the locked cabinet were an assortment of books—antique books. Books by authors like Herman Melville and Edith Wharton, with titles matching the insured list from FFM.

I'd found some of the missing books from the Biblio-phile B & B. I snapped a photo when Rita wasn't looking and left the shop without buying anything. It wouldn't have been the first time.

THIRTY-ONE

When I walked into the Bibliophile B & B, all hell had broken loose. Brenna was in the hallway moaning, her face slick with sweat and greener than a Granny Smith apple. I looked to the drawing room and saw Jordan stretched out on the settee with her eyes closed.

"Brenna, what's wrong? What's going on?"

"Food poisoning or the plague. I don't know which." She burped and ran to the bathroom at the end of the hall.

I went to the drawing room. Hal was holding Jordan's pale hand.

"What happened?"

Hal said, "After breakfast, everyone at the table got sick. I ate the same thing they did. And I'm fine. So we can't figure it out. Maybe it's a stomach virus?"

I put my arm up to shield my nose and mouth from any airborne germs. "What do you need me to do?"

"Ken went to the drugstore to get Pepto. Maybe you can

check on Allan. He crawled up to the Poe suite about an hour ago and I haven't seen him since."

"Of course." I felt Jordan's forehead. It was cool. "No fever."

He said, "I know. Strange. I'm starting to believe there is a curse on this house."

So was I.

The door to the Poe suite was open. I walked through the sitting room to the bedroom. Allan was lying on top of the red-and-gray geometric crazy quilt in the Dresden plate pattern with his arm draped over his eyes and his shoes still on.

I gave him a gentle shake. "You okay? Can I bring you anything?"

He mumbled, "The antidote." Then he turned on his side.

"Ken went to get something for your stomach. I'll send him up as soon as he gets back, and I'll check on you in a few."

He slurred, "Thanks, doll."

After I made sure Jo was okay, I went back to the drawing room. Jordan was awake and looked a tad better.

My phone rang. It was Elle. I went into the vestibule to talk.

She called to say she'd just heard from Detective Shoner. Toxicology reports confirmed Nicole Wolfstrum had been poisoned the night of the party.

"Say what?" I shouted into the phone. Then I told her what was going on at the Bibliophile. She promised to send the paramedics and her detective boyfriend immediately. Before I could mention that they might just have a stomach virus or food poisoning, she'd hung up the phone.

I went into the drawing room and whispered into Hal's ear about Nicole. He shot up, went to the settee, and picked up his wife, cradling her in his arms. As he charged out the door, he shouted, "I'm not waiting for an ambulance. I'm going to Southampton!"

"I'll phone and tell them you're coming."

The front door slammed.

I called the hospital and five minutes later three ambulances pulled up. Violet, Allan, and Brenna were carted off in two of them.

When Detective Shoner walked in with three officers, the first thing they did was go into the dining salon and look around. I followed. Ken stood by the sideboard holding a bag from Harbor Drugs. Detective Shoner told him what was going on and asked Ken to tell him exactly what everyone had for breakfast. Ken told him it hadn't been one of Brenna's special meals, just scrambled eggs, ham, and fresh fruit.

I couldn't help but think: *Green Eggs and Ham.*

Detective Shoner said to his officers, "Go into the kitchen and retrieve the trash. Is everyone who had breakfast accounted for?"

I looked at Ken and thought of his sister the beekeeper, the same person who mentioned that bees that feed on rhododendrons and azaleas produce poison honey. She had been wrong, because I'd looked it up when I'd taken my laptop to Sag Coffee. Bees might take nectar from a few rhododendrons and azaleas, but they usually like a smorgasbord of flowers to sup on, weakening the poison in the honey to almost nothing. But Kortney had mentioned the word "poison," and she'd also known the snakeroot I was holding when I saw her at the apiary was poisonous.

I said, "The only two people I haven't seen are Kortney and Ollie."

Ken said, "Kortney didn't have breakfast at the inn. She

never does. However, Mr. Hollingsworth was here and he had seconds of everything."

Now who was a glutton?

Detective Shoner told another officer to go down to the castle with the extra ambulance.

Ken went to find his sister, and I took Detective Shoner aside. "So, are you going to tell me what poison Nicole had in her system?"

"Digoxin."

"Where do you get it?"

"It's a drug used for heart patients. In the digitalis family."

"From the foxglove plant? I'm assuming Nicole didn't have heart problems."

"Digitalis comes from foxglove, but digoxin is synthetically produced for the same results. It's not as widely prescribed as it used to be. And no, Ms. Wolfstrum didn't have heart problems, just an infection. Her case was more severe because she was also on the antibiotic erythromycin. Erythromycin and digoxin don't mix too well. And then on top of that, she consumed a lot of alcohol. We still don't know what's going on at the inn. It might not be poison. Might just be a simple stomach virus. But you know Elle— better safe than sorry."

"Franklin had heart problems. Obviously, it wouldn't hurt to check out the cabin to see if he used that medication. How long will it take to get the tox results on the others?"

"That depends on the lab at the hospital. After we check every room for pills, I'll head to Southampton and see if I can move things along."

"And don't forget to have your team check the stables, castle, and even the boathouse."

"I know my job, Ms. Barrett."

"Sorry. Force of habit."

He raised a lush eyebrow. "I'll also find out what Hal Innes ate this morning. Ken Lerner had eggs, ham, fruit, and coffee with cream. In the meantime, stay out of the kitchen. By the way, why didn't you have breakfast at the inn?"

"Paddy's Pancake House."

"Oh, yes. Happy birthday."

"Thanks."

I did feel lucky Detective Shoner and two of his officers were on hand when the queen bed was delivered. It would have been seventy-five dollars extra for the deliverymen to cart everything up to the third floor. As a birthday gift, Detective Shoner even had his men set up the queen bed and remove the twin.

After Detective Shoner left, I went to check on Jo, making sure the loft door was locked behind me. Ken and Kortney were the only other ones on the Hollingsworth estate. Knowing there were possible poisoners on the loose, I couldn't think of a pair higher on my list.

Elle called every half hour. She told me Ollie had also been sick and was at the hospital. So far, everyone seemed to be recovering nicely, but there were no labs back yet confirming digoxin.

I spent the rest of the afternoon and evening barricaded in the loft, arranging the Emily Dickinson area so it would be ready for paying guests. Now that my cottage was up and running, I wanted to do the same: run.

The smalls (knickknacks) had been packed in boxes from when the Emily Dickinson suite on the second floor had to be moved to the loft. Emily Elizabeth Dickinson was born in 1830 at Homestead in Amherst, Massachusetts, and died in 1886. Dates that easily coincided with Ezekiel Hollingsworth's and Captain Isaiah Hollingsworth's lifetime. I was able to use some of the items I'd recently uncovered in the loft cupboard in the suite's décor. Unfortunately for Jo, the wooden horse had to go. Emily Dickinson never had children or married. There were rumors she'd had a love affair with a local judge, but it might have been a relationship in letters only. Just like author Patrick Seaton and me, penning verses on the beach without ever actually meeting.

Jo opened her eye only once. She was used to me unpacking and packing stuff, as long as I didn't disturb her naps or dinner hour.

I'd decided to focus on Emily's writing years for the décor, from when she was in her early twenties through her thirties. She was definitely a homebody and enjoyed all the home arts of her day, like cooking and gardening. I'd read that Emily Dickinson started gardening at eleven. Her garden was the inspiration for many of her poems. Her father even built her an indoor conservatory. She'd said all she had to do was "cross the floor to stand in the Spice Islands."

After I arranged the furniture, I was quite pleased with myself, until I looked at the two empty tiger's-eye maple-and-glass front bookcases against the southern wall. The boxes that held the books Franklin had chosen for the suite were missing. I went to the dresser and removed the copy of the list of insured books. Forty books, valued at two to five hundred dollars each, were missing. I got out my cell phone and looked at the photo I'd taken of the bookcase at Grimes House Antiques. Four of the books meant for the

Dickinson loft were in the photo: *The Marble Faun* by Nathaniel Hawthorne, *Middlemarch* by George Eliot, and two books from Charles Dickens. The other authors whose works were missing included: Washington Irving, Byron, Wordsworth, Longfellow, Sir Walter Scott, Tennyson, the Brontës (considered women's psychological fiction), and Elizabeth Barrett Browning. Also unaccounted for were early copies of Emily's poetry books, none of which had been published in her lifetime. All the authors of the missing books had been Emily Dickinson's favorites and had filled her bookshelves in Amherst. The missing books reminded me of Franklin and *The Heiress and the Light*. If the manuscript had been stolen from the book vault, and none of the other rare books were taken from the vault, then I doubted the person stealing the books from the Bibliophile and *The Heiress and the Light* were the same person or persons.

I had dozed off with the phone still on my shoulder after one of Elle's updates, when someone banged on the loft's door. I jumped awake and kicked Jo by mistake. She'd had all the room in the world on the queen bed but chose to lay her head on my ankle. She flew three feet into the air, but not before her back claws did a number on my legs. I had to scooch forward so none of the blood got on the quilted white coverlet.

They banged again.

"Hold on." I grabbed a brass telescope to use as a weapon and went to the door. "Who's there?"

"It's Detective Shoner."

"How do I know it's really you?"

"Don't be ridiculous, Ms. Barrett."

I opened the door.

"I need your help."

I looked at him. "I can tell by your face. They were poisoned. Please tell me they'll survive."

"Of course they'll survive. Yes, they had digoxin in their systems, but very low levels. Oliver Hollingsworth had the most, but he'll be fine. They'll all be released tomorrow. I think we've figured out what the poison was added to. Brenna Hollingsworth served rolls with breakfast. Hal Innes and Ken Lerner didn't have any."

"Honey twists!" I said.

"Yes. The theory is the digoxin was in the honey jar. Brenna Hollingsworth was out of honey in the pantry, so she went to the lounge to find a jar. In fact, she had to dig it out of the recycle bin. I think we should take a trip to where the honey is bottled to see if we find any digoxin. In the meantime, we wait for the lab results from the jars of honey we took earlier from the kitchen garbage."

We took the path to the apiary. The sky was darkening. We probably had an hour before sunset. As if her twin had warned her we'd be stopping by, Kortney Lerner was standing at the entrance in her beekeeper's suit. She held the combination hat and veil in the crook of her elbow.

Detective Shoner said, "We need to see where you bottle the honey for the Bibliophile Bed and Breakfast."

Kortney said, "What's she doing here? Don't you need a warrant or something?"

He said, "No. We have permission from Oliver Hollingsworth, your employer."

"Whatever. Knock yourself out. The door's open." Then she walked away. A little too quickly.

Carved in wood above the entrance was a placard that read HONEY HUT with a bee holding a flower in its mouth. We stepped in and Detective Shoner flipped the light switch. Everything was organized and clean. Even the steel garbage cans near the entrance. There were only six full jars of honey on a shelf. The hut was much deeper than it looked from the outside. Also on the shelves were candle molds and cans of furniture wax. The hut had a small kitchen at the back; all the appliances were stainless steel, including an industrial-sized stove and counter. On the wall was a chart with the dates the honey was harvested, processed, and bottled. Bolted to the wall was a dispenser that held a roll of labels with the Hollingsworth Honey insignia: two H's intertwined in the middle of a hive.

Detective Shoner said, "My grandfather had a couple of hives. I remember visiting his farm in the summer." He picked up a screen-like thing in a wood frame and looked at it. "These 'supers' would be covered in honey. I'd put them on a retractor and turn a crank. The centrifugal force would spin the honey off. A sticky mess. But fun."

I couldn't picture Detective Shoner as a boy. Especially a sticky one. He dressed so formally, I pictured him wearing a suit and tie from his christening onward. Even though Elle called him Arthur, he would always be Detective Shoner to me, and I'd given up that he'd ever call me Meg.

Just as I started to admire Kortney for her beekeeping, I saw two red tail feathers sticking out from a galvanized flower pot in the corner of a closet. The tail feathers belonged to two yellow arrows. They were the same arrows that I'd found sticking out of my Jeep's tires.

I didn't have a chance to tell Detective Shoner about the arrows because just then he received a call. One of the honey jars taken earlier from under the kitchen sink tested positive for digoxin. He grabbed the six jars of honey off the shelf and flew out the door to meet the additional officers who would search the estate for honey jars. I wished them luck. Honey jars were plentiful on the Hollingsworth estate.

I followed him out. "If I were you, I'd get ahold of Franklin's body. The viewing at the funeral parlor is scheduled for tomorrow evening. That's where his body will be. Oh, and I also remember that Brenna told me she had a bad heart. That it runs in the family. I'd check out her meds, too."

Later that night, I realized I hadn't reported the books I'd found at Grimes House Antiques that were stolen from the Bibliophile. I texted Elle and she texted me back that she'd notify FFM and see if they could find out from Rita who had sold her the books. Maybe that person was the poisoner?

CHAPTER THIRTY-TWO

Tuesday morning I was woken by my phone vibrating under my pillow. It was Elle, leaving a message to make sure I was still alive.

The sky outside the window reminded me of the day of the hurricane. Even sleeping beauty Jo was unnerved by the thunder and the wind that rattled the shutters. Jo opened her eye with each new crack. I was one of those weird people who loved a good thunderstorm, especially one with a Dr. Frankenstein-esque light show over the Atlantic. Thunder was a sound I could *feel* without my hearing aids

Per another one of Elle's texts, Violet, Brenna, Allan, and Jordan were due home from the hospital any minute. Hal had spent the night in Jordan's room. Ollie, however, might have to stay another night. I jumped out of bed, put in my hearing aids so no one could sneak up on me, and hurried down to the bathroom. I hoped Brenna planned to give a discount on the Dickinson loft because it didn't have an en suite bathroom.

I couldn't wrap my head around the fact someone had added digoxin to the honey. Why? For what purpose? Could it have been an accident? I didn't see how. If it wasn't an accident, then killing Franklin would have been the obvious motive, but the results hadn't come back yet. Franklin could have just passed away from a bad heart. Then I remembered something. If Franklin was poisoned and his poisoning was related to the manuscript, then I might be considered a suspect. I was the only one who'd set off the alarm to the book vault. *Please let him have died from natural causes. Please.*

When I returned to the loft, a cavalcade of thunder spurred me into action. I took out my suitcase. It was time to start packing to go home. "Home." What a wonderful word. I emptied the drawers and then remembered the bag of clothing I'd picked up from the Wash n Dri. I loosened the drawstring and reached inside. In a baggie on top of the folded clothes were two pieces of paper Paula must have found in my shorts pocket. One was a piece of paper I'd forgotten about that I found under the log on the day of the hurricane. It was a letter addressed to Randall McFee from Peyton's Auction House in Key West, Florida. The letter was questioning the validity of the Ernest Hemingway manuscript *Before the Scourge*. They wanted Randall to provide detailed notes and citations on the research he'd done. Maybe Randall had been suicidal. If the Hemingway proved to be a fake, then the Fitzgerald might also be.

I unfolded the other paper. It was my signature from

when Violet had analyzed my handwriting during the hurricane. Above my signature was an imprint in the notepaper from the page above. I went to the Emily Dickinson writing stand, opened the drawer, and pulled out a sharpened pencil. Then I did a trick my father and Nancy Drew taught me when I was eight. I took the side of the pencil and went back and forth over the page until another signature appeared—Randall McFee's. And the date he'd written was the same as mine.

Randall had been at the teahouse before me on the day of the hurricane. The same day he fell off Widow's Point. Why hadn't Violet mentioned it? Randall must have been another one of her graphography subjects. Violet had told me the empty teacup in the sink at the teahouse had been Franklin's. Franklin hated tea, as he'd said on more than one occasion. Why would Violet keep it a secret that she'd seen Randall?

I didn't have to ponder things any further, because Elle pounded on the door, and when I opened it, she burst into the loft. "Franklin was poisoned with digoxin. He took another drug for his heart and the combination was lethal. Hal Innes has been arrested for the theft of *The Heiress and the Light* and the possible poisoning of Franklin and even Randall McFee's death!" She bent at the waist to catch her breath.

"Slow down. What are you talking about?"

"Just now. They took him away."

"Why? What proof do they have?"

Jo waddled over to Elle and gave her a couple of affectionate shin-butts. Elle almost fell backward.

"They found a bag of digoxin between the box spring and mattress in the Melville suite. And you won't believe this one: in the lining of Hal's suitcase was an original page from *The Heiress and the Light*. The second page."

"A single page?"

"Yes. And remember, he's the only one who didn't get sick yesterday at breakfast."

"Him, Ken, and Kortney. What was his motive for poisoning everyone just a little? Even his wife, Jordan? I know his love for her isn't an act. Didn't the police search yesterday for digoxin? It doesn't make sense. Unless . . ."

"Unless what?"

"He put poison in Franklin's bee's knees in the lounge, then threw the jar in the trash so no one else got poisoned. He wouldn't know Brenna fished it out and used it for her honey twists."

"Good thinking. But then why would Hal avoid eating a honey twist, if he didn't know Brenna had used the poisoned jar in her recipe?"

"I remember Hal telling me he was trying to lower his carb intake. It could've been a coincidence he didn't eat one. Something else doesn't make sense. Why poison Franklin? What did Hal have to gain if he already had the manuscript? And what about Nicole? She was poisoned the night of the party. Why would Hal do that? Let's go see Jordan. Maybe we can figure this out together."

Jordan was in the parking lot, about to get in her Prius. She looked better than before her trip to the hospital—but not by much.

Elle called out, "Wait, Jordan!"

When Jordan turned our way, she raised her hands and placed them on either side of her open mouth. She resembled the main character in the Munch painting *The Scream.* "I don't know what to do! Call a lawyer? Or go to the station? Do I take out money for bail?" Then she stood straighter and jutted out her jaw. "This is ridiculous. Hal is innocent. I'm not letting them get away with this!"

When we reached her, I said, "Tell me exactly what he was charged with."

Lightning flashed.

Jordan looked up at the sky. "I don't know. It happened so fast. We'd just returned from the hospital and we were in the dining salon. Two Sag Harbor officers charged over to Hal. They asked him all these questions like, 'Where were you on such and such a day?'"

I said, "Did they read him his rights?"

"No, I don't think so."

Elle asked, "Was he in handcuffs?"

"No."

I said, "Then I don't think he was arrested. They probably just want to question him."

"They searched our suite and found a page from the original manuscript in Hal's suitcase. They also found some pills I'd never seen before in a plastic bag between the mattress and the box spring. What's going on? They even took Hal's phone."

My normal response would be to believe in Hal's innocence. But I'd learned to not jump to conclusions, but rather to wait until all the facts were compartmentalized. I wished I had one of my large storyboards and some index cards. Most crimes followed a certain progression, and to solve one, you needed to step back to see things in a different light—the trees for the forest, instead of the forest for the trees, as my father would say. With all that said, I felt in my gut that Hal Innes was innocent. Everything in the Melville suite could have been planted by Ken or Kortney.

I said, "Elle, why don't you go with Jordan. She doesn't look well enough to drive. There's something I need to check that might help Hal's case. Keep in touch."

Elle gave me a strange look—well, maybe not that strange, because I'd seen it before. It was the *What are you up to, Meg Barrett?* look, followed by the arch of an eyebrow. She said, "Okay, Jordan. Let's go."

They pulled away and I went through the back gates toward the apiary. It was time I confronted Kortney Lerner about the arrows I found in the honey hut.

Halfway to the apiary I got a call from my father. After yesterday's discoveries about the poison, I'd given him a list of everyone at the Hollingsworth estate. First and last names.

"Hey, Dad. Things are going down here like you wouldn't believe."

"Okay, my little sleuth, I'll be quick. It's about Brenna Hollingsworth. I was able to find out she was in a gang in Newark in her late teens. There was an initiation incident where someone died. She and other gang members were charged with felonies. But somehow Brenna got a big-time lawyer who managed to plead it down to a misdemeanor. Ms. Hollingsworth lived with her mother at the time, and shortly afterward, her mother died. The mother's death coincides with the time you said she came to Sag Harbor."

"Wow." That explained the creepy tattoo. I told him everything Jordan had just told Elle and me. I also filled him in about Hal and Jordan Innes's large bank account that Greg had alluded to.

"I think it's time for you to get out of there."

"I plan to. You don't know the half of it." I went on to
tell him about Violet lying about seeing Randall on the day
of the hurricane. He was very impressed with my pencil-
shading trick.

I said, "I'd better go before I get zapped by lightning."

"Did you know more people are killed by lightning than
by terrorism?"

"That's a charming statistic."

"I'm going to call Doc. He should come by and check
on things. If you don't think Hal Innes is a murderer, that
means one is on the loose."

That's what I loved most about my ex-homicide-
detective father. He was always on my side.

"Don't worry. As soon as I talk to a few people, Jo and
I are out of here. I can't wait to move into my cottage."

"You deserve the best. I'm happy it worked out. Have
you thanked Cole yet?"

"No, but I will, very soon. Love you. Say hi to Sheila."

"Be careful! Love you."

As I passed the path to Scrimshaw House, I tried to
organize my thoughts about what my father had just told
me. Brenna's involvement in a gang explained her tattoo,
and it also explained her and Ollie's conversation at the
book fair. Ollie was holding Brenna's past over her head
and possibly using emotional blackmail to get her to do
things she normally wouldn't. He was the one who'd probably hired her lawyer after the gang incident. Ollie made
me appreciate my parentage even more.

I remembered what my father had said earlier about
following the money when it came to the stolen *The Heiress
and the Light* manuscript. Jordan and Hal had a lot of

money in their account and Hal hadn't been poisoned, only his wife.

Violet might not inherit Franklin's rare book collection, but what if he had a substantial life insurance policy and she was the beneficiary? I couldn't see how she would benefit from stealing *The Heiress and the Light*. Could the theft of the manuscript and Franklin's murder have been committed by two separate people?

Allan Wolfstrum had been the last one with Nicole the night of the party. Had he given her poison? Allan had told me Franklin's entire rare-book collection would be going to the Princeton Library. It also seemed Franklin had been Allan's meal ticket since his divorce from Nicole. I'd read his lips asking Franklin for a loan, and Franklin had agreed. Brenna told me Franklin had taken out a loan against the Bibliophile, the reason my check from the inn bounced. If Franklin was murdered by Allan, what would Allan's motive be? From what I understood, all of Franklin's inheritance was tied up in books, ephemera, and the Bibliophile B & B.

What would Brenna have to gain by poisoning her uncle? Maybe what she'd said about the loan her uncle took out wasn't true and she was stealing the money Franklin had given her and he found out? Or possibly her father, Ollie, made her steal the money. Until the will was read, I wouldn't know what Brenna, Ollie, and Violet stood to inherit. And what had Nicole consumed that had honey laced with poison? Ollie hadn't served bee's knees at the party. I knew, because I'd asked for one. But I could tell from her breath, she'd consumed a boatload of alcohol.

As I got closer to the apiary, I walked faster. The rain

hadn't started, but the sky was black. The thunder and lightning Jo and I witnessed from the loft had been tame compared to now. I wasn't about to put off my little meeting. It was time for Kortney Lerner to face the music. I just hoped her bees were corralled in their cozy hives and not frightened by the electricity in the air.

When I walked through the opening of the boxwood hedges, I saw Kortney, dressed in shorts and a T-shirt. I didn't have to announce myself because a flash of lightning and clap of thunder did it for me.

"What do you want? Where's your cop friend?"

So much for my rule about having backup. "He's on his way. He wants me to ask you a few questions. Question one: why do you have arrows similar to the ones that were found in the tires of my Jeep?"

"What are you talking about?"

I strode past her and went to the honey hut. I made a point of pushing the door so hard it banged against the inside window frame. Then I went to the closet where I'd seen the arrows. I grabbed them and charged out of the hut, metal tips pointing forward. "This is what I'm talking about!"

She stepped back a millimeter. "So?"

"So, you used these to flatten my tires. What else are you up to? Poisoning honey jars?"

"Why would I poison my own honey?"

Someone dressed in a white beekeeper's suit came from behind the honey hut carrying one of those "supers" Detective Shoner told me about. I realized whoever was under the beekeeping veil was the person I'd seen the night of the hurricane, because he or she was four inches taller than Kortney.

Ken Lerner removed the hat and veil. "What's going on here?" He looked from me to his sister.

Kortney shrugged her shoulders.

I said, "Your twisted sister is the one who put arrows in all four of my tires."

He said, "Is that true, Kortney?"

"Maybe."

I said, "And she might be the one who put poison in the honey that killed Franklin."

Ken moved closer to me. "What are you talking about? Franklin was poisoned?"

"Yes."

Kortney went to her brother and grabbed his arm. "You know I would never do that to Mr. Hollingsworth. Why would I do that? All I did was flatten her tires and steal a dress."

He said, "You did what?"

I said, "You did what?"

Kortney stuck out her bottom lip in a cutesy gesture. It must have worked in the past with Ken, but it didn't work with me.

Ken said, "You told me Meg was out to get you because of Byron. What else have you done?"

She said, "That's it. I swear. I couldn't stand seeing Byron kiss and fawn all over her. Since our affair, he hasn't even said, 'Hello. How are you?' I followed her to the antique junk shop, broke a window in her ugly Jeep, took her dress, and sold it to Rags to Riches in Bridgehampton. I'll give the money back." She started crying.

So that was how Tara had gotten my dress for the party. For once she hadn't told a lie.

Ken took her by the elbow and sat her on an iron bench.

"We've been over this, Kortney. You've been doing so good since Ollie. Byron never took you on a date. He brought you a frozen hot chocolate from Chocolat when you helped him dig the koi pond."

I turned to Ken. "So that explains her exploits. But how about you skulking around in the beekeeper's suit the night of the hurricane and Randall McFee's death?"

Kortney said, "If I had to come clean, so do you!"

He looked at me. "I'm writing a book and screenplay based on the possibility of an Underground Railroad connection with the Hollingsworths and a slave plantation on Shelter Island. It's based on the true story of a sugar-and-slave trader from Barbados, Nathaniel Sylvester. Sylvester Manor on Shelter Island is the only intact slave plantation north of the Mason-Dixon Line. Some of the whale-ship owners in the mid-1800s turned away from whaling because their ships could be gone for up to three years, stockpiling whale oil and traveling to dangerous locales, and they found it more profitable to use their ships for the illegal slave trade. The waters were safer and there was a quicker turnaround of their cargo and, more important, they made more money on the slaves. I've already talked to a few Hollywood producers interested in the project. There's a tunnel that runs from the keeping room in the inn all the way to Scrimshaw House. I've found papers and ledgers in the cellar of Scrimshaw House, including a list of slaves and their monetary value."

I said, "So you're the reason for the lights at Scrimshaw House. Not Sarah's ghost." Instead of a ghost in a white dressing gown, people were seeing a man in a white beekeeper's suit.

He said, "I don't believe in ghosts, but I have felt a certain energy, even a presence, around Scrimshaw House."

"Ken, what did you hand that dealer at the book fair in the brown paper bag? Cash?"

"As a matter of fact, yes. Even though it's none of your business. It was for a book I'd given to him on consignment that I'd found in Yanio's. I paid twelve dollars and fifty cents for it and sold it for six hundred. I've learned a lot working for Franklin." His eyes teared at the mention of Franklin. "My sister will reimburse you for the tires and the dress, won't you, Kortney? And we apologize for any feeling of animosity toward you. Don't we, Kortney?"

She batted a few eyelashes at him. "Of course." Then she pasted on a smile for his benefit, not mine.

I said, "I'm leaving today. Slip the money for the dress and the tires under the door to the Emily Dickinson loft. And I want cash, not a check."

CHAPTER

THIRTY-THREE

I counted the time between the lightning and the thunder. There was barely a "one Mississippi" between them, but still no rain. The thunder seemed one continuous sound. A couple hundred feet ahead of me, I saw Violet coming from the rear of the Bibliophile. She was dressed in a fuchsia oilskin parka. She hurried through the gates and turned onto the path leading to the pagoda. I was happy to see she'd recovered from her stay at the hospital. I was also happy, because now she could answer a few of my questions.

When I got to the intersection of paths before the iron gates, I took a left and followed her toward the teahouse. I waited before going over the stone bridge and up the hill. I tried to rehearse what I was going to say. I didn't want to tip my hand. I felt in my pocket for the paper with Randall's signature. There was no need to rehearse anything. I just wanted an explanation of what Randall had been doing with her on the day of the hurricane.

The rain started once I was over the bridge. Instead of waiting politely for Violet to let me in the teahouse, I slid the doors open and walked in.

Violet stood at the stove.

I said, "Sorry for just walking in. It's started to rain."

She turned, brandishing the copper teakettle like a weapon. "You scared me to death. There's a killer on the loose, in case you haven't heard."

"I've heard. If I were you, then, I'd lock the teahouse door."

She looked well. Her cheeks were pink under her two blonde curls.

"How are you feeling?"

She said, "I'm devastated and sad, Ms. Barrett."

"I meant from the poisoning."

"I'm recovered." She went to the cupboard and got out a cup and saucer. "Are you staying for tea? I think Da Hong Pao will calm me."

"No. I'm good."

"I'm not going to poison you, Ms. Barrett. But I can understand your worry."

Instead of taking loose tea from one of the large glass canisters, she went to the cupboard and took out a small blue-willow ginger jar, opened it, and spooned out some tea. "Not that I don't mind the company, but what can I do for you?"

She didn't seem too upset about her husband's death— check that, her husband's murder. But I'd learned you never knew how someone else handled grief. The Steinbeck head was on top of the kiln next to her, uncovered. On close inspection, Steinbeck's face had a few of Franklin's features. His nose and weak chin.

"I wanted to ask you about Randall McFee."

She turned quickly and faced me. Tea leaves floated to

the floor. "Go on." Lightning flashed and then thunder sounded and the spoon slipped through her fingers and landed on the sisal mat.

"The day of the hurricane, you said your husband was the one who came to see you earlier and had a cup of tea." I looked over at the bench by the door at the F. Scott Fitzgerald book I'd tripped over during the hurricane. "Yet, Franklin hated tea."

"Tea or coffee. They both use cups, Ms. Barrett. Maybe you misheard me because of your hearing loss?"

"That's possible. Do you even keep coffee in the teahouse?"

She didn't, because the day she sent me for the jar of tea, I'd searched her cupboards for clear plastic Ziplocs. I never saw coffee, instant or otherwise.

"Ms. Barrett, what is your real question?"

I reached in my pocket and took out the piece of paper. "I have this notepaper where you had me sign my name with the date from when you were analyzing my handwriting during the hurricane. I found an impression in the paper from the page above with Randall's signature and it had the same date as mine. He was the one who came to the teahouse on the day of the hurricane, not Franklin, like you said."

She shot over to me, her hand reaching out. "Let me see that."

Instinctively, I stuffed it back in my pocket. "And that book I tripped over, it belonged to Randall McFee, didn't it? Not your husband."

Violet looked out at the rain sluicing down the windows. "Yes. Randall was here. He often came for readings. I didn't tell anyone because my readings are private."

As she talked, I sidled over to the bench and casually picked up the book, holding it by its spine. An envelope had been used as a bookmark and it naturally opened to Fitzgerald's short story that took place in Montauk, "The Unspeakable Egg." The envelope was addressed to Randall McFee from Peyton's Auction House. The same envelope that matched the letter I'd found on the day of the hurricane. I closed the book. Violet strode toward me and grabbed it from my hand.

She said, "Yes, this was Randall's, he was very upset about something, but I never found out what. And when he left, he was despondent. I didn't say anything because I felt guilty I hadn't stopped him from leaving the teahouse, knowing his frame of mind. I think he planned to kill himself. If you look at his signature, you'll see his handwriting trails downward at the end. A sure sign of depression. I read it in his leaves. They were in the shape of a Japanese hari-kari dagger."

The specificity of a Japanese hari-kari dagger in the tea leaves seemed a little ridiculous. Just a dagger or knife would have sufficed.

I said, "Did he share with you that the Ernest Hemingway manuscript *Before The Scourge*, which he authenticated, was being questioned and you realized the authenticity of *The Heiress and the Light* could be questioned as well? "

"No. He never did. I had the feeling it was something in his love life. Here, let me loan you my parka. It's possible we'll lose power and I'd rather be alone right now."

I could take a hint. "Thank you. And I'm really sorry about the loss of your husband."

"I hope Hal Innes fries."

Lightning stabbed the tree line outside the window. Then she pushed me out the door.

I flew down the hill from the teahouse and ran all the way back to the inn—daggers, ghosts, and ravensnakes hiding behind every tree.

CHAPTER

୶

THIRTY-FOUR

Instead of entering the inn via the front or back door, I followed a brick walkway embossed with SAG BRICKWORKS that led to the side of the Victorian. On both sides of the path was Brenna's kitchen garden. There were neat rows of assorted lettuce, herbs, and edible flowers, all getting pummeled by the rain. I hoped for a chance to get Brenna alone to ask how she was doing; it would be an extra bonus if I could segue to what I'd overheard between her and her father at the book fair.

I entered a small mudroom and wiped my feet on the mat. I kept Violet's raincoat on and went into the hall that led to the kitchen. When I passed the pantry, Brenna was slumped over the farm table, her elbows leaning on top, her head in her hands.

I went to her and touched her shoulder. She looked up. I asked, "How are you feeling?"

"I've been better. Honestly, it's not the poison that's got

me sick. It's the fact my uncle was murdered. And the murderer was one of my guests. Someone I thought was my uncle's friend. What if Hal also killed Randall?" She broke into a sob and then pointed to a box of tissues on the shelf.

I handed her the box. "Has Hal been arrested?"

"He hasn't been arrested for murder, but until they get results from Randall's body, they're holding him for a traffic violation. Jordan's in the morning room. I can't even look at her."

"Can I ask why you used the honey from the recycle bin in the lounge to make your honey twists?"

"A simple explanation I've repeated too many times. I went to make the honey twists and couldn't find any honey. So I checked the lounge, the room where more bee's knees are consumed than any other. The shelf under the bar didn't have any jars, but below it, in the recycle bin, there was a half-used jar. I grabbed it, thinking it had been thrown away by mistake or had fallen from the shelf into the bin."

I left her staring at the shelves of Ball jars filled with the fruits and vegetables of her garden's bounty. The timing wasn't right to question Brenna about her and her father's nefarious undertakings, so I went to the morning room to find Jordan.

Through the French doors I saw Jordan sitting next to the desk. On her lap was a stack of sightseeing brochures. I opened the doors, stepped inside, and sat next to her. "How are you holding up?"

"Hanging on by my fingernails." Her usually sparkly eyes looked dull. She bit at her lower lip, licking at dots of blood with her tongue. She picked up a brochure and waved it at me. "Instead of my husband being held in jail, we should be looking through these pamphlets, planning the next few summer days filled with fine dining, shopping, and leisure sports."

"Brenna told me they're holding Hal."

"Yes, and they've managed to add one more nail to his coffin." She swallowed. "There were phone numbers in Hal's cell phone of some of my exclusive bibliophile clients. Why would he have those numbers? He must have taken them from my phone. I can't think of another explanation."

As she spoke, I looked up at a scowling portrait of Captain Isaiah that took over the entire space on the wall above the fireplace mantel. I'd never realized how close in appearance Franklin had been to his ancestor Captain Isaiah. I put my hand on Jordan's shoulder. "Why don't you go upstairs and lie down. I'll check on you on my way out."

"Your way out?"

"I'm leaving. My cottage in Montauk has water and power."

"I wish I could leave."

I helped her upstairs and onto the bed in the Melville suite. Then I hurried up to the loft. Jo was waiting expectantly by the door. Ready to vamoose. So was I.

I looked over at the bed. Jo's cat hair covered the clothing at the top of my suitcase. I laid Violet's raincoat on a chair and went to my purse and got out the lint roller. It was a must-have accessory since I'd adopted Jo. After nine fur-covered sheets from the roller, it was hard to tell that a twenty-four-pound Maine coon had been anywhere near the suitcase. I hadn't weighed her, but I added an extra pound based on her physique. I walked to the desk and turned on the lamp. The thunderstorm, which had quieted,

revived itself. Jo leaped back on top of my clothes in the
suitcase. "Miss Josephine, you're right. Let's get out of
here. I'll de-hair later, once we're home. Home. Get used
to that word, Jo."

A few minutes later, I was under the bed looking for my
other tennis shoe when there was a pounding at the loft
door.

I slithered out and called, "Who goes there?" thinking
it was Elle or Detective Shoner.

"It's Violet Hollingsworth."

I opened the door and Violet stepped inside. She was
soaked from the rain. Her gauzy floral tunic stuck to her
like a second skin. The blonde curls at her cheeks were
pointed downward, resembling men's sideburns. She looked
over to the bed and the suitcase with Jo on top. Good thing
it was my last day at the inn with my illegal pussycat.

"Mrs. Hollingsworth, I'm so sorry. I'm sure you want
your coat back."

Violet pushed the door closed behind her and looked
around the room. "So, this where you found Sarah's
diary?"

"Yes. Inside an old rocking horse in the cupboard over
there." I pointed.

She went to the cupboard, then turned and faced me. I
took her raincoat off the chair and brought it to her. She
wrenched it out of my hand. A single white pill fell from
a pocket and skipped across the hardwood floor.

I looked at it. She looked at it. No one moved.

"Are you leaving us, Ms. Barrett?"

"Yes. I'm finished here. What do you think of how the
Emily Dickinson loft turned out?"

"What I think is, you're one nosy little girl, who isn't

long for this world. You should have heeded your tea leaves, Ms. Barrett." She pulled out something from her pocket. She cupped it in her hands, then opened them, palms up, exposing a mother-of-pearl-handled switchblade. In what seemed like slow motion, I watched as she pressed the silver button. The blade flipped out with a swish. It was the longest, sharpest-looking thing I'd ever seen. Nothing like my Troop 413 Girl Scout knife.

I said, "What's with the antique knife? Do you want me to put it in one of the suites?"

"Thank you, but that won't be necessary, Ms. Barrett. The only place this knife is going is in your heart. I'm sorry, but you're not ruining my plans."

"What plans?"

"Shush. Let's go."

I went toward the door, but she got there before me. Her and the knife. I looked over at Jo. She was fast asleep.

"No, Ms. Barrett. Not that door." Violet nodded her head toward the door leading up to the cupola. Lightning flashed, illuminating Violet's face. Her mascara ran from her lower lashes in downward streaks. She resembled a macabre Raggedy Ann doll. An agile Raggedy Ann doll, because she had the tip of her knife pointed at my back in seconds.

She prodded me through the door to the cupola and up the narrow, twisting staircase. I turned the key in the lock and we stepped into the storm. She must have known what I was thinking, because she said, "If you scream, it will be your last."

I doubted anyone would hear me over the shrieking of the wind. "It seems kind of silly that you plan to kill me without me knowing why."

"Hand me the paper with Randall's signature. Now."

I reached in my pocket, then extended my arm to give it to her, but instead made a fist and clipped her in the jaw. She fell backward on the slippery rain-slicked deck. The knife flew out of her hand and skidded out of reach.

We both dived for it.

I was the victor. I stuck the point of the knife under her jawline, near the jugular. "Don't move. I want you to stand slowly."

Violet stood and I forced her to the other side of the deck, toward the railing that overlooked the Bibliophile's parking lot. Someone stood below in a black-hooded raincoat. I shouted but the rain, wind, and thunder drowned me out.

I turned to Violet. "So, you stole the Fitzgerald manuscript and framed Hal Innes. Did you plan to sell the manuscript, then collect the insurance on top of that?"

She laughed. "Oh, Ms. Barrett, you have no clue what's going on." She headed for the door.

I followed. "Yes, we're leaving and you're going straight to jail."

"Who do you think they'll believe? A Hollingsworth or the woman who set off the alarm to the book vault? The same person who punched me and whose prints are all over that knife."

"I think they'll believe me when I show them the paper with Randall McFee's signature and date."

"And what will that prove, Ms. Barrett? That I'm guilty of not saying I was with a man who had an accident in a hurricane? Get over yourself."

"Then why did you want to kill me?"

She put her hand on the doorknob. Someone on the other side pushed it outward and Violet fell on her rear end.

Allan Wolfstrum walked out. He reached out his hand and helped Violet up. "What's going on?" He looked at the knife in my hand. "Violet?"

I said, "I'm so happy you're here. This lunatic tried to kill me. She came at me with a knife and had a pill in her pocket that I would guess is digoxin. Plus, she saw Randall the day he died."

For some reason, Allan didn't look surprised. Maybe everyone had known Violet was off her rocker and hadn't bothered to clue me in.

Violet stood and pushed Allan aside. "It's about time you showed up. Where were you? With her?"

Allan said, "Calm down, Violet."

She pointed to her jaw. "Look what she did to me."

He grabbed Violet by both shoulders and turned her toward him. "Violet, why is Meg here?"

"She knows," she hissed. "It's only a matter of time before she stops us."

I said, "As you just pointed out, I know nothing."

Violet said, "She knows the Fitzgerald manuscript might be a fake. What will we do if word gets out?"

Allan said, "Hush."

I still had the knife. Could Allan and Violet be partners in crime? Lovers, even? Poisoners? "Look, out of the way, both of you. I'm leaving." I strode toward the door, but my sandal hit a wet patch on the deck and my leg gave out.

Allan rushed over to help me. Or at least that's what I assumed. He grabbed my arm and karate-chopped my wrist. The knife hit the deck, slid under the railing, and fell sixty feet to the ground. I staggered up and went for the door. Violet blocked me.

He said, "Violet, you idiot. That switchblade was a Davy and Sons staghorn drip-point swing guard dirk!"

She moved away from the door and stuck her face inches from his. "I found your stash. Things you stole from my husband's family. That's the same knife you used to get Randall to fall off Widow's Point. I let Franklin ignore me for years. I'm not letting you get away with leaving me for a two-bit actress."

He pushed her back. "You are deranged. If I hadn't been with Nicole at the hospital when she got the news she'd been poisoned with digoxin, we wouldn't have been able to plant evidence against Hal."

I was dying to see how things played out, but I was more concerned with saving my life. Lightning splintered the sky. When the thunder sounded, I ran to the door. Two large hands grabbed fistfuls of my hair and pulled me backward.

Allan shoved me against the railing. "Don't move. Meg, I'm sorry."

Violet came toward us, her teeth clenched, her eyes narrowed to slits. Instead of going after me, she slugged Allan in the ribs, then kneed him between his legs.

He clutched his chest and bent forward.

Violet shouted, "Yes, I poisoned your precious Nicole, darling. Surprised? Not hard to do. Are you saying it's okay to poison my husband, but not your ex-wife? I didn't plan to kill her, just get her good and sick and make her look like a loser in the press. I won't let you use me, then leave with my money to be with that trollop. You are warned."

"You're unhinged," he said, moaning as he stood. "You poisoned Nicole, yourself, and half of the people here. You were lucky Hal didn't eat one of those rolls made with poisoned honey."

She swiped the rain out of her eyes. "How was I supposed to know Franklin's niece would dig through the garbage for the jar I used on your precious Nicole?"

Allan put his hands around her neck.

She choked out, "You kill me, you get nothing! All we have to do is silence Ms. Barrett by pushing her off and then Hal Innes will take the blame for the rest."

While Allan's hands were welded to Violet's neck, and Violet's hands were pulling at his ascot, I trucked it out the door and down the stairs.

When I burst through the door to the Emily Dickinson loft, Doc was standing in front of me with Jo in his arms. "Oh, am I happy to see you! I'm calling nine-one-one. You barricade this door and don't let anyone out."

Doc opened his mouth to speak, but thought better of it.

I locked the door, took the key with me, and hurried to the box of things going to the whaling museum. I removed the cannibal-head letter opener and brought it to Doc. My hand shook so badly, he had to grab my wrist to keep me from stabbing myself. He put Jo on the floor and backed up to the door, holding the letter opener. Jo stood sentry at his feet.

I thought of Violet's twisted face and felt the throbbing in my wrist from Allan's assault. "Don't be afraid to use that." Then I grabbed my phone and called for help.

After I hung up, Doc said, "Your father sent me. He said he talked to the judge in Key West and the Hemingway book Randall authenticated is back on the shelves, deemed authentic. He also checked Allan Wolfstrum's medical records. He was prescribed digoxin five years ago, then his doctor switched it to another drug. Randall McFee didn't have any poison in his system. The autopsy report on Randall came back that he was killed by the fall. But they also found a small wound in the center of his abdomen. It barely broke skin."

"The point of a switchblade, I bet." I reached behind and rubbed a spot on my back, then looked for a heavy piece of furniture to barricade the door.

It was then that we heard a scream, louder than thunder, and saw a body fly by the loft's window.

CHAPTER

✌︎⤳✍︎

THIRTY-FIVE

It was the third week in September. All the tourists and summer people had left the Hamptons. I wasn't sad to see them go. The weather was still warm. It had been a month since Violet Hollingsworth fell to her death from the top of the Bibliophile Bed & Breakfast.

The loudspeaker at the Long Island Railroad train depot in Montauk announced that my father's train was on time. He sat with his usual straight posture, dark hair a little grayer than the last time I'd seen him. Even at fifty-six, he'd managed to turn more than a few females' heads during the past week. It wasn't just his outward appearance that was attractive. He oozed calm, confidence, and control, "The three *C*s," my mother used to joke. We shared the same blue eyes but the rest of my fair coloring came from my mother's side of the family.

He said, "Looks like everything's tied up. I'm happy the Fitzgerald Family Trust is going ahead with the novel's publication. I can't wait to read it. Especially knowing it takes place in your new hometown. I assume the light in the title *The Heiress and the Light* refers to the Montauk Point Lighthouse."

"Yes. Doc told me it has a lot of local flavor—the lighthouse and bootlegging. I can't believe he and Sully got to read it."

"You and me both."

The past week with my father had been spent going to top restaurants, a few failed attempts at surfing, and lots of fishing. I think my father was surprised at how savvy I was with a fishing pole.

I said, "I also can't believe Violet killed her husband so she could collect the insurance on the Fitzgerald manuscript."

"Follow the money!" We said at the same time.

A few people waiting on the platform turned our way.

My father laughed. "From what you've told me, I think Allan Wolfstrum is the one who wanted the money. Violet Hollingsworth wanted her husband's love and attention. When he couldn't give it to her, she turned to Allan."

"I'm happy Hal Innes will be putting *The Heiress and the Light* into novel form."

After Hal had been cleared of all charges, he'd presented Jordan with a tenth anniversary gift, a first edition signed copy of *A Tree Grows in Brooklyn* by Betty Smith. It was Jordan's grandmother's and mother's favorite book, as well as hers as an adolescent, and the reason why Hal had copied her contacts into his cell phone. The large amount of money in Jordan's business account was also explained. One of Jordan's clients had transferred the money to the account so Jordan could purchase an entire library of rare books anonymously. Elle and I had inspired the couple to add vintage décor that could be purchased in their Brooklyn bookstore, Carpe Librum. Hal and Jordan also planned to sell coffee, tea, and finger desserts for their patrons, using some of Brenna's recipes. I couldn't wait to stop in—not for the coffee or tea, but for the vintage smalls. Brooklyn had the perfect eclectic vibe that Elle and I fed on.

Everything turned out well for Hal Innes, but that wasn't the case for Allan Edgar Wolfstrum. When Violet told Allan *The Heiress and the Light*'s authenticity might be called into question, they'd panicked and stepped up their plan to steal the manuscript for the insurance money and kill Franklin before anyone could take a good look at it. Allan and Violet knew Franklin had taken out a substantial business loan and second mortgage on the Bibliophile B & B. When Franklin died, Violet would get nothing, because Franklin's will stipulated his collection be donated to Princeton University. She and Allan decided the only way Violet could inherit anything liquid was through the insurance on the stolen manuscript. Franklin had even borrowed against his own life insurance policy. They had been slowly upping the digoxin in Franklin's bee's knees for weeks.

What they hadn't counted on, or at least Allan hadn't, was Violet having a jealous fit over Allan taking care of his ex-wife, Nicole, on the night of the twenties cocktail party. Violet snuck up to the Edith Wharton suite and had Nicole chug down a digoxin-laced bee's knees. The half-filled jar Violet had thrown away in the lounge in a hurry held the poisoned honey used in Nicole's drink, the same jar Brenna used to make her honey twists. Violet never thought she'd end up poisoning herself.

The loudspeaker announced the train was about to arrive.

I said, "Are you sure I can't drive you to LaGuardia in my new wheels?"

We both looked over at my new black hybrid Jeep Wagoneer with its wooden side panels—the perfect combination of function and form. My father had driven it from Detroit to Montauk. It paid to have friends in the Motor City. I'd donated my old Jeep to charity.

"No, I'll be fine. You stay here and get ready for your guests." He winked. "Two to be exact, a man and his beast. Next, it's your turn to come home. Sheila wants to fawn all over you. She never had children and all I do is tell her stories about you."

"You're both welcome here anytime. You know that, don't you?"

He took my hand. "I miss her every day."

"Her" didn't refer to his new wife, Sheila, but my mother. "Me too."

"I have something for you." He reached in his pocket. "It's her wedding ring. I should've given it to you sooner." He handed me a thick rose-gold band.

"Thanks." I slipped it on the ring finger of my right hand. It fit perfectly. I kissed his cheek.

"How are you feeling about your friend Byron and Nicole Wolfstrum?"

"I'm okay with it. They're a better match. We'll always be friends."

He stood as the train pulled up. "Take care of Jo. I froze

and labeled some of her dinners. And there might be a few goodies in the fridge for you. Give your old dad a hug and a kiss."

I did. Not wanting to let him go.

The train doors opened.

I called out, "Watch the gap!"

His long legs had no problem with the space between the platform and the train. It was like our roles were reversed. I was the parent and he was the child. Before the train left the station, I missed him. It disappeared down the track and became a pinprick on the horizon. Then something hit me square between the eyes like a freight train.

I took out my cell phone and called Elle. I told her to call Detective Shoner and Pete Wagner from FFM, then to meet me at the Bibliophile B & B.

Was it possible?

My new Jeep Wagoner performed beyond my expectations. It had three times the space to transport my precious junk and, at the same time, the car had a vintage feel to it because of the retro "wood" side panels. I reached Sag Harbor in record time.

I pulled through the front gates and into the gravel parking lot at the side of the Bibliophile B & B. Elle, Detective Shoner, and Pete Wagner were waiting on the front veranda. Brenna was also on the veranda. But no Ollie. After Violet's death and Allan's confession, Brenna had also confessed. Her lovely father, Ollie, had been blackmailing her into stealing books from the Bibliophile so he could pay for his gambling debts. He had threatened to tell Franklin about her past and convinced Brenna her uncle would kick her to the curb if he found out. Unfortunately, Ollie, like his big brother Franklin had with the Bibliophile, had put a second mortgage on Hollingsworth Castle. His only recourse was to put it up for sale. Brenna made her father sell one of his horses in order to pay me what I was owed for my work at the Bibliophile. I figured if what Byron had told me was true about Ollie's mishandling of his horses, the horse would be better off in a new home. Brenna reassured me, now that Ken was working at the stables, that the remaining horses were flourishing. Another thing to strike off my worry list.

Brenna had been named Franklin and Violet's beneficiary. Because the Fitzgerald manuscript was a recent purchase, it hadn't been included with rest of the items to go to Princeton after Franklin's death. Brenna would receive all the insurance money from *The Heiress and the Light*. The rest of Franklin's books and ephemera were already on a secured van bound for Princeton University. Brenna planned to open the Bibliophile the first of October.

Elle ran down the steps. "What's up? What's with all the cloak-and-dagger shenanigans, Megan Elizabeth Barrett? This case has been solved."

"Not exactly. What about the missing manuscript?"

Detective Shoner, Brenna, and Pete joined us.

Pete said, "Allan Wolfstrum said Violet burned *The Heiress and the Light*."

I said, "Follow me and bring a hammer."

"A what?" Brenna asked.

I said, "A hammer. You'll see."

Ken Lerner came toward us from the back of the inn.

Brenna called out, "Ken, bring a hammer and follow us to . . ." She looked at me. "Where are we going?"

"The teahouse."

When we reached the teahouse, Brenna put the key in the lock and slid open the door. Everyone filed in. The fountain no longer gurgled, the goldfish were gone, and so were the potted orchids. I couldn't help but think of my Mad Hatter tea party with Violet.

I walked over to the kiln. The head bust was still on top, a black cloth draped over it. Brenna must have wisely realized there wasn't a big market for art created by a murderess. I grabbed the corner of the cloth and exposed John Steinbeck.

Ken said, "He kind of looks like Franklin. Look at the nose and chin."

"Exactly," I said. "Hand me the hammer, please."

He did.

I held it with both hands, but before I swung, I looked at Brenna. "Do I have your permission?"

"Of course."

The first wallop caused a fracture. The next sliced the scalp straight off horizontally. It fell to the floor and shattered. Then I took the bottom part of the head off the top of the kiln and tilted it toward the others.

There, in all its glory, was Fitzgerald's *The Heiress and the Light.*

Elle said, "How did you know?"

"On the day of the hurricane, I watched Violet hollow it out after she sliced off its scalp. When I held Violet's other sculptures at Sag Art, I realized how light they were. The reason being, they were hollow. Why would Violet burn a potential five-million-dollar sale to a private collector somewhere down the line if she learned later the manuscript was legit? It was just a theory."

Pete said, "A pretty good theory." He came next to me and removed the manuscript.

I said, "Pete, I only ask one thing."

He looked at me.

"I get to read the original manuscript. Under your supervision, of course."

"Ms. Barrett, you've got it. And, of course, you get a reward."

"That will be reward enough."

Pete said, "No, we insist."

"Well, in that case, I'll donate half to SAIL—Save America's Invaluable Libraries. I have one other request for Brenna: when she sells the manuscript, she gives it to Jordan Innes to broker the sale."

"Done," Brenna said.

As I was leaving the Bibliophile B & B, I looked up at the cupola. The arrow on the whale weathervane pointed southeast . . . to HOME.

CHAPTER

❧

THIRTY-SEVEN

I threw the stick farther than planned. Tripod bounded after it.

I said to Cole, "I can't believe how fast he is for only having three legs."

Cole was breaking ground for our first clambake on the beach. Shovelfuls of sand flew behind him in waterfalls. He said, "You'd better keep an eye on Tripod or he'll be in Amagansett before you know it."

One of Cole's eyes was covered with a glossy lank of dark hair, the other bleached a Tiffany blue in the autumn sun. I couldn't tell if he was serious—one of my problems with a guy who could be so intense one moment, then teasing the next. I wasn't complaining.

I took off west down the beach, climbing over large boulders and beached tree trunks, calling out Tripod's name.

Instead of Tripod, a large greyhound charged toward

me. It put on its brakes and stopped inches from where I stood, sand spraying my jeans. The greyhound wore a collar with a rabies tag. Its pale gray body was scarred with raised welts.

I stuck out my hand for the dog to sniff or lick, whichever it chose. "Well, aren't you a friendly pup! Who do you belong to?" As I spoke, a stick of driftwood came hurtling toward me, landing next to the dog. Tripod came galloping after it. The greyhound beat him to it and a game of tug-of-war commenced.

At the top of a dune, advancing toward me, as if in slow-motion, was Patrick Seaton. I'd never seen him without a hood hiding his windblown dirty-blond hair. He wore an ear-to-ear grin, another surprise—I never pictured him smiling.

When he reached us, he said, "Don't let Charley scare you. She's a little rambunctious, not used to having free range."

I looked at the scars on her body and knew there was a tragic story there somewhere.

Patrick stuck out his hand. "I don't think we've been formally introduced. Patrick Seaton."

"Meg Barrett." I shook his hand and looked into his eyes. They were green. No, they were steel-gray. A cloud covered the sun and they changed like the sea itself. Eyes that told volumes—a portal into his poetry-ridden soul.

Our hands were still clasped when I heard Cole shout, "Good! You found him."

I sure hoped he meant Tripod . . .

Meg and Elle's
Think Outside-the-Box Guide
to Repurposing Vintage Finds

Meg: Repurpose vintage and antique books with torn and damaged covers by taking off the covers of two or more books, leaving the title page on top, then tie the books together with a string or lace ribbon to display on a table or bookshelf. You can also attach a feather or small key to the string for extra adornment. Remember well-worn books mean well-read and well-loved—share their bliss.

Elle: Use a lint-free cloth, or a soft tooth or paint brush to clean rhinestone costume jewelry. Liquid will cause the glue between the stones and the mounts to weaken, especially in foil-backed rhinestones. Excessive heat can also cause the glue to weaken. If you lose a rhinestone, Internet sellers offer an assortment of different rhinestones you can buy in one lot. You never know when you might need a replacement in the future.

Meg: Frame an entire vintage or antique illustrated garden or children's book behind glass and display on an easel or hang on the wall. Instead of destroying an entire book by cutting out a separate print, just spread open the book to the desired colorfully lithographed illustration and center it on top of a complementary solid background or mat. Thin books need a standard frame while thicker books can use a shadowbox frame.

Elle: Take Grandma's small gold-filled wind-up watch, that no longer keeps time, and replace it with a miniature photo of a loved one and wear the watch as a bracelet. Just pop off the glass crystal, remove the hands from the face, glue in the photo and replace the crystal. A keepsake that keeps on ticking with memories.

Meg: Cover worn hardcover books with sturdy wrapping paper, vintage wallpaper, or shimmery marbleized scrapbooking paper in assorted prints. Be sure to leave the top and bottom of the books showing for vintage appeal.

Elle: Think of different ways to display your vintage jewelry. Pin vintage brooches to a piece of velvet or vintage fabric then display your collection in a shadowbox.

Meg: Hollow out the center of a thick, past-its-prime vintage book, line the bottom with a small plastic container and plant succulents or indoor plants inside. Let nature jump right off the page.

Elle: Use vintage tartlet baking tins in assorted sizes and shapes as a fun, organized way to display and separate your jewelry in a dresser drawer.

Meg: Make a lamp out of a stack of vintage hardcover books by drilling a hole in the center of each book, string lamp wire through each book in the stack, then glue a socket to the top book and finish with a lampshade. You can either have all the spines facing the same direction or twirl the books so the spines are facing every-which-way. Now you have a double-entendre reading lamp.

Elle: Organize and display your jewelry in a vintage printer's tray. Paint the printer's tray white and glue pretty papers at the back of each cubby. Screw in brass hooks from the hardware store to hang your jewels. Now you have a utilitarian piece of art that is one of a kind. If you need to make room for larger pieces, just tap the slats with a hammer and remove.

Meg: Display vintage and antique cloth-covered books on a book shelf in a single color family. You can also tie a small stack of books that have similar hues and lay on a table or shelf for an interesting statement. Stock guest rooms with good reads and let your visitors know they are free to take home any books they want. And remember, a modern home can meld perfectly with that little touch of vintage or antique. Wishing you great finds!

Recipes

❦

JEFF BARRETT'S
TOMATO TART APPETIZER

This crowd-pleaser is uncommon and relatively easy to make. You should be done in 45 minutes time, including the baking.

1 sheet of Pepperidge Farm frozen pastry dough (they come in packages of two, 17.3 oz total; to use both sheets, double the recipe for the filling)
parchment paper (to bake on)
baking sheet

FILLING:

2 tablespoons butter
1 tablespoon brown sugar
2 ¾ lbs Roma tomatoes (or any small tomato around 2 inches in diameter)
1 tablespoon balsamic vinegar
1 tablespoon chopped fresh oregano plus one sprig for garnish
salt and pepper to taste

Preheat oven to 400.

Take one sheet of the pastry dough and roll it out gently into a flat rectangle, then place the dough onto the parchment paper lined baking sheet. (If you don't have parchment paper, lightly grease the bottom of the baking sheet.)

In a large skillet, melt the butter over medium heat, then add the sugar and cook to dissolve it. When it begins to caramelize, add the tomatoes and cook for 15 minutes.

Add the balsamic vinegar and cook two more minutes. Remove the tomatoes, leaving the juices in the pan. Place the tomatoes on the pastry dough, sliced-side down. Sprinkle with salt, pepper, and oregano. You should have enough tomatoes to completely cover the dough in a single layer, except for the edges.

Place on the middle rack of your oven and bake the tart for 30 minutes, or until the pastry is golden brown on the bottom. Remove and allow to cool for at least 5 minutes. Cut into squares and enjoy!

♒︎

JEFF BARRETT'S LABOR DAY GRILLED CHICKEN

This grilled chicken is super-flavorful and will always have folks asking how you did it. You can reveal your secrets or not—totally up to you. But remember, you should always leave them wanting more.

You're using chicken thighs for this, not the whole chicken. Thighs are the most flavorful part of the chicken; they can handle grilled heat without drying out, and are generally of similar size and density, so they tend to cook uniformly. These are skin on and bone in. The skin helps protect the meat during grilling and as it cooks, the drippings add to the smoky flavor.

There are two steps involved here: prepping the chicken and grilling it. First you make a marinade and let the chicken parts soak up the flavor for at least an hour or two. You then remove the parts from the marinade and add the spice rub. You're then ready to grill.

Okay, let's go.

8 chicken thighs (this assumes two thighs per person); skin on, bone in

MARINADE:

1 gallon-sized Ziploc plastic bag
1 large clove of garlic, minced
2 tablespoons of lemon juice
1 cup extra virgin olive oil
½ cup dry sherry
½ cup chicken stock
1 tablespoon dried rosemary
1 tablespoon dried thyme
1 tablespoon curry powder
1 teaspoon dried sage
1 teaspoon ground cumin
1 teaspoon salt
1 teaspoon ground black pepper

SPICE RUB:

salt (Lawry's Seasoned Salt if you have it)
black pepper

paprika
chopped fresh Italian parsley for garnish

Heat your grill to medium high.

Place all the marinade ingredients in a non-reactive bowl (plastic, glass or stainless steel). Whisk or otherwise thoroughly combine all the ingredients. Place the marinade, along with the chicken thighs in the Ziploc bag and seal it up. Try to remove as much of the air in the bag as possible. Place the chicken in the refrigerator for at least an hour, preferably two or three. The longer it marinates, the more flavorful it will be.

When you are ready to grill, remove the chicken thighs from the marinade and place on a platter. Discard the used marinade. Season the thighs with all the rub ingredients. Starting with the bottom (non-skin side), season with the salt first, then the pepper, then the paprika. Don't be too shy about the seasoning. When all the bottoms are seasoned, flip the thighs over and season the skin side in the same order.

Place the seasoned thighs on the medium hot grill skin-side down first. Immediately reduce the heat of your grill to medium low; if you are using charcoal, raise the grill to reduce the heat. Cover the grill and cook the skin side for 15 minutes, then turn the chicken over. The skin should be crispy and golden, not charred. If it looks less cooked than golden crispy, leave it skin side down until it is, probably another ten minutes or so. Cook meat-side down for 20 to 30 minutes. Flip back over to re-crisp the skin for five minutes, and the chicken should be fully cooked. Remove to a clean platter, skin side up. Garnish with chopped fresh Italian parsley.

Serves four people

MEG'S STRAWBERRY SOUP
(NO COOKING INVOLVED–YEAH!)

*1 quart strawberries (slightly past their prime are the
best), washed and hulled*
1 cup white wine
2 teaspoons grated lemon peel
1 cup sugar
4 tablespoons lemon juice

Place all the ingredients in a food processor or blender and
blend until smooth. Cover and chill overnight or for several
hours. Serve in chilled bowls and garnish with strawberry
slices, a dollop of whipped cream or vanilla yogurt and a few
mint leaves.

Serves 6—can be served as an intermezzo or dessert

Keep reading for an excerpt from
the first book in the Hamptons Home
& Garden Mystery Series

BETTER HOMES
AND CORPSES

Available now from Berkley Prime Crime!

CHAPTER

ONE

It seems I'm always at the wrong end of the stick. The pointy end. The one you can't see until you trip over it and it pokes your eye out, or worse yet, your heart. I got the flat tire at the intersection of Old Montauk Highway and Route 27. Earlier, my spirits had scaled the upper limits of antique-picker heaven. Now I'd be late, and Caroline Spenser would never tolerate lateness.

My rescuer came in the form of a PSEG power grid worker in a cable truck. When I offered him my last ten-dollar bill for a job well done, he refused and said, "But I'll take that woody golf club in the back of your Jeep."

I'd scavenged the club the day before from the front of the demolished Tiki Motel, along with a set of what I prayed were ivory mah-jongg tiles hidden in a moldy suitcase.

"Well, if you're ever on the lookout for any more clubs, give me a call." I handed him my business card.

"'Meg Barrett, Cottages by the Sea,'" he said, reading the card. "What are you, some kind of home builder?"

"No, more like a nest builder. Sorry, I have to run. I'm sooo late." I glanced at his ring finger. Darn. It would be nice to meet someone with the same collecting bug I had, instead of the cheating jerk I'd been engaged to who hated all things old. The only thing Michael and I had in common was *Jeopardy*! and an obsession with home décor magazines—he loved minimalist modern and I was more of a vintage upcyled-trash gal.

At the sight of the East Hampton windmill, my pulse quickened. Only a few rain-drenched souls trudged along Main Street. It was March, but come June, the beautiful people would descend and the east end of Long Island would morph into the American Riviera, double-cheeked air kisses on every corner and celebrities in every café. *National Geographic* voted East Hampton "America's Most Beautiful Village," and it was easy to see why, with its clean, tree-shaded streets and quaint storefronts.

When I veered left onto a narrow blacktop lane, I got occasional peeks at mammoth estates hidden behind tall privet hedges. My palms itched, forecasting good things around the corner—or disaster. I hoped the flat tire wasn't an omen for my upcoming appointment. After all, it was just a casual meeting with one of the most important antique and art collectors in the Hamptons, scratch that, Long Island, scratch that, the entire East Coast. Now I was really nervous.

The road dead-ended at Seacliff, the Spensers' estate. I passed through open iron gates and followed a long, curving driveway. Poplars, even without their foliage, guided me toward a jaw-dropping nineteenth-century Greek Revival manor house set on a bluff overlooking a tremulous Atlantic. Once upon a time, Seacliff had been the nineteenth-century summer "cottage" of industrialist and robber baron Thaddeus Spenser. Designed by architect Richard Morris Hunt, Seacliff was rumored to be the prototype for the Vanderbilts' castle, Marble House, in Newport. Even against the dark-shrouded sky, its largeness and whiteness took my breath away.

Caroline Spenser was Seacliff's twenty-first-century occupant, a former London socialite and fine art connoisseur with bloodlines to the Queen of England, hence her nickname, "Queen Mother of the Hamptons." Caroline, now widowed, had married Charles Spenser, our very own American royalty. She lived alone with her daughter, Jillian, whom I hadn't seen in fifteen years. Jillian and I ran into each other on Thursday, at the library in East Hampton. We'd only been roomies at NYU for a short half of a semester My schedule left us little time to bond. I was a teaching assistant for the head of journalism during the day, and a waitress at a dive bar in Greenwich Village at night. When I had hung out with Jillian, she'd seemed introverted, always seeking others' approval. Never had an opinion of her own. An odd duck. I chalked it up to her privileged upbringing. But it was thanks to her, I was allowed a short viewing this morning with her mother, the Queen, to discuss a business proposition that might give my fledgling interior design firm a much-needed shot in the arm.

I parked next to a boxwood maze and went up the wide marble steps. Under the sweeping portico, I pressed the button for the intercom. No response. Had I gotten it wrong? Was my appointment for *next* Saturday? Maybe I was too small a fish to fry, a minnow, a tadpole—oops, that's an amphibian. Time to get a grip. This wasn't my first trip to the rodeo. Actually, I'd never been to a rodeo, but I'd dealt with the snobby upper crust before. They weren't any better than me. Then I thought about yesterday's cocktail party. And the underwear.

I rang the buzzer again. With one last effort, I raised the brass knocker and let it thud against the door. To my surprise, the door groaned slowly inward.

"Hellooo, anyone home?" I stepped inside. The cathedral-ceilinged foyer had pale marble floors, dark early American furniture, and artwork even a first grader would recognize. I was admiring an enameled vase the size of my Jeep Wrangler when a sound came from behind the staircase.

I tiptoed toward it. Prickles of sweat formed on my upper lip.

Then I found them.

Jillian Spenser sat on the floor, rocking her mother's limp body. Caroline's mouth gaped open, oozing a pinkish froth. Her nightgown was a study in crimson—a macabre Jackson Pollock painting.

I skated across the blood-slicked marble and got down on my knees, gagging on the stench. "Jillian! What happened?" My father liked to recount tales of grisly homicides from his days in the Detroit PD, but he'd never warned me blood had such a sweet, sick odor.

Jillian pulled away when I tried to embrace her, cradling her mother closer. I felt Caroline's wrist for a pulse but couldn't find one. I crawled to the next room so Jillian wouldn't hear my call, dialed 911 on my cell phone, then vomited into a Ming Dynasty vase.

When I returned to the hallway, I said, "Let's go outside and wait." I was worried Caroline's killer might still be inside. "Everything's going to be fine, I promise." *Who am I kidding?*

Jillian wasn't about to let go of her mother's body. She mumbled, "Col . . ."

I draped my jacket on her quaking shoulders and noticed a lump on the back of her head. Jillian stuttered, "Col . . ." one last time then transferred her glassy stare to a nearby closet door.

Taking my best *Charlie's Angels* stance, I twisted the knob to the closet and pulled. My feet gave way and my tailbone hit marble just as the front door opened and a sea of law enforcement rushed in.

CHAPTER

❦

TWO

Two hours later, I was seated in an East Hampton patrol car. A young policeman, his face shielded by a hat, sat next to me entering data into his tablet. The estate around us buzzed. There were no sirens or flashing lights. Even in the off-season, the police were careful of making a spectacle of themselves in the prestigious Hamptons community.

"You okay?" the officer asked.

No, I'm not okay and never will be again. All that came out was a hiccup that sounded more like a beer belch.

Caroline Spenser's body remained inside. The paramedics carried Jillian out the front door, her thin body wrapped papoose-style in a navy blanket. Before she disappeared inside the ambulance, Jillian's pleading eyes found mine. I'd let her down.

After the ambulance pulled away, the officer extended a well-muscled arm. His smile revealed chalk-white teeth—a welcome contrast to the gruff Detective Shoner I'd met inside. "I'm Officer Bach."

"Meg Barrett."

"Where to, Ms. Barrett?"

I pointed to a bumper sticker on the back of my Jeep that read, MONTAUK—THE END, referring to the town's location on Long Island.

Up until this morning, I'd always thought of Montauk as the beginning.

"Can't I take my car?"

"Evidence. Needs to be processed."

Officer Bach put his tablet in the backseat and we pulled away from the estate. After a few wasted attempts at chitchat, we continued in silence. In Amagansett, undulating sand dunes played peekaboo with the ocean. The Seafood Shanty, a shell of its former self, was covered in two-by-fours and hidden behind straggly beach grass. In a few months, cars would line both sides of the highway for a chance to sample the Shanty's pricey lobster roll. Delicious, but three bites later you were done. I'd discovered better places to score fresh seafood without breaking the bank.

When we reached Montauk, I exhaled. Even though the small town was only a short distance from East Hampton, it felt like I was miles from civilization. Montauk was the un-Hampton. Unpretentious and untamed.

We passed the IGA, the only full-service grocery store in town, which stocked my basics: milk, bread, and Ben & Jerry's New York Super Fudge Chunk. After what I'd just seen at the Spenser estate, the thought of food, even Super Fudge Chunk, made me queasy. I closed my eyes and thought back to my first trip to Montauk. I knew I was

home when I saw a sun-faded sign in a restaurant window—
HELP WANTED—PIANO PLAYER WHO CAN SHUCK CLAMS.

Officer Bach left me at my door. I walked in and dropped
my keys and cell phone into a yellowware bowl—a thank-
you from decorating guru Molly McPherson after I worked
with her in my former life on an *American Home and
Garden* magazine spread. Like Molly, Caroline Spenser
had a grand passion for collecting. Did that passion have
anything to do with her murder?

At the French doors I looked out at the beautiful
seascape and thought back to Thursday, when I saw Jillian
Spenser at the East Hampton Library. It had been so long
since we'd shared a dorm room that, to be perfectly honest,
the only time I thought of her was when I read an article
in *Dave's Hamptons* about her mother, Caroline, and her
legendary collections.

After I'd filled Jillian in with the reason I moved to
Montauk, she asked, "Are you sure your fiancé was cheating?"

"Sure enough to leave Manhattan with a packed U-Haul
of 'vintage crap,' as Michael called it, and move to the
easternmost tip of Long Island."

"Oh, Meg, you're so hot, you'll have no problem finding
a guy. Mother's having one of her cocktail parties tomorrow.
I'd love for you to come. She's invited her usual stable of
men. Hopefully they'll swarm around you and leave me
alone."

I accepted, thinking of all the advantages of rubbing
elbows with Jillian's mother and her elite group of friends.
It would be the perfect opportunity to pass out my Cottages
by the Sea business cards. Only I, woman of big kahunas
and little capital, would try to erect an interior design
business in the glitzy Hamptons.